JUDGE Z

Irretrievably Broken

JUDGE Z

Irretrievably Broken

A Novel

TIM PHILPOT

Judge Z: Irretrievably Broken

ISBN-13: 9780692634967
ISBN-10: 0692634967
Library of Congress Control Number: 2016933555
Chilidog Press, Loveland, OH

For information, contact the author:
Tim Philpot
4837 Bud Lane
Lexington, KY 40514-1415
859-227-3093
judgezbook@gmail.com
www.JudgeZBook.com

Published by:
Chilidog Press LLC
6367 Waverly Hill Lane
Loveland, OH 45140
513-677-5254
pbronson@fuse.net

Cover design:
Chad Crouch

*This book is dedicated to
all the children of irretrievably broken families.*

"In the days when the judges ruled, there was a famine in the land."

— *RUTH 1:1*

TABLE OF CONTENTS

Chapter 1

FAMILY COURT

God puts the lonely in families.

— *Psalm 68:6*

MOTION HOUR
October 31

"All rise!"

The voice of Deputy Sheriff Clarence Palmer was loud and clear. As he spoke the command with authority, everyone stood—some in reverence, some confused, some just following the crowd. The judge walked in, black robe swirling. Everyone understood it was time to sit down and shut up.

"Oyah, oyah, all ye who have pleas to make or causes to prosecute, come forward and ye shall be heard," Palmer intoned. "Fayette Circuit Court is now in session, Judge Atticus Zenas presiding. God bless the Commonwealth and this honorable court. Please be seated. Turn off all cell phones. Remove all hats."

Judge Zenas, simply "Judge Z" to most, took his seat at the bench, just a little higher than everyone else. Judge Z was an increasingly obsolete model— a white, middle-aged, male judge. He sat at the head of a big, rectangular room facing swinging doors at the other end, through which came all the dysfunction, misery, anger, frustration and desperation of Lexington, Kentucky.

The courtroom had high ceilings—probably to make room for all the hot air, curses and prayers, Judge Z thought. It was a big room—too big for most days. But they needed the space, especially on Fridays for "Motion Hour," when lawyers and people without lawyers filed motions to be heard by the honorable judge. The room had to be big to keep the husbands and wives apart, to keep the victims away from the "perps," to keep order in the court.

Extra sheriffs were needed as well. This was family court, where emotions ran especially high. Where parents refused to talk to each other and where lawyers told the truth, but not the whole truth. Certainly not "nothing but the truth." Family court was a place where people should be embarrassed just to be there. But they were not. It was a place where children were often forgotten in the chaos of personal agendas.

Today was standing room only—over a hundred people of all types. Young and old, black and white, Asian and Hispanic; blue-suited lawyers and well-dressed ladies next to men and women wearing T-shirts, jeans, sideways caps and the human graffiti of tattoos. Unless invited, nobody was allowed past the front railing except lawyers and court workers. Lawyers arrived early to get the best seats, to be seen by each other and to impress potential clients.

It was a typical Friday at 8:30 a.m.—the hour set for Judge Z to listen to lawyers and litigants embarrass themselves in front of a big room full of people.

Today's docket could include truly destitute couples, the poorest of the poor, seeking a simple divorce. Or perhaps millionaires arguing over the gated winter estate on the Gulf Coast in Florida.

In Motion Hour, lawyers file motions asking the judge for something. Then opposing lawyers file responses and replies. It was a bit like prayers: They all asked the "higher power" to bless their humble requests. So sayeth the antiquated legalese at the end of each pleading: "Prayer for Relief."

"Our father, who art on the bench, hallowed is Thy courtroom. Please reduce my child support by fifty dollars. I got laid off last month."

Or some such thing.

Once upon a time this was for lawyers only. But after many years of "access to justice" reforms, the paperwork became available over the internet to file motions without high-priced lawyers—or even low-priced ones.

If television had not been invented, Motion Hour would be the greatest show in town. It would be Lexington's version of the Colosseum, with crowds gathered to watch mortal combat. Judge Z would be as well-known as Judge Judy. Instead, he was just another judge in another courtroom, on another crazy Friday morning in family court.

STIRLING v. STIRLING

The judge wasted no time starting a docket that would last three hours. Case after case after case. Some were routine requests for trial dates. Others required more substantive hearings. Wives wanted husbands to leave the house. Husbands wanted payments reduced. Unmarried couples argued about which freezing parking lot they would use to drop off the two-year-old on a winter night. Would it be the McDonald's on Broadway or the Wendy's on Richmond Road? "It's not fair for me to have to drive all the way over there," he would say. And she would reply, "Maybe we should meet at the police station so you won't make a scene."

Judge Z would think many thoughts, usually unspoken: *Yeah, and it's also "not fair" that this sweet little girl has you two for parents,* he often wanted to say. More and more he would say it out loud.

After ten years on the bench, he did not like messing around. He was losing patience. So he just dove into the docket. Today, thirty-seven cases. Only a few would be "heard." He would run through every case quickly to see who needed an actual hearing for five to fifteen minutes.

"*Stirling versus Stirling,*" said Judge Z as he looked out over the crowd, knowing this was a case with no lawyers. Slowly, a well-dressed and uncomfortable middle-aged man stood and announced from his cheat-sheet, "Your Honor. This is an uncontested divorce. All the paperwork is in the file. We need a date for final hearing please." He was hoping to get it done today, in fact.

"Sure," said Judge Z. He got his schedule book and offered November 10 at 10 a.m. "My office will prepare an Order for both parties to appear." Puzzled, Jack Stirling offered that his soon to be ex-wife had signed everything and they were told she would not have to appear. Technically correct, said the judge, but he always wanted both parties to be present for uncontested divorces with children, just to be sure all is in order. This divorce had only been filed fifty days ago. Kentucky's sixty-day waiting period for cases with children was often ignored. But Judge Z was old-fashioned and thought people should actually wait the sixty days before finalizing everything.

Satisfied, Jack Stirling turned and left the courtroom with a nervous smile, sure that his marriage was over. The judge had been cordial. The system seemed in place to end his marriage. His girlfriend's young lawyer helped him with the paperwork and promised him it would be easy. So far, so good.

The new girlfriend was in place.

The two kids would adjust.

The ex-wife would eventually move on.

As he hurried out, he was met by his girlfriend, who was there to make sure her new man actually followed through on the divorce he promised her.

The judge didn't think she looked attractive enough to make a man leave a wife of twenty-two years and abandon three children. But he shrugged it off. He had learned long ago that love is not logical.

"*Hopper versus Hopper*," the judge announced.

"Your Honor, this case needs to be heard at the end of the docket," said a young lawyer in un-pressed khakis and a worn blue blazer that probably fit him better when he started law school than when he graduated, which the judge guessed was probably last week. The kid was nervous, reading from a script prepared by his senior-partner boss who had bigger carp to fry than a family court motion for a client who might not pay anyway.

Judge Z tried to be nice to nervous young lawyers. He remembered what it was like. Young lawyers didn't even care about winning, they just didn't want to be embarrassed or yelled at. Losing with dignity was a good day.

"Okay," he said, "I'll mark it to be heard. Have a seat and we will get to you shortly."

The young lawyer looked grateful and sat down with obvious relief. He was feeling successful already. He was now part of the bar. He had survived so far without anyone finding out that after three years of law school he knew almost nothing.

ELEANOR AND HARRY

"*Lee versus Chapman.*"

Eleanor Day stood, smoothed her long, straight gray hair back over her shoulder, looked over the John Lennon bifocals on her nose and reported, "Judge, we just need a trial date in that case. Perhaps thirty days from now. We will need half a day."

Often the judge would grill the lawyer about why they needed so much time or why they hadn't settled, but Eleanor, now on the far side of seventy, was one of the first female lawyers in town. She was a legend. And the judge genuinely liked her. Nobody would say it, but she was over the hill. Yet many divorcing husbands still tried to hire her before their wife did. Smart men would pay her a thousand-dollar "consultation" fee just to stop her from being the wife's lawyer. Eleanor knew how the game was played, and was well aware she was being paid to do nothing, like farmers paid to not plant beans, but she gladly took their money anyway and even doubled the fee when she could.

A quick trial would be no problem. Judge Z kept his docket up to date. In fact, he would often set a trial before the lawyers were ready. Some of them speculated behind his back that he didn't have enough to do. He was too efficient, which is almost a felony for government work.

"And what are the issues?" he asked Eleanor.

"Your Honor, as you may recall, these parties were never married. They have one child, age two. The issues are custody, time-sharing and child support. I am afraid to tell you we could not settle in mediation—not even the name of the child."

"Okay. I remember a little bit. This is the one where mom planned to name the baby after the father, John Thomas Lee Jr., and went ahead and put it on Facebook while she was pregnant. But then she named him John Thomas Chapman, after her own family. Is this the one where she even denied John Thomas Lee was the father after a few weeks? And am I correct that Mr. Lee is still married to another lady?"

"Yes, Your Honor, that's correct. You have a good memory."

Flattery was one of the perks that went with the robe. But it was never as sincere as what they said about him over drinks after work. Judge Z set a date four weeks away.

Eleanor and her honorable opponent, Harry Wolff, looked at their calendars and pretended to out-busy each other—the lawyer version of bragging. For anyone listening, it was also a good way to justify their fees of three-hundred dollars an hour.

"Your Honor, I have to be in federal court that day," said Wolff, as if announcing that he was personally invited to a state dinner at the White House. Something about a habeas corpus for one of his rich and important clients whose divorce became criminal due to false tax returns. His smirk added that he would make a lot more money than the judge that day. Wolff was one of those lawyers who would occasionally brag that the only reason he was not a judge was because he couldn't take a pay cut.

Eleanor also had conflicts, mostly due to her semi-retirement. "Your Honor, I will be at the beach with my grandkids that week."

After two more tries at a date, Judge Z said with just a hint of sarcasm, "Counsel, perhaps you could let me know what dates are suitable for you?"

Wolff missed the hint. "Your Honor, would the court have any time available after the first of the year?"

"Sure. No problem. That's over two months away. Although your client, who seems to want this matter concluded, may not want to wait that long. Perhaps she needs another lawyer?" Judge Z was talking to himself, but out loud.

The client, Miss Chapman, looked peeved. Her very expensive lawyer was not only making her mad but also annoying the judge. Even she could tell it was not going well. Wolff had seemed to forget she was even there, watching it all from three feet away.

As much as Judge Z liked to be nice to young lawyers, he also quietly enjoyed embarrassing puffed up roosters like Wolff who thought they were more important than their clients.

"I have an idea," the judge said. "You guys call my secretary if any times open up on your important schedules in federal court, and the Supreme Court, and the United Nations, and beach vacations which I seem to have missed this year, and if we all get lucky, we'll hope it works. In the meantime, I will set this case down for a half-day on May 15. That's after the first of the year. Have a nice weekend."

His big smile said it was time for the next case.

HOSTILE TAKEOVER

By 9 a.m. Judge Z was ready to actually hear some cases. Half of the initial crowd was gone, having taken care of their routine business of getting trial dates and saying "Your Honor, we'd like to pass this motion to next week." Today was the usual conglomeration of divorce and custody matters, with some contempt issues for those who had failed to pay child support or comply with various orders. Some had no lawyers and some had the expensive kind, who never tell their clients that nobody really pays retail at three hundred dollars an hour. Some of the poor souls had seen the judge fifty times, and some had never been in court.

First up was Bernard Bates, one of the richest men in town—at least for the moment. He had been served with divorce papers on Monday night. Now, three days later, the lady who told him twenty-three years ago that she would be his wife "until death do us part" was asking the judge to order him out of his own house. He hadn't had time to get a lawyer, although the phone book was filled with dozens of hungry sharks. His corporate counsel had recommended a few good names but he had not had time to interview them. He was staying at the Hyatt Regency after his beloved wife hustled him out of the house with an Emergency Protective Order, alleging he was a danger to the family.

Judy Bates had handpicked the nastiest divorce lawyer in town. It was the same guy who couldn't find time for a trial date ten minutes ago, Harry Wolff—a man who thoroughly enjoyed plotting a hostile takeover by Mrs. Bates. Their play could be called "The Death of a Marriage." It was an old script.

Mr. Bates never knew what hit him. His wife had been so nice over the past ninety days that he had begun to hope things were getting better. The sex was good. She had started to cook again. This was the best they had gotten along in years. She seemed to have forgiven him for all of his misdeeds, which were many.

But to his surprise, their joint bank account was no longer joint. He would need an apartment now and might see his two kids every other weekend, plus one two-hour dinner on Wednesdays. Meanwhile, he would write big checks every week. His assets were all "marital," which meant she would get half. If he had seen this coming, he might have been able to hide some assets. But it was too late now.

Mr. Bates would pay for the X-rated sins he had confessed to his priest. And family court wouldn't order Hail Marys. Allegations of domestic violence were scattered among twenty-five pages of so-called facts. He drank too much, she alleged; he had an alcoholic girlfriend; he was a danger to the children.

Affidavits from three neighbors he thought were his friends added salt to the wounds. He had even been drunk at Holy Communion one Sunday, said Mrs. Shirley Payton, who never missed church and happened to be the best friend of Mrs. Bates.

The allegations were so serious and outrageous that Judge Z had no choice but to grant the temporary relief sought by Harry Wolff and his client, who was doing her best to look pitiful. He knew there was another side to the story, but today was not the day to hear it. As they all turned to walk away, the judge wondered what would happen to the Bates family.

Many of the stories in family court were like walking in to the middle of a movie, then leaving before it was over. The Bates divorce might or might not come back to his courtroom. Judge Z seldom saw endings, and almost never happy ones. That was part of the job on the justice assembly line—or maybe it was the opposite of an assembly line. Families came in to the courthouse factory in one piece and were slowly dismantled, piece by piece. He didn't know what would happen to the Bates family, but he knew Mr. Bates would need a very good lawyer. Next case.

It was fitting that on Halloween, Mr. and Mrs. Garrison were ready to fight over nothing again. Judge Z remembered them well—a couple in their 60s, married for forty years. Mrs. Garrison had been part of a "Pagans" rally in front of the courthouse a year ago, complete with witches, warlocks and wiccans. Mrs. Garrison led the chants to worship Satan in a crowd that looked like rejects from a Grateful Dead concert.

The divorce was final. The separation agreement said they would equally divide the silverware and other personal items. But they had failed to agree, and now they wanted Judge Z to divide up the silverware. It had been a happy day for both of their lawyers when the Garrisons fired them. They were now both representing themselves.

The settlement looked like the work of lazy lawyers and stupid clients. *If they can't get along in their marriage, how can they get along to divide their property?* Judge Z wondered. And in this case, one was a real witch.

"If I rule, it will be this," he explained. "I will send the sheriff out to take possession of the silverware and give it to the Salvation Army."

He invited them to step out to the hallway and work it out. They returned a few minutes later. "Thank you, Your Honor, we settled the case," Mr. Garrison said. The former wife nodded agreement but was not happy. But that was nothing new.

ADOLPH AND BILLY

Other than the lousy football team, October was always a great month in Kentucky. Horse racing at Keeneland. Good weather. Beautiful leaves—especially in eastern Kentucky.

But mostly, basketball season was hyping up. In fact, Midnight Madness was tonight. Students had been sleeping outside for three days to get tickets to a basketball practice. A *practice*. In front of 23,000 adoring worshipers.

So this was a good day to settle the Jones case.

The couple had settled all the routine divorce issues. They had been married for twenty-two years. He would keep his pension plan. She would keep the house and equity therein, which roughly equaled the pension plan. They would have joint custody, but their two children would mostly stay with Mom, who had given up her teaching career to stay at home. Dad would pay child support and maintenance for ten years and then she'd be on her own. Mr. Jones would give up nearly everything to keep his girlfriend. Mrs. Jones already had her eye on a divorced man at church.

They were in motion hour to let the judge know that everything was settled, except the two common disputes in divorces in Lexington. Never mind the kids and the house—the big question was who would get the dog and the UK basketball tickets? This was urgent, since basketball season was coming up in November. "Your Honor, this is an emergency. If you can find a day, we'd like to be heard this month," said attorney Frances Stone with a straight face. "The first game is November 15."

Mr. Jones' affidavit said that Adolph, the well-bred pug, always came to him first when called. As far as he was concerned, Mrs. Jones could keep "her dog," the mixed poodle, Billy. She wanted Adolph, too. They explained that their dogs had always been named for Kentucky basketball coaches. Joe B had been a lovable old hound dog. Eddie, named for Coach Sutton, ate too much, got too big and was returned to the pound when he bit a neighbor. Ricky P was a snappy miniature fox terrier, much loved until he ran away one day. Mr. Jones especially loved Tubby, a wonderful lab. He had been given a real funeral with a real preacher when he passed away too early of cancer.

Billy came home from the pound on the same day that Billy Gillespie was hired. He peed on the carpet, pooped in the kitchen and barked all night. Mr. Jones wished he could get rid of him, just like UK had fired his namesake after he was arrested for DUI.

Adolph, however, was a Hall of Fame champion pug. He was smart. He seemed to enjoy the UK games on TV, but that might had something to do with the Milk Bone victory celebrations. The dog custody hearing would be almost as serious as the UK tickets.

Judge Z warned everyone that he would likely order joint custody of the beloved pooch. "I normally order therapy for the dogs, but Adolph seems to be OK," said Judge Z. Everyone got the joke except Mr. Jones, who looked relieved that he wouldn't have to pay for dog counseling.

The basketball tickets were more complicated. Attorney George Tackett claimed the tickets were non-marital property. He produced Mrs. Jones' affidavit, which claimed they were her sole property since they came from her parents, who had been big donors and alumni. Mr. Jones countered that she never attended the games and only wanted them now out of spite, whereas he needed them for business entertaining. The UK Athletic Department submitted an affidavit that assigned a fair market value of the four season tickets at $300,000. UK had a waiting list of hundreds of people lined up to pay that much for the right to purchase tickets.

"Looks like fans who worship Big Blue have to sacrifice some big green," Judge Z commented. Mr. Jones didn't think that was funny, either.

The tickets were marital property, according to the attorney, Ms. Stone. The Joneses paid for them every year from joint marital funds.

Judge Z would enjoy this hearing. He already knew what he would do, but they didn't, and he was looking forward to the drama.

"How about November 14 at 1 p.m.?" he asked. "That's the day before the first home basketball game." They would be ready.

Next, Dr. Gupta Patel was back making his annual cameo appearance to try to stop his six-thousand-dollar monthly maintenance payments to his ex-wife. Born in Mumbai, India, he had fallen madly in love with the cute American girl at the hospital where he did his residency in 1979. Rejecting his family's marriage traditions, he married her and they had three little kids. But he was a typical workaholic doctor at the University hospital.

Connie Patel put up with the doc because he made nearly a half-million a year. Interesting how thirty-five thousand a month can cover a lot of husbandly failure. But now the kids were teenagers. There was no longer any reason to tolerate his arrogance, affairs and silence.

In the beginning, Dr. Patel was proud to tell people that his marriage was different than the typical arranged marriage in India. It was a "love marriage."

Not anymore. On top of maintenance payments, he had to give up the million-dollar residence and half of their rental properties, plus child support. He could see his kids, but they hated him.

His motion, filed without a lawyer this time, was to reduce his maintenance to "whatever you think is fair, Judge." It was his third attempt. He claimed he had lost his job and didn't make the big money anymore. He had moved to a country hospital in Corbin, Kentucky, where Colonel Sanders got his start. He was pleading poverty.

Judge Z set it for a two-hour hearing—not because Dr. Patel had any chance to win, but just to be entertained by the doc's antics. He had already been to jail twice for failing to pay. Then, after screaming under oath, "I have no money, I have no money," he always paid to get out.

The first time, Judge Z put him into the jail holdover. And—surprise— he had the six-thousand dollars in his girlfriend's purse in the back of the courtroom. When he said, "I have no money," what he meant was, "My girlfriend has it."

The next time he stayed in jail the full sixty days, growing a mangy beard and claiming various religious convictions no one had heard of to set up a discrimination suit against the jail and maybe even the judge. He found out from Google that the judge was a Methodist and therefore must be biased against Hindus. But his wife had testified that in decades of marriage she had never seen any evidence of a devout Hindu living in her home.

He did have an orange dot on his forehead to go with his pitiful beard. But no lawyer would touch his lawsuit. And now he was "pro se," meaning he represented himself and had a fool for a client. He still owed money to his past two lawyers, and word gets around.

"Dr. Patel, I am intrigued by your motion to reduce maintenance and will set this down for two hours on February 8 at 9 a.m.," said the judge, pleasing Mrs. Patel and her lawyer, Charles Barker. They would enjoy grilling him and the lawyer would make a couple thousand dollars for the show.

"Bring all your proof with you about your inability to pay. Mrs. Patel's attorney will cross examine you about your current situation, of course, including vacations, girlfriends, cars and the new house you just paid cash for in Corbin. This should be interesting. See you then."

The judge was not supposed to make up his mind until all the evidence was in. That was a hard rule to follow.

Motion hour was finally and mercifully over. The only souls left in the courtroom were Deputy Palmer; Judge Z's secretary, Karen Martin; and the judge's staff attorney, Clay Henderson. It was 11:30 a.m. Another one in the books. "You can't make this stuff up," said Karen for the umpteenth time as she shut down the computer and smiled.

IRRETRIEVABLY BROKEN

Judge Z left the courtroom and went straight to his office, where a couple was waiting in chambers for a simple, uncontested divorce. Judge Z, like all the judges, had a conference room with a camera and recorder for routine or confidential matters. He divorced people in this room several times a week. Five minutes was usually scheduled for couples with no disputes. They could end their marriage in less time than it takes to vote or pick up a meal at Burger King.

His conference room was the death chamber for marriages.

Or maybe more like the funeral parlor.

In most cases, the marriage had been dead for years. This was just the formality of making it official.

As Judge Z briskly walked into the conference room, Mr. and Mrs. J. Morton Hemlock were already sitting there. No lawyers were needed for this hearing. Mort had put on a tie for the occasion, looking like the banker he wanted to be. Melanie was dressed as if she was headed to Sunday school. Judge Z had done this thousands of times. But this was a big deal for the Hemlocks. They were fidgety and nervous. They stood, but the judge quickly motioned for them to sit down and relax. "This won't take long," he assured them. "I have already reviewed your documents and all is in order, so raise your right hands." They swore to tell the truth.

They gave the right answers to all his questions: no domestic violence, yes they had a property settlement, etc. He got to the point.

"Mr. Hemlock, is your marriage irretrievably broken?"

"Yes."

"Is there any reasonable prospect for reconciliation?"

"No."

The judge turned to the wife and saw that she was reaching in her purse for a Kleenex. He waited as she wiped her eyes and took a deep breath, then asked, "Mrs. Hemlock, do you agree?"

She was quiet. The silence stretched.

He asked again, "Ma'am, do you agree that your marriage is irretrievably broken and there is no reasonable prospect for reconciliation?"

Silence filled the room. The husband gave his wife an angry glare, but she would not look at him or the judge. She was blocking the divorce assembly line and pretty soon the couples waiting for their turn would back up.

Judge Z was in a hurry, in no mood for tearful women. His job was to divorce people, not counsel them and hand out Kleenexes. "Ma'am," he said, "the law is clear that if one party says the marriage is irretrievably broken with no prospect of reconciliation, the divorce will happen. I see that this day is making you sad, and for that I am sorry, but Mr. Hemlock has a right to this divorce and so, frankly, your answer doesn't matter. You have signed the agreement. Unless you can tell me something I am not hearing, this marriage will end with my signature today."

Melanie Hemlock nodded, but still wouldn't look up or say a word. The great Judge Zenas had spoken. The Wizard of Oz had laid down the law.

Judge Z uncapped his pen and signed the papers that declared that the marriage was dissolved.

Irretrievably broken.

No prospect of reconciliation.

The agreement signed by the parties was, by legal definition, "not unconscionable," meaning it was fair to both. The twelve-year-old son would bounce back and forth like a Ping-Pong ball, one week with dad and his latest girlfriend, and one week with a depressed, lonely, over-indulgent mother. Statistically speaking, Junior's chances of success in life were being radically reduced. Even the child's lifespan was going down five years, statistically, thanks to divorcing parents.

But none of this was Judge Z's problem. He was just there to sign the papers. "Karen, next case, please," he said. This was the cue that it was time for the Hemlocks to leave. They did. As single people.

Chapter 2

WELCOME TO SADIEVILLE

Do everything you can to help Zenas the lawyer.

— *Titus 3:13*

GOD-FEARING GREEK

One of the problems with being a judge is the loss of a first name. No one feels comfortable calling a judge by their first name, even if he is your best friend from third grade.

"Hi, Judge," they say with a smile and fake cordiality. Lawyers have a lot more to say about a judge outside the courtroom. But the judge never hears the truth, except at home, where Judge Z was still "Atty." The irony that his nickname was also the abbreviation for attorney was lost on most people.

But the judge was not even "Atty" at home anymore. Not since Angelina died last year. And home was not really home anymore. Instead, home was a cold condo where he rarely stayed for long. In many ways, the real "home" was with his mother, Beulah.

The story of how she named him Atticus had been told by Beulah a million times. Atty was tired of it, but had to admit he liked it.

Beulah Knox was a country girl from Scott County, Kentucky, near Lexington. She met Johnny Zenopoulos at a dance when she was eighteen, at Joyland, an old amusement park, bowling alley and roller rink.

Johnny was born in the USA, but his parents were from Greece. He was an inch over six feet, with a permanently tanned complexion and the classic features of a Greek god. But his accent was a cross between Kentucky "briar" and Greek—like a Greek country music singer. His mother could barely speak English. His parents ran a restaurant in Winchester, Kentucky, The Grecian Diner. His father, Gus, had worked night and day, while Helen stayed home and raised Johnny and his three older sisters.

When Johnny turned nineteen, four years before he met Beulah, he decided to change his last name. He was tired of everyone calling him "the Greek boy." So when he joined the Navy in 1950, just in time for the Korean War, he filled out the paperwork with a shortened version of his Greek name, which was butchered by the Navy and came out as Johnny Zenas. He liked it. He didn't know anyone with a name like Zenas. And nobody could tell exactly where he was from.

Johnny took great pleasure in making stuff up. One day he was from Italy. The next he was from Lebanon. His dark skin and love of olives made either story believable. On some days he was even Greek.

He fell hard for Beulah. She was a cute little redhead. Smart as a whip. Straight A's. Opposites attract, and she fell for Johnny. Maybe it was the uniform. He was just back from Korea. It was 1954.

Johnny's family was disappointed by his choice. A marriage had been arranged with Anastasia Collis. Her parents, Nick and Lydia, operated the Georgetown Restaurant, where the smells of feta cheese and olives and baklava and lamb lingered all day long. This was to be a Greek-style arranged marriage of restaurants as well as children.

But Johnny married the little redhead after just four months of courtship. Beulah was nineteen. Johnny was twenty-four. They walked down the aisle of Sadieville Methodist Church in Scott County. His parents would not attend the wedding. Beulah's parents were there, but not too happy either.

Beulah had to overlook some things about Johnny. Her parents were Methodist teetotalers. So was she. Johnny drank a little bit—maybe even a little bit too much. Beulah knew that he would get drunk on weekends sometimes. But she was sure she could change him. Surely love and marriage would settle him down.

Surely her good cooking would keep him home at night. Surely her bedroom would satisfy him. Surely her hugs and smiles and compliments would be all he ever needed. Men hope their young bride never changes, and women are sure that their new husband will change. Both end up disappointed.

Beulah exchanged her maiden name, Knox, for one that was more exotic, with Greek roots: Zenas. She took some solace in the Bible's story of young Timothy, whose mother was a devoutly Jewish believer in Christ. Timothy's father was a "God-fearing Greek," according to the Book of Acts.

She hoped Johnny would be a "God-fearing Greek." But nine years into the marriage, they were childless and Johnny showed no sign of changing. So she started dreaming and praying for her own son, who would be God-fearing. She even thought of naming him Timothy. Timmy.

She often prayed the prayer of Hannah in First Samuel, Chapter 1: "*Lord Almighty, if you will only look on your servant's misery and remember me, and not forget your servant but give her a son, then I will give him to the Lord for all the days of his life…*"

But no children came. And Johnny's rebellion continued. Most Greek kids grow up to be doctors or lawyers, or run the family restaurant and made more money than the doctors and lawyers. But Johnny wanted nothing to do with that. He started selling dental equipment and began to make a little bit of money. To the young couple, it was a goldmine.

He refereed some high school basketball games in his spare time and made a few bucks as a bookie on the side. What Beulah didn't know wouldn't hurt her. And being a dental equipment salesman was a great front for a bookie. It was especially lucrative on games he refereed. He would suffer through some boos for a few bucks.

They had a nice little house in Sadieville, just fifteen miles from Lexington. Johnny only drank too much about once a month, and that was tolerable to Beulah.

MOCKINGBIRD

Sunday mornings were spent at the small Methodist Church in Sadieville. The Greek Church in Winchester was for baptisms, weddings and special family occasions. The chanting of a Greek priest was still pleasant to Johnny's ears on occasion, as long as it didn't last too long. Like Bluegrass music after the third twangy tune, Greek chanting soon began to drag.

Beulah kept praying for a baby. And then, after nine years and several doctor visits, Beulah was pregnant. She was reading her Bible during her first trimester when she came to the obscure book of Titus—and things got spooky. Titus 3:13 sounded like God Himself talking: *"Do everything you can to help Zenas the lawyer."*

Wow. Her last name was in the Bible. She heard the Lord telling her that she would have a son and he would be a lawyer. Maybe even a "God-fearing lawyer," if there was such a thing. But she dared not say anything to Johnny. He hated lawyers. The ones he knew in his big, extended Greek family were on the way to being disbarred. Cousin Mike "forgot" that a fat escrow account did not belong to him. And Uncle Bill missed a statute of limitations, then lied about it to his client for two years.

So Beulah kept her secret. *To Kill a Mockingbird* was a big hit movie that year, starring Gregory Peck as Atticus Finch, who would do the right thing at the right time and be a hero, if not to the city, at least to his own kids. Beulah was raised as a proud Lincoln Republican and she liked the civil rights message. It convinced her that a lawyer should be someone who cares about real people. He should solve problems, not cause them.

Atticus Zenas. What a name. Surely a boy named Atticus could become a lawyer. Maybe even a judge. So Atticus Timothy Zenas was born on January 27, 1964. Johnny did not really like his son's name, but some things are beyond a man's control.

Beulah hung onto the dream that her boy would be a lawyer. Even when young Atty got in so much trouble at age fourteen that they had to ship him off to a military school in Connecticut. Even when he came home again and got caught smoking marijuana in high school.

Even when he barely got into the University of Kentucky, finished with a 2.9 GPA and applied to law school only because Beulah told him to at least apply. He ended up as the last alternate to get in, selected the day after classes started.

As much as Beulah loved the story, her son found it too complicated to explain how he was named after a guy in a movie. Judges had no first names anyway. So now, he was just Judge Z.

EMPTY CONDO

Sunday mornings meant church with Beulah. At age fifty he was not the devout man Beulah prayed for, although he was a faithful churchgoer, especially since Angelina had passed a year ago. She had kept him straight. Now it was Beulah's turn again.

His mom had always made sure he went to church when he was growing up, and also sent him to Camp Meeting every summer—a ten-day affair in July for serious Christians and their children. For teens, it was a place for girls and boys to meet behind the barn to smoke a first cigarette or sneak a first kiss.

The camp meeting they attended was in Eldorado, Illinois—ironically named Camp Beulah, a reference to the "land up yonder," heaven itself or at least the land leading there. Maybe it came from "Beulah Land," one of the most popular hymns of the 1800s, still beloved by many churchgoers, including Beulah Zenas. It would certainly be played at her funeral. It was a song about heaven.

The camp had special family significance. Johnny Zenas, an unreligious, small-time alcoholic and secret bookie, met God there in 1963. He wept like a baby as he knelt at an altar to pray and confess his sins and seek forgiveness. The change was immediate. He quit drinking and eventually started teaching Sunday school, so his son only knew the new and improved version of his dad. In fact, one of Judge Z's favorite speeches was his "used to be" speech. He would tell fathers, "Make sure your kids only hear stories about how you 'used to be.'"

Johnny liked to say that marriage must be difficult because he was married to Beulah, the "perfect" woman, and it was still hard. As he got older, Judge Z understood his dad better and realized he was right about marriage.

As a senior at UK, he met the love of his life and his future wife. After twenty-eight years of marriage, Angelina was still beautiful. They had no financial problems, the house was paid off, they had no children to cause trouble, their love life was still good, and yet—Johnny was right—marriage was still difficult. Happy wife, happy life. It was true.

And then, without much warning, cancer found his only love. And he was soon alone again. He had nobody to make him sad, mad or glad. If not for missing Angelina, he had no emotions left at all.

So most Sundays he escaped the empty condo and went to his momma's house for church and Sunday dinner—always fried chicken, Greek hillbilly style.

Johnny had died five years ago, at age eighty. The funeral was at the Sadieville Methodist Church, where Johnny and Beulah were official members. Beulah still taught a Sunday school class of people her age. She had been doing it for fifty years.

Judge Z had been raised in a house where God was almost a member of the family, but he wasn't really sure what he believed anymore.

He believed in Beulah. He knew her faith was real. She could be trusted. She was sincere. Perhaps she was wrong about heaven and everlasting life and all that, but probably not. And her faith kept her son coming back for more.

Belief usually started with believing in someone else's belief—true for politics, baseball and religion. Presbyterians, Methodists, Baptists, Catholics, Buddhists, Muslims of all kinds, Hindus, communists, socialists, fascists, Republicans or Democrats—they usually started by believing in someone, not some idea. Judge Z was a Cincinnati Reds fan because Johnny raised him that way.

Angelina had grown up Methodist and probably married Atticus because she knew that anyone raised by Beulah had to be pretty decent. Sort of the way horses are chosen at Keeneland—based on breeding first and looks second. Beulah and Johnny provided a sound lineage.

Atticus and Angelina tried to have children for fifteen years, then finally decided to just love each other as a husband and wife should, and be happy without children. It seemed to work. They were proof that a marriage could be happy without children.

ROOKIE REVEREND
November 2

The church was half full, as usual. As the opening hymns came to an end, the young preacher announced a new series on marriage.

Oh boy, thought Judge Z, *just what I need. Marriage advice from a kid. And I'm not even married anymore. Get me out of here.* But he had no choice but to listen as Pastor Billy Hughes dove in.

Rev. Billy was the latest in a long line of student pastors at Sadieville. He was in seminary at Asbury Theological Seminary nearby, appointed to Sadieville and their one hundred and forty members at the Methodist conference in June. On a good Sunday, only fifty people would be sitting in their seats, waiting on all the wisdom a young preacher could locate. If they were fortunate, the young pastor would repeat some good stuff he learned that week from a learned professor.

"You should first know how this series started," he told the sleepy-looking crowd.

"First, marriage is finally in the news, thanks to the same-sex marriage battle, but this is not about that. This is not about what marriage is 'not.'" He paused to make sure they understood.

"This also will not be about how to be a better husband or wife. Men, don't worry. This is not another version of a marriage weekend where you will be asked to look into the eyes of your spouse and tell her how much you love her." That brought soft chuckles of relief to several husbands.

"Instead, it will be about how marriage is keeping the human race alive. It's about why marriage is important. It's about how marriage is a 'divine conspiracy,' as John Eldredge has said in one of his books, to make us who we are supposed to be.

"We will see what the Bible says, starting with the Book of John, Chapter 2, which deals with a wedding in Cana of Galilee. Then John 3 covers Jesus declaring Himself to be the Bridegroom. John the Baptist was the best man at a wedding.

"John 4 is the woman at the well with five husbands. John 8 brings adultery into the conversation. John 14 gives us insight into Jewish marriage in Jesus' day. And then Jesus Himself is asked about divorce in Matthew 19. It is hard to discuss marriage without also talking about divorce.

"We end the New Testament study in Revelation 19, the wedding supper of the Lamb. And then we will back up to the Old Testament, and see how God's perfect plan has always been, from Genesis, for one man and one woman to be the foundation of this world. The family. God's best idea."

Okay, thought Judge Z, *I'll come back for more of this. You never know.*

ONE COURT, ONE FAMILY, ONE JUDGE

The new young preacher and his bride of six months, Susie, were invited for Sunday dinner at Beulah's country home: fried chicken, of course, with mashed potatoes and white gravy, green beans, and sweet tea.

Judge Z had skipped church most of the summer with golf and fishing trips, so this was a chance to get acquainted.

"Pastor, that was good this morning," said Beulah. "I'm glad you are staying away from the same-sex mess. I think the greatest tragedy is not that gay people want to get married, as much as I disagree with it. The real tragedy, seems to me, is that straight people don't get married anymore. Or at least that is what Atty says. "

Pastor Billy nodded agreement, then asked Judge Z what he did every day in family court. "What is that exactly? Sounds like an oxymoron to me," Billy said, holding hands with Susie.

Judge Z thought, *Look at that. Now there's something I don't see much. A couple in love.* It reminded him of Angelina, in the old days when hand-holding was their normal. And that made him think about how sometimes it was just ridiculous how much he was alone. Even now, with plenty of other people in the room, he felt alone.

"Billy, you are totally right," he said. "It is an oxymoron. The words don't really go together. 'Family' should be the most satisfying word in the English language."

Beulah jumped in, "Psalm 68:6 says 'God puts the lonely in families.'" Only Beulah would quote scripture to a pastor. But Billy liked it.

"I might have to use that one," he said. "Mankind's primary problem is being alone—and God's answer for loneliness was the family. Nice."

"But from what I see," said Judge Z, "we've messed up life so much that not only is family not the answer to the problem, family sometimes *is* the problem. In fact, the family is such a problem that we have to make special courts for it. Almost half of all the litigation in Lexington involves families. Sometimes I wonder if maybe God missed this one. Maybe the creation of man and woman, and all the mess that followed, wasn't such a good idea after all."

"That sounds like you handle a lot of divorces?" Billy asked.

"Sure. But there's more than just divorce. There are actually seven types of family court cases. The basic theory is one court, one judge, one family. Every family in the system keeps the same judge no matter what the case is. That way the judge is familiar with the issues, like a member of the dysfunctional family. Probably should be in their Christmas card.

"So first, we get the divorces. Men and women who stood before a judge or a priest and told them they would live together forever are now saying, 'No more.' Sometimes they're simple. Sometimes complicated. Young and old, rich and poor, children or not, all are eligible for a simple no-fault divorce in Kentucky.

"Second are the custody battles for people who are not married. In fact, marriage is virtually meaningless in family court. Unmarried people get all the same advantages and disadvantages. We've gone to great lengths to make sure unmarried couples with children have all the rights of married people. We don't want them to feel guilty or bad about anything."

Billy said, "What was I thinking to preach the next eight weeks on marriage?"

"Beats me," said the judge with a smile. "Third," he continued, "are the DNA cases, which have nothing to do with proving paternity—that's another story. DNA stands for Dependency, Neglect and Abuse—where children are removed from their parents. The state of Kentucky takes over. The children usually go into foster care or grandparents' homes. There are some horrific cases of abuse and neglect. Drugs or alcohol are involved about ninety percent of the time.

"Fourth, related to DNA cases, are the TPR cases: Termination of Parental Rights. When a DNA case goes bad and the parents can't get their act together, the legal rights of the biological parents are terminated, opening the way for adoption. It's the 'death penalty' of family court. It can take six to eighteen months. At the conclusion, we tell the parents, if they show up, that they are no longer the parents. The parents are either missing or weeping. They are often in jail.

"Fifth is the only happy part of family court—adoptions. A TPR is often followed a few months later by an adoption to give neglected and abused kids a happy home—or at least a better home. And hang on to your Bible, because about half the adoptions I do are adoptions by gay men and women."

Susie's eyes popped with shock and dismay.

He explained, "Gay couples can't conceive, so they are prime candidates to adopt. By definition, they are 'barren.' My choice is usually simple. The biological mom is on drugs, dad is in prison, and the only one stepping up is Sally the nice lesbian schoolteacher and her partner Molly. They usually take parenting quite seriously, or at least that's what they tell me."

Beulah shook her head. She had heard it all before, but still found it disturbing.

"Sixth is paternity court, where we determine who is the father, which is done these days by blood tests that can show that the possibility that Bobby is not the father is only one in seven hundred and twenty million. Then, collection of child support begins. Paternity Court is still confidential because girls used to be embarrassed to be pregnant and make the father pay. Now it is totally routine, without one ounce of shame. Embarrassment is a thing of the past.

"Finally, domestic violence court—often the courthouse version of the *Jerry Springer Show*. Again, two words that don't go together. Domestic. Nice word. Violence. Not nice. In the family. While some cases are quite serious, involving injury or even death, the saddest part is that a significant number of the women want their cases dismissed."

"Oh my. How do you do all that?" Susie asked.

Judge Z had to admit to himself that he wasn't doing it very well anymore. He was wearing thin. "Statistics show that family court judges last about seven years," he answered. "It's a little bit like soldiers in combat: Too much time on the battlefield causes PTSD. Constant family strife causes judges to lose their patience and sanity. I do it by compartmentalizing my life. I almost never take a case home."

Judge Z smiled at his mother and added: "And I come back here for Sunday dinner as often as I can."

It was true. Her chicken, her common sense and her wisdom kept him sane. And her prayers.

After ten years on the marriage battlefield, he was three years past his expiration date—definitely not the same man who eagerly took the job with a missionary's idealistic vision. At first he believed he would change the world. Now he settled for an occasional changed life.

Maybe, in a few cases, he had made a difference. But now it was all chaos and casualties.

"Reverend Billy, would you pray for us?" asked Beulah. He prayed his thanks for the chicken, but also for a judge who was feeling pretty fried himself.

Chapter 3

FOR RICHER, FOR POORER

*Two are better than one, because they have
a good return for their labor.*

— *Ecclesiastes 4:9*

THE FERNANDO FAMILY
November 3

Judge Z tried to schedule most of his divorce cases for Mondays. He had discovered that after a Sunday of rest with Beulah it was easier to dive into his week. He actually enjoyed what he called "real trials" that lasted a few hours, with "real" lawyers and "real" witnesses. He had been a trial lawyer working jury cases for fifteen years, and he missed the action.

There were no juries in family court. Judge Z was judge and jury.

Today's case featured one of his favorites: the Fernando family, divorced seven years ago but back again for the umpteenth time.

Generally speaking, poverty and family court go together. But even the rich and famous show up now and then. Augusto and Peggy Sue Fernando had been married in a spectacular wedding over three full days that cost a half-million dollars. She was a country girl with a downhome accent. She had a teaching degree but stayed home after the children came along. He was second-generation Venezuelan with a pipeline of oil money. The first rule they broke was the quaint custom of having the bride's family pick up the wedding tab. So a simple Baptist ceremony in Laurel County was followed by a private jet to Venezuela for a Catholic ceremony with a cast of thousands.

Judge Z smiled every time he thought of the Fernandos. He pictured "The most interesting man in the world" married to Ellie Mae Clampett.

The issue today was the mother's motion to let the children explain why they should not be ordered to visit their father. Both children said they wanted no part of him. Augusto Jr. was seventeen and played on his private school's tennis team. Lydia was fourteen, with a future in volleyball.

Augusto complained that his ex-wife had alienated the children from his affections. It was true. But she had done it with the truth, not lies. He was a womanizer, a gambler, a classic playboy. The court file contained pictures from a yacht in the Caribbean: Augusto with an arm around a well-known actor on one side and a porn star on the other. He held a bottle and a glassy-eyed, angry stare.

Maybe the kids had a point. But Judge Z hated talking to kids. For one, he didn't know what to say. And he dreaded listening to them tell a judge that they hated their dad. It was too sad. Peggy Sue pleaded, "They deserve to be heard."

Augusto pleaded, "I just want to see my kids."

Even bad dads have a right to see their kids, Judge Z told himself. And that led to a question that had no answer: Better to have a bad dad or no dad at all?

Augusto was not embarrassed. He just couldn't understand what was wrong with "partying" as long as the kids were not there. His dark eyebrows scrunched and his smooth tanned forehead was furrowed in disbelief. He loudly insisted he had spent $700,000 on attorneys' fees during the ten-year battle, as if that proved he cared more about his children than anything in the world. "If I didn't love my kids so much, why would I spend so much money on lawyers?"

The kids were tired of weekend visits going to the Super Bowl or the Final Four on a private jet. They were sick of their dad.

Judge Z had told Augusto, "All your kids want is for you to sit on the couch with them at night and watch a movie. They'd like to be normal." Augusto seemed to understand, but two weeks later he took them to ski in Vail—with his current girlfriend, who looked like she was barely out of high school.

Peggy Sue had hired a private investigator in the beginning, but now Augusto made it easy by putting pictures all over Facebook. His adventures were posted for the world to see. He was clueless why pictures of him with porn stars were a problem.

The case had been to the Court of Appeals and the Kentucky Supreme Court two or three times on various issues—custody, attorneys' fees. But the result was the same: the trial judge has great discretion. It's almost impossible to overturn a family court judge.

Judge Z decided to talk to the kids one last time. "Can you bring them in Friday, November 14 at 8 a.m.?" Peggy Sue was happy to do so.

PAPA WAS A ROLLING STONE
November 4

Tuesday morning was the usual steady stream of fathers who had not paid child support. It was Paternity Court, which was not always what the name implied. Before child support could be collected, the county had to first prove who was the daddy.

First up today was Anica Washington, twenty-one, a mother of three. Her "baby daddy" was Xavier Bradshaw, known as "X." The judge called the case first because he knew Anica had three crying babies in the hallway, plus the jail wanted X back in the slammer where he belonged. Crying babies got priority.

X was on the docket only because of his arrest for "failure to appear" and "failure to pay." They had found him at his favorite location, Anica's "crib"— an especially fitting name for an apartment that was crowded with babies and a baby daddy.

"X, where've you been? We've been looking for you," said the judge to the young man in an orange jumpsuit who was tugged forward by a deputy sheriff.

"I caught a charge, Judge."

"Really? I caught a cold last week but nobody arrested me."

Xavier smiled and chuckled, although he had no idea what the judge meant. He smiled a lot. Maybe it was the marijuana in his system. He was twenty-six and had thirteen kids with eight women, so the judge had seen him a lot. He might catch a lot of charges, but he would never catch up on child support. Never.

"X, did you ever think about getting married?"

X was speechless. He had never considered it. No one in his family had been married. Ever. There was no reason to think about it. He could not name one person in his life who was married.

So he just nodded and smiled when the judge went off on one of his speeches about marriage. He had no clue what the crazy man was saying.

Xavier was from the streets, down near Race Street and 3rd Street. The judge was an old country boy from Scott County. They barely spoke the same language.

Finally, the judge made his ruling, agreeing as he often did with the recommendation of the prosecutor, Brian Ackerman. All Xavier heard was "... thirty days in jail. You can purge out with two-hundred dollars, X. Your next date will be November 22, back in child support court."

Next up was Janet Guy, a typical young lady who got pregnant and became eligible for government benefits. Government benefits made it automatic that the system would file a paternity action to collect child support.

Janet knew the father was in jail. A drug addict, with six kids by five women. And married to one of them. She never planned to be anything other than a single mother, just like her own mother. She had been taught well that a single woman is perfectly capable of raising a child. After all, didn't it work well for her?

The old man in the black robe was just working for the system. So why cooperate?

But today, her latest "baby daddy," one Darius Barnhart, was brought out from the jail holdover. Brian, the prosecutor, had been a lawyer for the county in this court for thirty years. "Your Honor, the DNA test has been returned. It shows that Mr. Barnhart is probably the father. By probably, I mean 99.99999 percent. It is a one-in-one-billion chance that he is not the father."

"Mr. Barnhart, would you like to stipulate that you are indeed the father?"

"Sure, I knew he was mine all along."

"Okay, child support will be set at $207 per month."

"Judge, hey, that's a little outta my range, if you know what I mean."

"That actually is the amount established for everyone on minimum wage. It's about seven dollars per day. Do you think you could live on seven dollars per day?"

No comment.

In about a hundred cases like this one each day, the fathers lined up three hours before the judge's appearance to cut deals with the prosecutor. Brian knew all the tricks. Dads who showed up with no cash and no prospects got a hearing with the judge and often went to jail. Brian, whose age and slow drawl often made people underestimate his subtle wit, had become a hardened cynic.

The docket usually included a dozen or more men in green and orange jumpsuits, color coded, stashed in the jail holdover, picked up for failing to appear in court. Some knew the judge so well that they just called him "Judge Z" or "Zenas." Some even liked the judge, who gave them what they deserved, but also showed mercy if they had jobs. Brian and the judge were good cop and bad cop for ninety minutes each Tuesday.

On some days the sadness was overwhelming. When most or all of the men in orange jail jumpsuits were African-American, the judge would ask himself, *Where are all the black pastors? What happened in the African-American culture that led to this day, when nobody seems to be married, children are born to single moms and the fathers are not working, not educated, and often not caring? Where's Jesse Jackson? Where's Al Sharpton? Is this my fault? Am I a racist for even having these thoughts?*

Hopeless was the only word that came to mind.

Judge Z hated sending people to jail for failing to pay child support. "If anyone could solve the problem of putting people in jail for not paying child support, they should win the Nobel Peace Prize," Brian said during a break. And that was the prosecutor.

The judge agreed. "This makes no sense whatsoever. The county spends fifty dollars a day to put someone in jail. Thirty days adds up to fifteen-hundred dollars to squeeze out three-hundred dollars in unpaid support. No wonder the government is broke."

But they were just talking to air. There was no time to fix the world.

Tuesday was also Election Day. Judge Z stopped by the polls on the way home. The lifelong Republican had become an Independent when he became a judge, thinking that it made sense to be non-partisan. This year he would vote for himself. Judge Atticus Zenas was on the ballot for re-election to an eight-year term. He gave it no thought because he was unopposed. But that didn't mean he was doing a good job. It just meant that no sane lawyer wanted his job in family court.

The qualifications were simple. You must have been a lawyer for eight years to be a family court judge. And you had to be half crazy to take a job at half the money good lawyers make, with no raises from the tapped out state budget.

Judge Z had already planned his victory party. He would read reports from social workers for two hours and be in bed by 9 p.m. so he could be rested and ready for a wild Wednesday in DNA court with ninety-three cases on the docket.

NEGLECT AND ABUSE
November 5

The Dependency, Abuse and Neglect docket was every Wednesday morning at 9 a.m. Today's load would be almost a hundred cases, including seven new cases, with social workers firing the opening shots. Lawyers were appointed at the end of a five-minute hearing, where the judge approved taking the children away from whoever committed the abuse or neglect. The judge would spend four or five hours sorting through the mess of their lives. Almost always, it included drugs and alcohol.

First up was Althea, a heroin-addicted mother, twenty years old, with her third baby in her arms, born six days ago. Her second cousin appeared and the state had every intention of granting temporary custody to the cousin, who already had Althea's other two children.

Next was Patricia, who took heroin and pills during her pregnancy. She didn't show for court, but the baby's grandmother appeared. Grannie already had custody of four grandchildren and had no idea where her daughter was. Judge Z remembered her from last year because she actually had an eerie and striking resemblance to Beulah. The Judge asked the social worker, "Are we sure this lady that raised the missing drug addict mom is really okay to raise the grandkids?" The social workers all knew that was a common question from Judge Z.

Candace, next, was a young bleached-blonde mother of two on drugs. Prostitution charges were pending.

Then a single black dad, Anthony. His child was now at the grandmother's because the mother had disappeared—on drugs again. Anthony was just out of prison two months and insisted he and his girlfriend could take care of his four-year-old son. But the record showed that his girlfriend was on a list of "Most Wanted" in Kentucky, and he was five thousand dollars behind on child support.

Redhead Jennette was only eighteen and probably weighed ninety pounds. Two children, ages four and one. The report showed that she was heavily into drugs and prostitution. Judge Z had done the math and asked, "Are you telling me that you had a baby when you were fourteen?" She nodded. It was obvious that she had been abused. Her grandmother, who looked like a sweet little Sunday school teacher in a Baptist church, was there to take custody of the kids.

Cindy had just had a baby two weeks ago. She snorted pills during her pregnancy, but claimed she didn't do it for the past four months. "And who is the father? Have we found him?" Judge Z knew the research showed that fatherlessness is perhaps the number one current social issue. So even when it seemed hopeless, he had to ask. "Where's the father?"

The social worker said they had done an "absent parent search," a procedure to look for missing dads. They usually failed. The judge was getting numb to all the stories.

The initial hearings were over in about an hour and the docket moved on to Pre-Trials and Dispositions and Reviews.

Lowlights included Scott Kendall and his girlfriend, Sherry. She had filed her tenth domestic violence petition against him last week. Scott had allegedly poured Clorox down the throat of the woman of his dreams. And now her three kids—not his—would be going to foster care because she had taken him back into her home. He was out of jail on bond and back in her bed.

That was followed by another shocker, even for Judge Z. He would never forget the Darlin children. A little girl, age three, had been sold for drugs and abused repeatedly. She was one of eight children in two combined families.

The two fathers were first cousins who looked like brothers. The mothers looked sixty years old but were actually in their mid-thirties. Meth addicts.

Pictures of the three-year-old were horrendous. She had been sold to sexual predators and beaten when she cried about it. Judge Z thought, *I may believe in the death penalty after all.*

Both sets of parents would spend decades in prison if there was any justice at all. He signed an order that they would never again see their children. Ever. Drugs had ruined another family.

Hippie mom Tulip was back for a pre-trial. She was allowed initially to keep her three children despite the report that they had been living in a parked car. Tulip looked like Janis Joplin and seemed reasonable at first, so the social workers let her keep the children: Earth, twelve; Rain, ten; and Fire, eight. Fathers unknown. None of them had bathed in months.

But a drug test showed that Tulip tested positive for cocaine and marijuana. She had a long story. Something about eating a cupcake. That was a new one. Creative.

Judge Z put the children in foster care. At least they would get a bath, hot meals and a safe place to sleep. They would be back in six weeks.

The rest of the cases included "Baby Boy Roe," who had been abandoned at a hospital, and a couple caught selling drugs with three small children in the house. The children and the abandoned baby were remanded to foster care. On and on it went.

The day finally ended at 5:40 p.m., with a motion from DeJuan Wilder hoping to get custody of his daughter. He'd just gotten out of prison, but since the mother was on drugs and the child was in foster care, he appeared to be a decent alternative—until more facts came out. Judge Z decided to drug test him, and when he was asked who he lived with, he pointed out his girlfriend in the courtroom. She would need to be drug tested. The girlfriend got so loud and angry that the judge booted her out of court. On the way out, she called the judge a racist in a profanity-laced parting shot. Judge Z thought that was odd, since she was as white as he was, but he brought her back into court and asked her if she would rather apologize or go to jail. She reluctantly mumbled "I'm sorry" and the overcrowded jail was spared one more big mouth to feed. Just another day in family court.

Katy Beth, a middle class nineteen-year-old intern from Asbury University, watched the whole thing. It was her first day. She was in shock. "Was that a normal day?" she asked.

"Normal is hard to define around here, but for me, yes," Judge Z smiled.

"I expected to see lots of married people getting divorced."

"Oh, that's another day. You'll see that soon enough. But on Wednesdays, no one is married. Marriage died about two generations ago." He was exaggerating. But not much.

NO CHANCE
November 6

Status Court was for juvenile, non-criminal cases: runaways, skipping school and "beyond the control" of their parents or school. Judge Z hated Status Court.

Kids in court. Kids going to jail. They softened the language by calling it "juvenile detention." But it still had bars and the kids had to wear shackles on their legs. It was a necessary wake-up call for many kids. But it was always sad.

Naqueen Busby, seventeen, was back in court to dismiss everything. But that did not mean all was well. At one time, Judge Z almost considered Naqueen as his "buddy." At age thirteen, he had appeared before the judge for the first time. He was a routine runaway and "beyond control" of his mom. So Judge Z sent him away to a home for kids in trouble. It seemed to help.

But now his Status case was being dismissed because he was sitting in jail waiting on a jury to decide if he was a murderer. He would be tried as an adult. The prosecutors wanted to send him to prison for life.

"Naqueen, nice to see you again. It's been a while. You know the routine. What's your date of birth?"

"May ninth," he replied. He actually smiled. He had always liked this judge, who took his side when it came to conflict with his mom. In fact, Naqueen well recalled the day that Judge Z said in frustration, "I'd run away too if you were my mom. How can you complain about him smoking dope when you smoke every day? How can you complain about this kid doing anything when you and your boyfriend stay high and scream and yell all day long?"

But now Naqueen was out of chances. Judge Z spoke to him as if he was a grandson. It might be their last meeting ever. "Today, Naqueen, I am speechless. I honestly hope you didn't do what they said you did. Either way, your life is not over." But both of them knew it probably was. The sound of shackles on his legs was all the judge heard as Naqueen was ushered back into custody.

Naqueen was a textbook case for Trauma Based Therapy, the latest approach among counselors and social workers. Instead of starting with, "What's wrong with you?" it started with a better question: "What happened to you?"

Something usually happens to make people wreck their lives. In Naqueen's case, it was no dad and a mom who was awful by any definition.

Judge Z kept a copy of the Adverse Childhood Experiences, or ACE, test on his desk. The rougher the childhood, the higher the score and the higher the risk for drug use and bad health as an adult. Naqueen would not do well on this test:

1. Did a parent or other adult in the household often or very often swear at you, insult you, put you down, or humiliate you, or act in a way that made you afraid that you might be physically hurt?

2. Did a parent or other adult in the household often or very often push, grab, slap, or throw something at you, or ever hit you so hard that you had marks or were injured?

3. Did an adult or person at least five years older than you ever touch or fondle you or have you touch their body in a sexual way? Or attempt or actually have oral, anal, or vaginal intercourse with you?

4. Did you often or very often feel that no one in your family loved you or thought you were important or special? Or that your family didn't look out for each other, feel close to each other, or support each other?

5. Did you often or very often feel that you didn't have enough to eat, had to wear dirty clothes, and had no one to protect you? Or your parents were too drunk or high to take care of you or take you to the doctor if you needed it?

6. Were your parents ever separated or divorced?

7. Was your mother or stepmother often or very often pushed, grabbed, slapped, or had something thrown at her? Or sometimes, often, or very often kicked, bitten, hit with a fist, or hit with something hard? Ever repeatedly hit or threatened with a gun or knife?

8. Did you live with anyone who was a problem drinker or alcoholic or who used street drugs?

9. Was a household member depressed or mentally ill, or did a household member attempt suicide?

10. Did a household member go to prison?

The score was a total of the "yes" answers. Naqueen, waiting on murder charges at age seventeen, was a perfect ten.

Judge Z's own score was zero.

Most drug addicts scored from six to nine. But even a simple divorce put a one on the board. And if the family didn't make you feel important or didn't support each other, now it's a two. If mom was depressed, if dad was drunk and couldn't get you to school—it all added up pretty quick.

Absent father. Messed up mom. Naqueen never had a chance.

OXYMORON

Domestic Violence Court. Another classic oxymoron.

"Domestic" sounds like a cozy home. Mother in the kitchen. Father mowing the lawn. Tranquility. A little boy in the sandbox. A little girl playing with her puppy.

Then "violence." Somebody hit somebody. Someone is hurt. Blood. Weapons. Guns. Knives. Assault. Even murder.

It was one of the most common problems in the world. People hit the people they claim to love. Men, especially, for a myriad of reasons, hit women. They are bigger and stronger and feel the need to use their strength to impose their will—often aggravated by alcohol and drugs. The problem was so common it required a special court.

It wasn't just for husbands and wives, or boyfriends hitting girlfriends. It included brother versus brother, sister versus sister, mother versus daughter and father versus son. Gay couples were not a legal family in Kentucky—except in Domestic Violence Court.

The Kentucky domestic violence statute also covered unmarried couples living together. But it had to be a romantic relationship, meaning a hearing must sometimes be held to determine if the couple has had intercourse. Dating was not covered. Sex without living together did not count. Living together without sex did not count. It was complicated.

The parties must be married, formerly married, have children together, or live together "romantically." And now lawmakers were talking about adding "dating" to the group entitled to protection. But how would dating be defined?

Judge Z loved to ask people about that. No one could really say. The proposed definition included "a reasonable expectation of affection." What? It was implied, but not stated, that sexual contact must be involved. The idea that people could date without having sex was apparently unthinkable now.

First up was Tonya McDonald, asking for "no contact" with her latest boyfriend, Jerry Turner. This was her fifth petition against five different men who had fathered her babies. The petition, handwritten at the domestic violence office in atrocious spelling and painful grammar, said: "This Saturday he threaten me, he pull a knife, say I always going to be with him wherever I go he find me. He beat me. He took my stuff clothes dog etc., the police has stop him meny times. They told me to get a epo they even told him to stay away. I am scared of him. He drink and he hit me. I am in proses of put my life together an don't need the man. Thanks you. Tonya McDonald."

But in court, she had changed her mind, and no longer wanted an emergency protection order—an "epo."

"I exaggerated," she said. "Jerry would never hurt me."

"Tonya, is your petition true?"

"Yes, but he didn't mean it. Yes, he did pull a knife, but that had never happened before."

Judge Z warned her that dismissing the case could cause her to lose her kids, so she agreed to talk to Patti Coldiron from the prosecutor's office. After a brief whispered conference with Patti, she came back asking for a "no violent contact" order, which meant he could move back in but was prohibited from making threats or acting violently. Jerry quickly agreed. He appeared to be high and would have agreed to anything.

He was ordered to get a domestic violence assessment and follow through on the recommendations. But when he sobered up, he would likely be so mad he would not cooperate and probably would not be allowed to see his baby at all.

The Cranfords were back. Both parties were Fayette County police officers. They had an affair that lasted just long enough to divorce their previous spouses, have a baby boy to fight about, get married, and start all over again in divorce court. The Domestic Violence Order meant he could not carry or own a gun—which was quite a problem for a cop. Today was a motion to get his guns back. He argued that the DVO was ruining his career. He not only lost his motion, he had to endure one of the judge's speeches: "Sir, you are actually one of the scariest men I have ever met. I don't feel bad at all about you losing your job. Have a nice day," which meant the hearing was over. Judge Z could smell the creeps, even when they wore suits and ties.

Judge Z's domestic violence day ended with the Napier twins, Ned and Wilbur. Ned's petition said Wilbur threatened to kill him in a text message and a voice mail. It was a dispute about the trailer their mother left them in her will.

"Mr. Napier, I see that you and Wilbur are brothers?" It was obvious, since they were identical twins, about age forty, working class men who likely would not be able to tell you who the Kentucky governor was but would know opening day of deer season to the minute.

"Used to be," said Ned, staring a hole through his twin.

"What are you asking this court to do? Sign a No Contact Order?"

They both agreed enthusiastically.

"OK, then we can keep this simple. A no-contact order will be entered, effective for three years."

That was fine until Wilbur discovered it meant he could not possess or own a gun. He got so irate he had to be removed from the courtroom by Deputy Palmer. Wilbur was big, but Palmer was bigger. The scuffle was over before it started. Wilbur was told to stay put so Ned would have time to vacate the building.

As Palmer returned, straightening his tie and belt, Judge Z gave him a nod of gratitude. He loved Deputy Palmer.

J.J.'S WORLD
November 7

Another Friday round of motions, and another week of dysfunction and divorce, American style. Jackie Finley and Ben Keegan were back again.

Time-sharing battles had raged over five-year-old Emily since she was an infant. The mother was concerned about dad having adult conversations with the daughter, and rightly so. However, as the judge explained, the dad wouldn't need to have such conversations if the mom had not introduced the little girl to her live-in girlfriend.

So now Emily had two mommies, plus a daddy on the margins some-where with multiple girlfriends and drug problems. Plus a judge to help her parents resolve all their dysfunctional arguments.

Then "Dr. T." was back. The judge could not pronounce or spell his long African name. His first wife from Zambia, Veronique, was in court to ask for an increase in child support for the one daughter of the marriage, twelve-year-old Vanna. But what Veronique really wanted was an opportunity to stand up in front of fifty people and tell everyone what a lousy father and husband he was. Again.

She had done this many times and couldn't wait to replay the part where she shamed her husband and told everyone he had beaten her, cussed her and been unfaithful to her. In Africa, she would have been thrown out with the trash. The father would have "won" the case, gathered his children into his new home, and the mother would get nothing but misery.

But this was the USA. Women had the upper hand in custody cases, and Veronique loved it. She got her child-support increase by proving that Dr. T. had not been forthcoming about all of his income. Judge Z raised it from the minimum $207 monthly to $467.

When Judge Z took a lunch recess and got back to his office, Karen said, "Judge, J.J. called. Wants to know if he can come in to see you later." Jeremiah Jackson, or J.J., only called when he needed money or a favor now.

J.J. was nineteen, and had been mentored by the judge since he was fourteen through the Amachi program for kids whose fathers are in prison. His father was long gone, and his mother was a drug addict. He was raised by a friend of his mother who took him in as a baby.

The judge and J.J. both liked baseball. Common ground between a white middle-aged judge and an eighth-grade kid from the streets was hard to find. So Judge Z had taken him to a Reds-Braves game in Cincinnati. J.J.'s grandpa, now deceased, had taught him two things. One, to hate cops for no good reason and two, to be a Braves fan because of Henry Aaron. It was his first trip out of Fayette County ever.

J.J. thought smoking marijuana was normal. It was what everyone did in his world.

They usually met weekly for dinner at a fast-food joint. J.J. had failed the tenth grade twice, called in a bomb scare to Lafayette High School, got caught, and was charged with a felony by age seventeen. Soon after, his girl-friend got pregnant.

Looking at the results of his mentoring, Judge Z reflected that maybe God knew what He was doing when he decided not to give him any kids of his own.

When J.J. turned eighteen, the judge took him out to dinner and told him, "From now on, our conversations are man to man." They parted with a firm handshake that the judge had taught him. He had smiled a smile of happiness at being free and eighteen.

Taking the phone message from Karen, he went to his office and called J.J.

"Hey, buddy, I'm done today at 2 p.m. How about Bob Evans at three for a late lunch?"

"OK, but can you pick me up? I don't have a license or a ride now."

J.J. was still living with the same girlfriend who had kicked him out a couple of times.

As J.J. got in the car, the judge asked, "How's life working out, J.J.?"

The long answer could be summed up in two words: Not well. By the time they finished lunch and headed back to drop him off, J.J. had told it all: He was two-thousand dollars behind on child support, and he'd just lost his job at McDonald's. His baby mama, Kalie, wanted him in jail for unpaid child support. He never got to see his son. On top of that, a letter that week had informed him that he was the father of another baby in Mississippi, and his Lexington girlfriend was threatening to throw him out, again.

And now the brother of a young man killed two weeks ago was looking for him. "I had nothing to do with it, Z, honest," he said. J.J. loved that he could call the judge just "Z." They were friends.

"J.J., any one of the things you mentioned would keep me awake at night."

He bowed his head and was quiet. When he finally looked up, wiping a tear, he mumbled, "Z, I need help." That usually meant, "I need money."

"All I have is time. No money. Why don't we start meeting together again on Saturdays to talk and work through it all?"

J.J. nodded yes, mumbled his thanks, hugged the judge awkwardly, and off he went, back to the streets.

Chapter 4

HE SAID, SHE SAID

On the third day there was a wedding in Cana of Galilee.

— *JOHN 2:1*

FAMILY LAW 301
November 8

It was the first day of Professor Brad Bertram's advanced seminar, Family Law 301, entitled, "Marriage: What is It?" Three hours a week for five weeks. Fifteen class hours to know everything about marriage. Pass/Fail. One credit hour. The final would be a simple paper written at the end of the semester.

It was a miracle the UK Law School granted permission to include it in the curriculum. But Professor Bertram's class was partially in response to all the same-sex marriage cases in the news. Marriage was being legally re-defined, so why shouldn't law schools at least discuss it?

The problem that upset the UK Law School faculty was that Professor Bertram was known to harbor conservative sympathies, though he generally kept his opinion out of the classroom. And the notion that marriage could be studied also made them uneasy. After all, wasn't marriage just an infinitely malleable social construct, to be defined by each person or couple according to their individual lifestyle preferences?

Prof. Bertram announced, "This class is a seminar on the subject of marriage. There will be a fair amount of reading, so if you three-Ls are hoping to skate through without cracking a book, I would advise dropping this class. This is pass-fail, but still, I expect you to participate and read."

He went through the syllabus, explained the assignments and took questions about the required student presentations. The reading list was impressive: at least twenty cases covering two hundred years. Eight books would be offered to read. The students would be required to pick three of them to make a report.

Judge Z was there, invited to answer any questions that came up about how things really work in family court. He was more than a little excited to hang out with kids. He took a seat near the back of the small room, drawing a few glances from students who wondered about the "old guy."

Noticing the looks, Judge Z's friend Brad introduced him.

"Judge Atticus Zenas is here as a resource. Feel free to ask him anything. He has been a family court judge for ten years. He graduated from this school in 1986 and probably had classes in this classroom. He has likely forgotten more family law than I ever knew. He will be here as often as he can."

All twelve students turned around and stared, wondering silently if maybe they could get a clerking job with him next year. The job market was pretty thin.

"OK, so what is marriage?" Professor Bertram continued as the students shifted their attention back to the front of the room. "This is obviously the heated question of the day. We will examine the statutes and the current case law. But we will also go back into history and sample some sociology and philosophy.

"I have index cards here. In fifty words or less, I want your first-impression answers to define marriage. You will have two minutes. Answers can be anonymous."

As they filled out the cards, Judge Z examined the names and profanities carved into the wooden desktop, wondering if it could be the same one he slept on through most of a lecture in Property Law. On his own card, he wrote: "Marriage is your last chance to grow up. Marriage lets you know who you really are."

He felt like it should be more profound, but he had no better answer.

Professor Bertram collected the cards, shuffled them, laid them on his desk for later, and turned to the class. "Now tell me what you are thinking."

First to answer was Jason Farmer, seated by himself in the front row. Judge Z figured him for the kind of student who finished his term paper a week early. He didn't just raise a finger, his whole arm shot up like a precocious child in grade school. Judge Z smiled as the professor nodded to Jason.

"Marriage is just really a contract to love for as long as you can stand it. It involves inheritance of property to their children, but beyond that, I am not sure it's a legal issue at all. More like an informal contract between two people."

"Good. Who else? Don't be afraid. There are no wrong answers. Yet."

Sally Jennings jumped in. The redhead who never made anything less than an A said, "The word 'union' comes to mind. It has something to do with two persons making an agreement to be one entity for all legal purposes. It is supposed to be the foundation for children."

Chloe Hampton, in owlish glasses and a red bandana over severely short hair, declared her certainty that marriage was a relic of the male-authoritarian past, instituted to suppress women and treat them as property.

"Is anyone married?" Prof. Bertram asked. One hand went up, shyly. It was Nicole Mason, a mom in her thirties. Her husband was a teacher, coach and pastor at one of Lexington's biggest inner-city churches, and her father had been one of the first black judges in Virginia. She had two kids. "So what does marriage mean to you, Mrs. Mason?"

"When I got married, I thought of it more as a religious idea than a legal process," she said. "In our pre-marriage counseling, we learned that it's a covenant, but I don't know how that compares to a regular legal contract. I know that 'Till death do us part' is still in the wedding ceremony, symbolizing the union of two people in a pact of lifelong affection, loyalty, and protection."

Judge Z thought, *Wow. I need to hire her when she graduates.*

Michael Burch was openly gay. He couldn't resist quoting President Obama's tweet: "Luv is luv."

"Sure, that's a popular view. It's all about love," said Brad.

"Based on what I think I know today," said Jeff Faulkner, "it means nothing now. It really seems irrelevant. I know almost no one who is married. I honestly don't know why gay people even want to marry. I mean, seriously, I have been with my girlfriend for four years. We have never even had a conversation about it."

"So why are you taking this class?" Brad asked.

"I am almost done with this place. I needed an hour."

Everyone smiled including Professor Bertram. "I can see from your puzzled looks that it is not as simple as you thought." He leaned back against the edge of his desk. "Let's start with some history. Ms. Hampton is right about one thing: Marriage dates back to pre-historical times, before the appearance of any major religions. We'll get to the definition question later, but primitive marriage can be described as a stable relationship between a man and a woman that generally involved childbearing.

"Obviously, for any community to continue it needs to have offspring. Remember, there was no effective birth control. Children were born as a fact of nature. And once they reached a certain age, children were a crucial source of labor. We have to keep in mind how different other times and places could be. The idea of the normal family as a father who goes off to work and a mother who stays home with the kids is very modern, and relatively unusual in history. Women have always worked.

"There's no question that marriage has changed dramatically. What we know as modern marriage is different in several respects.

"First, people usually marry now out of romantic motivations. In the past, marriage was for economic and social reasons. 'Love,'" said the professor with air quotes, "only entered the picture over the last hundred and fifty years. It was virtually irrelevant in most of history.

"Second, marriage was the primary means of property acquisition. Property mainly came from inheritance after the death of parents, and in the traditional marriage dowry. Families arranged marriages primarily to consolidate properties. Questions?"

A few hands went up, starting a conversation that was mostly personal opinions. Finally, Brad said, "Okay. Now we know how little we know. So read the assignments for next week. Come ready to discuss all the statutory definitions of marriage."

Judge Z realized he had a lot to learn, too.

CANA OF GALILEE
November 9

Beulah sat in her usual pew on Sunday morning—fourth row, right side, next to her son, Judge Z. Reverend Hughes was going to share everything he knew about marriage. Judge Z didn't think it would take long, given that the kid hadn't been married long enough to miss an anniversary.

They stood to sing "The Love of God" and "Love Lifted Me." Pastor Billy motioned for all to be seated. "Turn to John, second chapter, verses two through eleven," he said. After a pause filled with the sound of rustling pages, he began reading:

On the third day a wedding took place at Cana in Galilee. Jesus' mother was there, and Jesus and his disciples had also been invited to the wedding.

When the wine was gone, Jesus's mother said to him, "They have no more wine."

"Woman, why do you involve me?" Jesus replied. "My hour has not yet come."

His mother said to the servants, "Do whatever he tells you."

Nearby stood six stone water jars, the kind used by the Jews for ceremonial washing, each holding from twenty to thirty gallons.

Jesus said to the servants, "Fill the jars with water"; so they filled them to the brim. Then he told them, "Now draw some out and take it to the master of the banquet."

They did so, and the master of the banquet tasted the water that had been turned into wine. He did not realize where it had come from, though the servants who had drawn the water knew. Then he called the bridegroom aside and said, "Everyone brings out the choice wine first and then the cheaper wine after the guests have had too much to drink; but you have saved the best till now."

What Jesus did here in Cana of Galilee was the first of the signs through which he revealed his glory; and his disciples believed in him.

Rev. Hughes paused as he closed his Bible, then said, "Jesus turned water into wine at a wedding feast in Cana of Galilee. This story is only told by the apostle John. Matthew, Mark and Luke were either unaware of the story or unimpressed. But John thought this story was important enough to be the second chapter of perhaps the most important book ever written.

"Why would Jesus pick such a meaningless act for his first miracle? Why not heal someone or raise someone from the dead? His opening act was to turn water into wine? That's it? Our wine drinking Episcopalian friends find this to be quite a cool miracle, but it's usually ignored in Baptist Sunday school classes. Even some Methodists skip through John 2 rather quickly."

Judge Z smiled. He was not a teetotaler. But ten years in family court and seeing the effects of alcohol and drugs had made him appreciate the ones he knew.

"Some preachers will make this all about a mother's power over her son."

Judge Z raised his eyebrows and tuned in. His mother had incredible power over him.

"Mary said, 'Jesus, go do it,' and rather than argue with his mother, he simply did it. Some scholars are convinced that Jesus had no plan to make this his first miracle. He was simply attending a wedding. People he knew would be there. Some of his own disciples had agreed to attend.

"But then his mother stepped in. She called him out. And Jesus responded."

Judge Z thought of Beulah, and all the times he simply did what she said. If he tried to say no, his father Johnny let him know that "no" was not an option. There were orders. And then there were Orders From Mom.

That led him to think about all the times he attended weddings only because his wife, Angelina, pressured him into going. He had not been to a wedding since his wife died.

Rev. Billy continued, "Maybe a mother's love and her son's obedience will be a sermon for another day. But today I'd like to make a less obvious connection. This miracle is not about turning water to wine as much as it's about when and where it happened.

"At a wedding.

"Why a wedding?

"Is it possible that God himself was saying that weddings are more important than we think?"

Judge Z thought about how he avoided weddings. They always made him cry. Eight years ago, as he wiped away tears during the wedding march for two kids he barely knew, he had vowed that he would never attend another wedding. Why did he cry at weddings?

Besides, most weddings are on Saturday afternoons, usually in the summer. What a waste of a perfectly good golf day, or fishing trip, or nap. He would open the invitation and say out loud to the dog, "Who is crazy enough to plan a wedding on the Saturday of the U.S. Open?" His law partner had once invited him to attend his son's wedding on the first Saturday of April, when anyone with half a brain knew the Final Four would be on TV and the Kentucky Wildcats would be there. The weekend of the Masters Golf Tournament was no better.

Rev. Billy was summarizing his three main points, most of which Judge Z had missed by daydreaming.

"Jesus seemed genuinely interested in making sure that the wedding celebration was a true feast. Jesus wants us to have good parties."

What? God wants good parties? I should have listened better on that one, Judge Z thought.

"And finally, this story is just a prelude to the day when this same Jesus would be telling us that he was the Bridegroom with a capital 'B.' This term 'bridegroom' meant something. Something important that we will ponder in the Sundays ahead.

"God's story starts with a wedding in the Garden of Eden and ends with a wedding in Revelation. God's ultimate invitation is not to obey Him, or follow Him, or serve Him. His loving invitation is simple: He asks, 'Will you marry me?'

"God is more than a King or Judge demanding obedience. He is Love, and He wants to marry you. That's why marriage on this earth may be more important than you think it is."

Judge Z was surprised. He said to himself, *You'd think that a family court judge who has gone to church his whole life would have heard all this. You'd think Beulah's son would have heard this.*

In fact, Beulah had said it before. But her son had no ears to hear. Until now. He was listening again.

BEULAH'S PROVERBS

"So, whatcha think of our new little preacher?" Beulah asked on the way home. The word "little" was thrown in a lot in rural Kentucky. Billy Hughes was not little. He was over six feet and two hundred pounds.

"I like him. He's better than the last guy who was a Louisville fan. He seems way better than your average seminary kid. I liked his sermon today. He got me thinking some. He said Jesus turned water into wine mainly because his mother told him to."

They looked at each other and smiled. They both knew that the judge might be in charge in his courtroom, but not in Beulah's house.

Judge Z offered, "In fact, it reminds me of a test the social workers use, showing adverse consequences for kids growing up." He explained the ACE test. He told her about Naqueen. But he also told her that the research shows that a mom who hugs and cares overcomes it all. "Motherhood matters. Even children with high scores on the ACE test thrive when they have a mother figure who really gives everything for the child. Almost every day I find myself saying out loud, 'Thank the Lord for Beulah.'"

After Sunday dinner, Beulah asked, "Anything changing at the court-house or is it the same old same old?"

"Nothing, really. The only thing changing is me. I've about had it. No one makes a commitment anymore to anything except their own selfish interests. Marriage is gone."

"Maybe our way is gone. Once upon a time, there was an order to life."

Judge Z had heard this before. Beulah was seventy-nine and starting to repeat herself, which was not all bad.

"A boy and a girl would see each other. They would like each other. At some point there would be handholding, and maybe a kiss, but only at the right place and the right time. And eventually, if it was true love, he would ask her to marry him. She would become his fiancée. The word meant there was a plan to get married. There was something to look forward to. The wedding night meant something. They waited. And it was worth the wait."

Even at fifty, he got uncomfortable hearing his mother talk about the wedding night.

"And so the wedding day was a glorious day with great meaning. It was the beginning of the possibility of children. Not a day sooner. Marriage always included the possibility of children. Marriage itself was sacred."

"I don't hear that word much anymore: 'sacred.' It is not a word we use in court. I know the Catholics call it a sacrament," Judge Z said.

"Well," said Beulah, "they seem to get it right on family more often than us Methodists. For sure, marriage has to do with children. And even if life got complicated and led to divorce, at least there were boundaries."

"Yeah, that's true. There are no boundaries anymore. It's obvious to anyone who spends a day in court. There are no rules about marriage that make any sense. No rules about when or how to have children. No rules about who to have sex with. Same-sex, no problem. Multiple partners, no problem. Creepy boyfriends, no problem. And of course, no job, no problem, either.

"But I have to live with this every day. Let's turn on the football game."

FAILURE TO COMMUNICATE
November 10

Zhiu v. Yang was an uncontested divorce. Ten minutes, maybe even five. The husband had filed. The wife had been served but never responded. Neither had a lawyer. Their law firm was Web, Google & FreeLegalAdviceDotCom. Judge Z enjoyed people who didn't hire lawyers, and he liked to help them finesse procedural problems.

As they sat in the judge's chambers, Karen started the videotape and announced, "We're on the record." The parties were nervous. But the judge had done this a thousand times. He wanted to make it quick.

"Nice to meet you both. I have briefly thumbed through the record and all seems in order. So, this shouldn't take long. Both of you raise your right hand." They obeyed, but only after the wife gave her husband a look of nervous disbelief.

"Do you swear to tell the truth, the whole truth, and nothing but the truth, so help you God?"

"Yes," they agreed.

The judge asked, "Can you speak English?" The wife nodded yes, but Judge Z knew he was stretching the law to take her word for it. She might speak English well enough to answer the phone and order lunch, but would she understand what was happening as her Chinese marriage was dissolved in a Kentucky courthouse?

"Sir, you are the petitioner so I will ask you some questions first. Your name is?"

His answer was impossible to understand, but the judge kept moving. Lots of cases today. "And your wife is?"

The judge tried to repeat it phonetically, butchering the Mandarin: "Duck Chow Yang?"

"Yes," said the husband, who dared not correct the ignorant judge. In China, being impertinent to a government official could land him in solitary confinement for twenty years.

The wife nodded, with one eye on her husband, following his cues. She was not just nervous, she was lost. The husband gave her a sharp look and she dropped her head to stare at the table. He would answer the judge's questions.

"And where is your marriage registered?"

"Shanghai, China."

"Is either party in the active military service?" Neither party was even a US citizen. Mr. Zhiu shook his head nervously, hoping this was not some American trick to get him into the army.

"Is the wife pregnant?"

"No."

"Are there any children of this marriage?"

"Yes. One daughter. We call her Meggie."

"Age?"

"Two."

"Do you all have a property settlement agreement that resolves all issues?"

"Yes," the husband answered.

"Is that your signature on the document, and do you recognize your wife's signature?"

"Yes."

"Ma'am, is this your signature on the papers?"

She looked and answered softly, "Yes."

Judge Z almost stopped and asked her to read it aloud, but he did not want to embarrass her. She probably wanted out of this marriage too. "Have either of you changed your mind since signing this?"

"No," they agreed.

Something about her was making the judge uneasy. But he moved on.

"Is it fair to both of you?"

"Yes," they said.

He asked the mandatory questions about domestic violence orders, and both agreed that was not their problem. They were almost finished.

"Ma'am, are the answers he has given so far accurate?"

"Yes."

"OK, sir, is your marriage irretrievably broken?"

"Yes."

"Is there any reasonable prospect for reconciliation?"

"No."

The judge turned to the wife and saw that she was upset. She had started weeping quietly. *Oh great*, he thought. *It's the Hemlocks on replay.* He paused and handed her a tissue from the box he kept handy.

After she wiped her eyes and took a deep breath, he asked, "Ma'am, do you agree?"

She was quiet. She looked at the judge with pleading eyes, and then at her husband. The silence stretched.

He asked again, "Ma'am, do you agree that your marriage is irretrievably broken and there is no reasonable prospect for reconciliation?"

She looked down at the table and said nothing. The silence filled the room. The husband gave his wife an angry look, but she would not look at him or the judge.

"Let's take a break," the judge said. Karen paused the tape. He sat back, conscious now that he had been leaning over the table to draw out her answer. His shoulders felt knotted. A tear fell from the woman's face to the legal papers in front of her, making a tiny splash.

He caught Karen's eye and made a little circle with his finger, like stirring a drink, and she started the tape again. "Back on the record," she announced. The wife looked up like a startled deer.

"Ma'am, do you understand the question?" he asked, gently.

"Not really. Can I ask question?" she almost whispered in broken English, looking down again. The slow drip became a light rain of tears. Her shoulders trembled. "What means ir-trievably broken?"

Judge Z was stopped in his tracks.

"Okay," he began, stumbling ahead into mostly unexplored legal territory. He grabbed a handful of legal jargon for support, talking now for the record. "It is obvious that the respondent is upset. The court is making a finding that an interpreter will be necessary to complete this case and be sure the respondent understands the ramifications of her appearance today and her answers under oath. And since the parties have a child, age two, this court will appoint a guardian ad litem to represent the interests of the child. I want the guardian to make a report and meet with the respondent, with an interpreter. If all is in order, the matter will be concluded in sixty days."

He turned to the surprised husband. "Sir, this is not unusual. It takes some time. It's not as simple as you may have thought." That was a fib. It was always very simple.

The husband politely put his papers into a small file, bowed, and told the judge he would be back at the appointed time.

Judge Z remembered the Hemlocks from a few days ago. Irretrievably broken. What did that mean in plain English? He was starting to wonder. He had divorced three thousand couples by now. Were they all irretrievably broken? With no reasonable prospect of being reconciled? He wasn't so sure.

Judge Z felt like the executioner at a death camp, pulling the plug on marriages that might be saved.

IVORY
November 13

Judge Z was excited to see Ivory Smith back on the docket in juvenile Status Court on Thursday morning. Her case would be dismissed today since she was now eighteen. An adult.

She'd been a regular in Judge Z's courtroom since she was thirteen. Today she was holding her one-year-old, Jeremiah, a fat and happy looking boy. Ivory had been in lots of trouble—runaway, drugs, and plenty more the judge never heard about. But now she was back with her grandmother and things seemed to be going better. Her clothes were neat, clean and carefully pressed. She was smiling.

In his mind, Judge Z had almost adopted Ivory as his own daughter. He thought back to the case two years ago when Ivory was barely sixteen. Her appearance that day had been a routine review for another rebellious teenager living with her grandmother.

Her young appointed lawyer, from the legal clinic, in agreement with her social worker, had asked for a continuance to work on "some issues."

"We'll see you in two weeks," said the judge, calling the next case. Then Karen had approached the bench and Ivory's case went sideways.

"Judge, would you like me to tell you what I heard in the hallway about Ivory?"

"Sure."

"She's pregnant, apparently. The social worker told her, and I quote, 'You've heard Judge Z before. He's religious, and he won't like you getting an abortion. We will ask for a continuance and help you make an appointment for the abortion, and by the time you get back to court it will all be done.'"

Judge Z stared at Karen. He dropped his reading glasses that were on a string around his neck and scanned the courtroom. "You've got to be kidding me. Are you serious? Remind me. How old is she?"

"She's sixteen. And yes, I am totally serious."

"And who was in on this? Her lawyer?"

Karen nodded.

"Okay. Call 'em back in. Right now."

"The social worker has already left the building."

"Then call her and tell her to come back. Now," he said with a voice like a slamming gavel. All hell was about to break loose, confirming once again the growing courthouse consensus that Judge Z was on the edge of crazy.

Ivory's social worker, Louisa Franke, was found in the parking lot and hurried back. As she entered the courtroom, Deputy Palmer was waiting and motioned for her to come to the bench.

"Is Ivory pregnant?" the judge asked her, getting right to the point.

Louisa was caught by surprise, but answered, "Yes, Your Honor, we found out yesterday."

"And you didn't think that was important to tell the judge?"

It was a question that had no good answer. So Louisa looked at the floor and said nothing. Young attorney Laura Mahoney stood next to her, speechless, hoping the judge would not look at her.

"Okay. This is simple. Everyone be back tomorrow at 10 a.m. We will have a special hearing. Grandma should be here. Ivory should be here. Lawyers should be here. You should be here. There's nothing I can do to stop an abortion, if all the proper legal procedures have been followed. In this case, that would include parental permission from her grandma, who is not even here right now. My guess is that she and her friends at the Consolidated Missionary Baptist Church are not going to be happy about all this. I could be wrong. I guess we'll find out tomorrow."

Tomorrow had come quickly.

The judge came in to Courtroom G quickly and sat down.

There were no wisecracks or friendly greetings. It was all business. Louisa Franke was fidgeting. Ivory sat with her lawyer, Laura Mahoney. Her supervisor at Legal Aid, a fifty-something man in a bow tie, sat in the audience in case his young staffer needed backup. Judge Z had never seen him before. The prosecutor for status court, Rachel Fielding, was present and nervous, worried that the judge may have thought she was part of the deception.

The social worker answered all the judge's questions forthrightly and confirmed what Karen had said. They had asked for the continuance so that Ivory would have time to "consider her options"—including an abortion that was already scheduled for later that morning. Yes, they presumed that it would upset the judge, so they did not mention it.

Judge Z asked Ivory's grandmother, "Are you in agreement with your granddaughter getting this abortion?"

"No, Your Honor. I was never in agreement with it," said Margaret Crenshaw.

"Well then, why are you allowing it? As custodial party, Ivory needs your permission."

"That's not how I understood it. I understood she was going to have it done and there was nothing I could do about it."

"Really? Who told you that?"

She pointed at a red-faced Louisa Franke, who shifted from foot to foot, looking very uncomfortable. There was a long pause. The judge opened the file and pretended to be reading something, but he was stalling for time to cool down and handle this right. One miss-step and he could be on Page One tomorrow: "Religious Judge Blocks Abortion."

"Ms. Mahoney, can I presume that you may have also given legal advice to this grandmother and sixteen-year-old girl about the abortion?"

The lawyer stood to speak, carefully, as if reading from a script: "I know that conversations with my client are privileged. And I know abortion is legal.

And I know that this court is not supposed to consider evidence of what happened in conversations in a courthouse hallway."

Judge Z was surprised. Her boss, a more seasoned lawyer, had given her good answers. The judge was now on the defensive. He took his time.

Mrs. Fielding confirmed that she had not been in on the 'secret' and apologized for requesting the continuance, never dreaming that the legal aid lawyer and social worker would cook up such a scheme. She would know better next time.

"Okay. This is where we are," he began. "I'm not here to micromanage anyone's life. But I wonder why some people are so sure that this baby is a mistake. I have no authority to tell grandma what to do. If she chooses to consent to this abortion, and Ivory chooses to have it done, so be it. And if grandma chooses not to consent, it is always possible that Ivory will find a way to do it anyway. Planned Parenthood. What a name for an organization that plans abortions for teenagers."

He shook his head and grimaced like he had just bitten a sour apple.

"This is one of my saddest days in this court, but there is not much I can do about it. I can stop appointing this lawyer to my cases. But what else can I do?" He paused. He shot a glance at the bow-tied legal aid supervisor who appeared to be plotting his next move already. "I'll see you in court two weeks from yesterday. I will expect a full report."

Ivory and her grandmother had decided not to have the abortion.

Now, two years later, she was finally eighteen and her days in juvenile court were over. And with her was a baby boy with lots of hair named Jeremiah. The rebellious, dangerous juvenile delinquent was gone, replaced by a proud mom with a very lucky little boy.

Judge Z told Ivory about his own Jeremiah. J.J. was his "little brother." Ivory reported that her son's daddy was still "not in the picture," so raising the boy would be a challenge.

He told her one good mom could make a difference, and that maybe she could even dream about a wedding someday when a man would make a lifetime commitment to her, just like Cinderella. Ivory thought it sounded good, but could not imagine such a thing.

On the way out of the courtroom, she asked her grandmother, "Who's Cinderella?"

"I don't know, child. Nobody we know."

JUST LIKE YOUR MOTHER
November 14

Mr. and Mrs. Bates were back in Friday's Motion hour, two weeks after Mr. Bates was kicked out of his house. He hadn't seen his kids since that first hearing.

But now he was lawyered up with Kirk DeMoss, a courthouse pit bull. Mr. Bates needed someone who could go toe-to-toe with Harry Wolff.

Their sixteen-year-old daughter, Melinda, had been in a car wreck, drunk driving, which showed that Mrs. Bates was not the great mom she pretended to be. And Mr. Bates testified that his wife was a dope smoker.

The judge ordered drug screens for both parties, just to be safe. And sure enough, she was positive for low levels of cannabis. Not a felony, but now she was a liar, having insisted in court she never used anything like that.

Her life was spiraling out of control, and her husband was thrilled. If he was going to pay for his philandering, heavy drinking and anger, then she should too. Divorcing couples often forgot that their spouse knows all of their little secrets.

Neither one seemed to care that the kids were headed for trouble. Melinda's DUI charge was bad enough. The son, thirteen, was flunking all his classes.

"Sir, you should never pull for your spouse to mess up," Judge Z told Mr. Bates. "You won't win this case by her screwing up. You will win, if there is such a thing, by doing the right thing. Wouldn't it be nice if these kids had two parents doing the right thing? And ma'am, same for you. Don't be too quick to tell me everything bad about Mr. Bates. Keep in mind that if I decide to believe you both, the result could be disaster. I might have to send the kids to foster care."

Also back were Augusto and Peggy Sue Fernando. The judge's talk with the kids had not gone well. Each told the judge how bad their dad was. He was always late or didn't show up. He brought along his alcoholic girlfriend. He seemed to be high on something at the last visit. And he texted the son to say, "You're just like your mother," not as a compliment.

Despite all of this, the judge told the kids there was nothing he could do to make their dad grow up and behave. The judge told them their dad loved them, which was maybe a lie and certainly an exaggeration. Then he told them they would have to see Mr. Fernando. He was a narcissistic fool, but he was still their dad.

When Peggy Sue protested, he told her, "You married him," with a raised eyebrow like a shrug. Next case.

The Jones family was back for a hearing over the dogs and the UK tickets. Judge Z quietly smiled for the entire two hours. These people were paying two hundred dollars an hour to mediocre lawyers to defend their canine rights and keep the tickets to UK basketball worship services all winter. After all the proof was in, Judge Z decided that the parties would share joint custody of Adolph, the pug. One week with daddy and one week with mommy. Mrs. Jones would keep Billy, the mutt who peed on the carpet.

The Kentucky basketball tickets would be split evenly. "Mr. Jones, you are welcome to negotiate with your ex-wife to purchase her tickets. Good luck." Even Rupp Arena, with 24,000 seats, would not be big enough for Mr. Jones' new girlfriend and Mrs. Jones.

Chapter 5

TILL DEATH DO US PART

My son Absalom! If only I had died instead of you.

— *II Samuel 18:33*

UNITED IN LAW FOR LIFE
November 15

The law students had settled into their desks and opened their notebooks. "If you learn nothing else, never forget this," Professor Bertram said. "When doing legal research, always start with the statutes. So with that in mind, what do the statutes say about marriage?"

Judge Z realized he wasn't aware that marriage was defined by statute at all.

Bertram clicked a PowerPoint: "In Kentucky, here it is." The screen showed:

"As used in recognizing the law of the Commonwealth, marriage refers only to the civil status, condition, or relation of one man and one woman united in law for life, for the discharge to each other in the community of the duties legally incumbent upon those whose association is founded on the distinction of sex. KRS 402.005."

"Anyone wish to explain this to me?" Bertram asked.

Silence.

"How about you, Judge Zenas. Help us out. Give us the word from family court."

"Other than specifying one man and one woman," Judge Z replied, "I have to admit I have no idea. Can I be honest? My law degree is older than your students. I have divorced thousands of people. I was married myself for twenty-eight years. I like to think of myself as an expert on family law. But I have never read this statute and I have no idea what it means."

The students laughed. Maybe they thought he was joking.

"You're not the only one who can't decipher the dead language of law-makers," Bertram said, as he passed out a handout with the definitions of marriage in all fifty states. None of them were any better. Half had already been ruled unconstitutional based on court rulings in federal same-sex cases.

"Now, let's go to some case law. You all read *Maynard versus Hill* from 1888. Someone, please, tell me what that is about."

Jason waved his hand, "The case was in Oregon. The underlying issue was whether a legislature could pass a bill to divorce a couple."

"Right. Just think about that for a minute. Unthinkable today. But common in our history. Divorce was so frowned upon that it took an act of the legislature to divorce someone. Marriage was supposed to be permanent. Till death do us part.

"By the way, it was mostly difficult to divorce, not as a way to trap women in marriage, but to keep men accountable. In case you haven't noticed, men like to run away."

That drew silent "amen" nods from even this young crowd., "Women's property rights were tied into her marriage to a man. The law did not want it to be easy for a man to just run away and leave her with nothing. Which is basically the system today in Africa and many Arab nations where women's rights are minimal. But I digress."

Professor Bertram clicked his PowerPoint to display the *Maynard v. Hill* definition of marriage, which said:

> "Marriage, as creating the most important relation in life, as having more to do with the morals and civilization of a people than any other institution, has always been subject to the control of the legislature. That body prescribes the age at which parties may contract to marry, the procedure of form essential to constitute marriage, the duties and obligations it creates, its effects upon the property rights of both, present and prospective, and the acts which may constitute grounds for dissolution."

> The students looked confused. He clicked to the next screen.

> "It is rather a social relation like that of parent and child, the obligations of which arise not from the consent of concurring minds, but are the creation of the law itself, a relation most important as affecting the happiness of individuals, the first step from barbarism to incipient civilization, the purest tie of social life, and the true basis of human progress."

"One more," Professor Bertram said. "*Black's Law Dictionary* says it is 'The formal union of a man and woman, typically recognized by law, by which they become husband and wife.'

"Simple—as long as we all agree on the definition of a 'formal union' and a 'husband and wife.'" By the end of an hour of reciting various court definitions of marriage, it was clear that nothing was clear.

Professor Bertram ended with a statement the judge would remember for a long time. He seemed to be quoting someone, maybe a Catholic priest, although he gave no credit.

"As you can see, the courts and legislators have had great difficulty defining marriage. So maybe, just maybe, marriage is something so sacred and holy that it should not be defined in law at all. After all, the Kentucky statutes don't define Holy Communion. They don't define baptism. The churches don't get permission for their activities. Why marriage?

"Now, before we leave, there was a Sixth Circuit Order just this past week which is relevant. By a two-to-one vote, the Federal Court of Appeals found the Kentucky definition to be legal and constitutional. Read *Bourke vs. Beshear* and come ready to discuss it too. It will likely end up at the Supreme Court. As I said last week, this same-sex issue has been healthy in the sense that we are discussing, for the first time really, what marriage really is."

As usual, law school was better at asking questions than providing answers.

As Judge Z left with the students, he was still thinking about the quote from Maynard. Marriage was "the first step from barbarism to incipient civilization."

Barbaric. Thought Judge Z. *That's it. My world is barbaric.*

COUSIN HANK, R.I.P.

Judge Z left the law school and headed straight to Denny's. J.J. had called the judge and left a message to confirm that he'd be there at noon. They would meet every week until J.J. decided he was okay. Free brunch and free wisdom from an old white judge. Denny's "Grand Slam" at $4.99. Or a burger.

But after twenty minutes, he finally had to admit that J.J. was back to his old habits—no show, no call. No explanation. Judge Z was sort of relieved. He would have an hour of silence and eggs and bacon while he read some pleadings from a case set for next week. He had learned to always bring something to read in case J.J. failed to appear.

Just as well, really, or he might be late for the funeral. He left Denny's, and went straight to Scott County for a 2 p.m. memorial service.

"A celebration for the life of Henry 'Hank' Clay Alexander," the fancy bulletin said.

Three days ago, Hank was the richest man in Scott County. The governor of Kentucky sat in the front row at his funeral. Even the UK basketball coach was present.

Hank's long battle with cancer was over. Judge Z was in the third row because Hank was his cousin. Hank's mom was Beulah's older sister.

The service was conducted in Hank's private airplane hangar at the Scott County Airport, big enough to house his three jets. He made his money in the coal and timber business. He came from nothing, never graduated high school and proved that education was overrated—that you can be successful with hard work and a little bit of luck. He believed that paying all your taxes was for fools.

Hank had loved his Aunt Beulah. He just didn't agree with her about a whole lot. He didn't really take women seriously. Whatever wisdom she passed along over Sunday fried chicken was forgotten by Hank no later than Monday morning. Like a lot of men, Hank missed the point of Proverbs that portrayed wisdom as female, such as, *"Blessed are those who find wisdom, those who gain understanding, for* she *is more profitable than silver."*

The funeral opened with "My Way" by Frank Sinatra, played through a surprisingly cheap sound system. Judge Z wondered if he was supposed to picture Hank and "Old Blue Eyes" together in the Members Only section of heaven. Instead, as he listened to the lyrics and the strings, he thought that "My Way" was an awfully lonely and empty road to take.

After Sinatra's crackly song came to an end, an opening prayer thanked the good Lord for all the good work done by Hank. Then a business buddy talked for five minutes about how smart Hank was. And a young girl, probably a friend's granddaughter, sang "Life is Like an Old Coal Truck."

Really? thought the judge.

The "dearly departed" had lots of mourners. He had been married three times, all ending in divorce. He had no children by his wives, but had a couple by other ladies. One of those sons, who would have been mocked as a "bastard" in the bad old days but was now a trust-fund millionaire, stood and said a few kind words about his dad.

"He taught us to work hard," he said—causing a few raised eyebrows because nobody could remember this twenty-something kid ever working a day in his life.

Judge Z could read between the lines. The kid didn't like Hank. Not really. He didn't like the way his mom had been treated and the way his father was never there.

The funeral ended with a short sermon by the pastor of a Scott County mini-megachurch. Hank was never seen there on Sundays, but he had donated two-million dollars to build a gym "for the kids," just in case St. Peter asked, "What have you done for me lately?" at the Pearly Gates.

Beulah missed the funeral. She said going to two out of three of Hank's weddings was more than enough. She said she would rather stay home and pray.

LIFE AND DEATH

After the funeral, Judge Z slipped out to the Keene Trace Golf Club for a 4 p.m. golf game. If global warming was true, he thought wryly, he liked it. He could play golf in November. He turned off his cell phone and for a quick nine holes he was free from all stress except four-foot putts that broke left to right. He played alone, like he did a lot of things.

He had politely said no to a wedding invitation that evening. The RSVP had been returned "with regrets," although that was a lie. He still hated weddings. Kentucky's lousy football team would play that night in Oxford, Mississippi. They would hope to beat Ole Miss, and after losing again, the airwaves would be full of why the coach was really bad. Or why he was not really the problem. Or how basketball practice was looking good.

Heading home from the golf course, he checked his voice mails. One message from 5:44 p.m. "Judge, this is Wanda, I'm sure you remember me. We haven't talked in a while." There was a pause, and what sounded like a choked sob. "I'm so sorry to tell you that J.J. was shot early this morning. I just got the call five minutes ago. Please call me right away. You're the first person I called." Wanda failed to mention if J.J. was dead or alive.

Judge Z hit the accelerator and headed straight for Wanda's place. As he drove he cursed God and everyone who had failed Jeremiah Jackson—especially himself. This was his "only child," a chance to make a difference outside the courtroom for a lost kid with a missing dad and a mom on drugs.

Wanda had done the best she could, raising him even though she was not his mother. Judge Z had tried to show J.J. that there was hope for a better life. But it was not good enough.

He was going sixty in a forty five when he dialed Wanda. There was no answer. Just the happy message that sounded jarringly out of place today. "Hello, this is Wanda. Leave a message and have a blessed day."

"Wanda, this is Judge Z. I'm so sorry I didn't call sooner and so sorry about J.J.," he said to the voice mail. "Please call me. I am on the way."

He didn't know what else to say and wasn't sure he could say anything else if he tried.

As he pulled up to Wanda's place at East Sixth and Chestnut Street, he remembered the first time he had been there four years earlier. Despite his standing in the community, or maybe because of it, he had been afraid that morning. Not physically afraid as much as anxious that this kid wouldn't like him. This was two worlds coming together. White and black. Rich and poor. Right side of town and wrong side of town. Behind the door was the unknown for Judge Z. And again tonight, the unknown awaited.

He rang the doorbell three times. Finally, Wanda came to the door, wailing and weeping. Her three-hundred-pound boyfriend was spread out on the couch, watching TV like it was just another Saturday night.

"Judge, J.J.'s dead. He's gone," Wanda cried.

He was at a loss for words, so he hugged her. Then they talked, and he found out she knew practically nothing about what had happened. He promised he would try to find out and get back soon. No funeral was planned. No money. No preacher. No hope.

A phone call to the coroner confirmed that J.J.'s body was sitting in a freezer at the coroner's office. "Yes sir. We have the body of Jeremiah Jackson," said the girl at the morgue. He played the judge card and she answered his questions. Yes, there was an autopsy scheduled. No, she didn't know where or how many times he was shot but the paperwork said gunshot wounds. As far as she knew, they were waiting for instructions from a funeral home. She gave him the number for the detective who was working the homicide case.

Driving home he turned on WLAP to catch the UK football game. He turned it off when the announcer said it was 33-7, Ole Miss. The commentator used the word "tragedy" to describe the game and the football program.

Judge Z silently yelled at the radio, *Tragedy? You people have no idea what tragedy means.*

BUILD AN ARK

Judge Z drove to Sadieville for 11 a.m. Sunday church. He met Beulah outside in the parking lot and told her the bad news about J.J. Beulah was speechless. She knew J.J. She loved him. She prayed for him daily. She also prayed for J.J.'s father, that he would choose to be a good dad someday. And his mom, that she would get off drugs and get involved with her son. But today, it seemed those prayers had gone unanswered.

Beulah and the judge found their spot in church.

Pastor Billy got started.

"It is a fact that Jesus chose a wedding to do his first miracle, as we saw last week. The Bible also begins with a wedding in Genesis. Adam and Eve. And the Bible ends with a wedding in the Book of Revelation. Jesus and His church. In between, the Old Testament is filled with wedding references. The Bible is actually a story of the human family. And much of that story is tragedy, pain and heartache.

"It was so bad at one time that God chose to start over again, through Noah, who was actually not asked to save the whole world. He was told to save his family.

"'By faith Noah, when warned about things not yet seen, in holy fear built an ark to save his family.' Noah built an ark to save his family, not the world.

"The human stories of families and weddings continue after Noah's day. They include Abraham and Sarah, Ruth and Boaz, Jeremiah's references to the bride and bridegroom, and the same for Ezekiel, the whole Book of Hosea, and the Book of Malachi. The Bible then goes silent for four hundred years.

"Then, finally, Jesus appears at a wedding at Cana of Galilee. In the New Testament, John the Baptist refers to himself as the best man at a wedding. Jesus calls Himself the bridegroom."

Reverend Hughes paused. "Maybe weddings are important. You think?" He looked up from his notes and smiled.

Judge Z was stopped in his tracks. He thought, *Maybe I've been a little harsh on weddings*. His mind wandered to his own cynicism. On average, five couples showed up at the courthouse each week, unannounced, looking for a judge to marry them. It was never Judge Z. No way.

Typically, they were low-income couples who had just enough money for a marriage license and no religious affiliation or pastor. They often had children tagging along, or an imminent baby that was obvious. The bride and groom would likely fail drug tests.

The couples always gave Judge Z a twinge of sorrow. They were not the weddings little girls dream about, with a white gown and a church full of family and friends watching her father walk her down the aisle. Her best friends weren't there in bridesmaid-pink, flirting with groomsmen in tuxedos.

Instead, the courthouse groom wore his finest tee-shirt and the bride showed off her tattoos while her—their?—children got excited about something they didn't understand. Did anyone have any clue what it meant?

Judge Z's antiquated view was that a wedding should be a grand ceremony, not a secretive affair conducted in the judge's hidden chambers. When he was first elected as a family court judge, he got a call from the receptionist: "There's a couple here that wants to get married. Are you available?"

"No, I'm actually not. I have a hearing in five minutes. But let me save you some time in the future. I don't do weddings. I do divorces. Thank you."

Marriage was supposed to mean something. Just showing up at the courthouse like the drive-through at McDonald's—"Two Big Macs, supersized, with two large Cokes and a side order of 'I now pronounce you man and wife'"—did not sit any better than a cheeseburger for breakfast.

Reverend Billy finished his sermon by explaining a verse from John, Chapter 14, commonly heard at funerals like cousin Hank's. "I go to prepare a place for you" was not about death at all, Reverend Billy said. It was about Jewish wedding traditions. A husband would go to prepare a place for his bride. When Jesus said in John 14 that he would be back for his bride, Jesus was telling his beloved disciples that He would be back. He was the bridegroom.

"A man and a woman in holy matrimony is the best metaphor we have of how we are to relate to God," said Reverend Billy. "And it is no accident that when he created mankind, he did it in families. His creation was deliberately man and woman, with the idea that from their love and commitment would come the survival of the human race."

Back at Beulah's, as Judge Z sat in Johnny's worn swivel chair and leaned back for some serious thinking, he and Beulah were strangely quiet. They were in deep waters this morning. The loss of J.J. was hanging over the judge like a dark cloud. He had failed as a father figure and big brother. There would be no more second chances.

As Beulah stood in the kitchen finishing Sunday dinner, she finally broke the silence. "Did you learn anything today from Reverend Billy?"

"I learned I need to build an ark to save my family. But now, honestly, I don't have much family. J.J. is gone. Too late to save him.

"Just you, Mom, and you look as saved as it gets to me." He smiled.

Beulah was quick with an answer. "Son, your family is a thousand or more families in family court." She turned from the fried chicken and smiled back.

"Yeah, I get that. I also learned a little bit about Jewish weddings, and that I may need to start going to weddings. In fact, you remember Ghuna, my lawyer friend in India?"

"Sure."

"He wants me to come to his son's wedding. I got an email on Friday. I think I might go."

"When is it?"

"January. Short, expensive trip. But while Billy was preaching, I kept hearing, 'Go to the wedding.' We'll see."

"That voice should not be ignored."

Judge Z knew his mom's voice. But this other voice was getting louder.

TALK TO MY FATHER
November 17

Breakfast with Reverend Billy Hughes was simple to arrange. 6:30 a.m. Monday at Cracker Barrel offered an opportunity for the judge to entertain one of his private pleasures and have a serious discussion at the same time. Judge Z wanted to know more about the Jewish weddings and John 14.

As they waited for their eggs and pancakes, he told Billy about J.J.

When Billy asked about funeral arrangements, Judge Z explained that the family had no money.

"You know, the church can help on things like this. I'd be happy to help with a funeral," Billy offered.

"Thanks. I hope to see his guardian, Wanda, tonight. I will let her know. She will appreciate it, I'm sure."

After their breakfasts arrived, Judge Z asked, "So where'd you get this betrothal stuff?"

"Well, Judge, maybe my own story will answer that. I'm twenty-seven. I went to UK. My grades were average. I fooled around too much. So I ended up in seminary. I could've gone home to work for my dad but I wasn't ready for work yet. So here I am. I had no desire to be a minister of any kind, and honestly I'm still not sure that I do. But I'm learning and for now it feels good."

"I think you're good at it," Judge Z said.

"Thank you. The important part of the story is that I was saved by a girl named Susie. For four years in college I did what everyone does. Date. Break up. Date again. Break up again. One night stand. Drink too much. Wake up in unknown places. Try to get serious. Break up again. One of my friends called it 'divorce practice.' Breaking up gets easier with practice."

"So college is perfect practice for divorce court?"

"I guess so," Billy continued. "Until I was invited to a little Pentecostal Church by a friend. I grew up going to church, and just got away from it. So the Pentecostal experience was interesting. Susie was there, singing in the choir. I could not get my eyes off her. I went back to the same church for three straight Sundays, pretending it was the sermons and the music. I even raised my hand to pray with the preacher and receive Jesus. I would have prayed to accept Kermit the Frog as my savior, but all the time I was going back for Susie, who I had still not spoken to.

"I knew she had been glancing at me too, so I worked up my nerve and asked, "How about a nice simple date? Maybe a dinner at your favorite restaurant?"

"She said, 'You'll have to ask my dad.' I did a double take and looked deep into her eyes to see if she was kidding. She just smiled and pointed to the program where her father's number was listed as a deacon. At first I thought, 'No way.' But there she was in the choir and I couldn't stop thinking about her. The service was a blur. But that Sunday evening I called him.

"After I introduced myself he said, 'If you're hoping to date my daughter, you passed the first test. She gave you my number.' We agreed to have lunch after church. That was not what I expected, either. It was friendly but there were some tests involved. Where did I work? What were my plans for life? How did I get to the church? Where was I from? Who were my parents and what were they all about?

"What he found was a sixth year senior in college, from a solid Methodist home in Owensboro, who majored in history, had a 2.9 GPA and a prematurely receding hairline. I would not improve the family gene pool.

"I only wanted one date. But he was looking at the future. I slowly realized I was getting aboard a very slow train. I picked up the twenty-dollar tab. I think he was impressed."

Judge Z had finished three eggs over easy with bacon while Billy told his story. He asked, "How did you ever get to a wedding date?"

"Well, I was invited over for lots of family events, which meant that Susie liked me. And every time I saw her, she looked better. My desire was turning from lust to love. She was different. This girl had been protected by her family, especially her father, and there was no doubt that if we got married I would be her one and only. There was something very exciting about that for me.

"On a fishing trip with my dad, I found myself telling him all about Susie. He could tell I was serious and gave me advice for the first time about women and life and marriage—and I actually listened. Six months later, we walked down the aisle.

"In short, I had gone away to 'prepare a place' for my bride, just like Jesus mentioned. The intentional process of courtship made it possible for us to be truly prepared for each other in marriage."

"Was she a student too?"

"Yes, she was in nursing school. I delivered pizzas. We didn't have much, but it was enough. Our way of marriage was the old way—what they used to call courtship—but it was the right way. And that's partly what got me so interested in the meaning of marriage."

Judge Z nodded, impressed. Billy knew a lot for a "kid" of twenty-seven—maybe more than some judges at fifty.

DARK DISNEYLAND

Judge Z seldom read the paper, but J.J.'s death caused him to buy a Monday edition as he left the restaurant. He was disappointed to find that the murder of a black kid was barely news in Lexington. On page B3 was a three sentence paragraph. Another gun homicide on East 6th Street. The victim was named. Details were sketchy. The police had no suspects.

The obituary was on Page C5.

"Jeremiah Jackson, age 19, of 370 2nd Street, Lexington, Ky. died unexpectedly on November 15. Survivors are a son, Da'Juan Greene, his guardian, Wanda Overstreet, his mother, Maria Jackson, and his father, Charles Morton, as well as several siblings, nieces, nephews and cousins. Funeral arrangements are undetermined."

That was it. Nineteen years of a troubled, sad life in two sentences.

Later in court Deputy Palmer told him there were no funeral arrangements. J.J.'s body was still lying in a deep freeze at the coroner's office, waiting for instructions from someone in the family. He knew the family better than Judge Z. Used to go to church with J.J.'s grandma before she died.

"They don't have the money," Palmer said. "They don't know what to do. They can't afford a funeral, not even a casket. The mother is missing and the father is, as you know, nowhere in the picture. Still in prison. Wanda has nothing."

If no one stepped up, he would eventually be buried in a pauper's grave called Hillside Cemetery, ten miles out of town on Paris Pike. The government would chip in the five hundred dollars to make it happen, but only if no family took care of it within thirty days.

"I asked around," Palmer said. "It was a drive-by. Nobody's sure if he was the target or just standing on the wrong corner at the wrong time. He didn't have drugs or a gun on him, but he tested positive for marijuana, for what that's worth. You know how they say one death is a tragedy and a million is a statistic? Well in that neighborhood, J.J. is a statistic."

There was a bigger headline in the paper over a very different story: "Eight Dead in Perry County 'Disneyland' Trailer-Park." Top of B-1.

Underneath the big headline was a small one: "No Foul Play." The story quoted a fire marshal who said there was no evidence of arson. No "cause" had been discovered.

Even Judge Z was shocked by the story. In Perry County, deep in the mountains, eight people died in a fire, not counting an unborn baby. Killed by smoke inhalation was Johnny Disney, twenty-six, a boyfriend who was soon to be a father. He was found in bed with Kim Brown, twenty-three, the pregnant mother of three, ages three, two and one. Their father, Jack Brown, still Kim's legal husband, "was visibly upset about the death of his three children," the story said.

It seemed to have never occurred to Jack Brown that his three children might not be safe in the care of Mom and her boyfriend.

Barely mentioned were three more kids, ages five, three, and two, who had been over for a sleepover, according to the news story. These three children were not named, "pending notification of family."

Family? thought Judge Z.

So, six kids and two adults, not counting the unborn baby. Dead.

The fire broke out early Sunday morning—about the time other children headed to Sunday school. The adult victims were still asleep because they had "partied" until 3 a.m., according to a Disney family member living nearby.

"The area of the fire is known as Disneyland," the story said. "It's a real close family," one of the Disneys told the reporter. The cause of death was being investigated.

"Is it that hard to understand?" the judge wondered aloud to his staff attorney Clay Henderson. "Maybe it was a bad heater that caused the fire or someone forgot to put out a cigarette. But the real cause is a total breakdown in the family. Marriage means nothing. A father who is not there to protect his children is so common nobody even mentions it. How can any man find it okay for another man to be in bed with his kids and their mom?"

Clay nodded. "Those kids never had a chance. And the three kids over for the sleepover, there was not even any mention of their names or parents."

Judge Z had heard it often. "Judge, I got no problem with her new boyfriend. Seems like a good guy to me. The kids like him just fine."

No problem as long as dad gets to be with his girlfriend. Let someone else take care of the kids.

Judge Z had not even been to court yet and already it was a bad week.

J.J. was gone. Just another statistic. And Disneyland was not the fairytale version.

'GO SEE THE JUDGE'
November 17

The work week started with a couple from Kuwait. Mr. and Mrs. Dawid were American citizens, in court for a pre-trial hearing on their contested divorce. The American dream included an American divorce for the Dawid family. He had stopped paying support five months ago. Judge Z had put him in jail for ninety days or until he paid nine thousand dollars arrearages. He was out in four hours. One of his brothers "loaned" him the money.

During a break, Karen mentioned a book she had read about Muslim marriage and divorce—a real eye opener. She offered to loan it to him.

The next morning it was sitting on his desk. He looked at the cover. Only a girl's eyes could be seen peeking out from her burka. Under that was the title: *I Am Nujood, Age 10 and Divorced*. He flipped it over and read the back: "Marriage is a prison for a lot of women," it said. "There is legal, systematic child abuse and domestic violence."

It turned out that the girl, Nujood, was the first child bride in Yemen to win a divorce. Ever. "Nujood Ali's childhood came to an abrupt end in 2008 as her father arranged for her to be married to a man three times her age."

With harrowing detail, she told of abuse at her husband's hands and of her daring escape. With the help of local advocates and the press, Nujood won her freedom—an extraordinary achievement in Yemen, where almost half of all girls are married under the legal age.

Her courageous defiance of Yemeni customs and her own family had inspired other girls in the Middle East to challenge their marriages.

The judge put the book in his briefcase and headed home. That night he sat by the fire and read the whole book. The part that really got to him was the advice she got: "Go to the courthouse. Ask to see the judge—after all, he's the government's representative. He's very powerful, and he is godfather to all of us. His job is to help victims." The words stuck in Judge Z's heart like a knife.

"Go to the courthouse. See the judge. Godfather to us all.

"He can help you."

Some people might read the book and think, "Marriage sucks in the Middle East. It is a tool of a male dominated society to systematically abuse women and girls." And there would be truth to that.

But the judge saw another message: Nujood survived because a judge did his job. He protected her. He used his government power to save her.

Okay, he thought, *maybe I do need to stick around for a while. Noah built an ark to save his family. For me, that's the children of family court.*

Chapter 6

FOR BETTER OR WORSE

The friend who attends the bridegroom
waits and listens for him.

— *John 3:29*

PURE GOLD
November 19

The judge thought he was having a decent Wednesday for DNA court. He spent three hours seeing sixty cases of child abuse and neglect. By 4 p.m., the judge was ready to go home. As usual, he had learned something new today. He learned from one mom that twins can have two fathers. Even that one raised the judge's eyebrows.

The day finished with Allie Gomez. She had two kids. Typical drug mom. Dad was from Mexico and long gone. She had worked her case plan, according to the report, got her kids back, and then relapsed three months later. It seemed hopeless. She knew the questions but had no answers.

The dispositional report said the kids were in temporary custody of the state, with a goal of RTP, or "Return to Parent." Everyone hoped Allie would get her act together. Again.

The best option for the kids, said the social workers, was mom's sister, Sheila Cassity, who had not had any criminal problems for more than ten years. Her husband had no felony convictions, just an old DUI. He apparently had a job. The placement looked good.

Then Karen whispered, "Judge, do you know about the Cassitys?"

"You mean the aunt and uncle? No, tell me."

"The cabinet placed these kids with the people who run Pure Gold."

Judge Z stared at Karen to see if she was joking. She nodded, as if to say, "Oh, yeah, it's true."

"That sleazy strip bar? You sure? Where the big drug bust happened last year?"

Karen nodded again.

The judge turned to the social worker. "Ms. Carlson, I didn't see in the report where the aunt and uncle are working?"

Glenna Carlson glanced at her paperwork, stalling.

"Umm, let's see... here it is. Manager at Pure Gold."

"The strip club?"

"Yes, Your Honor. The report says 'adult nightclub.'"

"And the mom works there as a waitress?"

"Yes sir."

"You think that's appropriate?"

"Your Honor, I have never been there, so I can't say."

Judge Z stared a hole through the social worker.

"Is it not true that we never, and I mean never, allow a mom to continue to work at a strip club?"

Ms. Carlson looked around but got no help. "Well, yes. That would normally be true. We encourage them to find another place to work if they want their kids back."

"Why is it okay to place kids with the man who hires these sad moms, almost all on drugs, almost all broken, almost all abused in some fashion? This man participates in their downward spiral. The man who hires them is okay as a 'custodian,' but the women he hires are not?"

No answer.

He continued. "I cannot tell the Cabinet where to place children, Ms. Carlson. But this makes me crazy. Is there any doubt in anyone's mind that the man who hires the strippers is more of a problem than the women who do the stripping?" Judge Z went on and on and on. Ranting and raving. This man was a creep. A sleazebag. He cited statistics on porn shops and strip joints and the crime and drugs that surround them. He didn't have to exaggerate. The facts alone were stunning. But no one wanted to listen.

The next court date would be in six weeks. Most likely, the social workers would be looking for another home, but maybe not. The judge could not micromanage the state workers.

'CLICK'

Karen didn't even say good morning on Thursday. She looked up as he walked through the door, all business. "Judge, I think you better listen to the voice message we got overnight."

Apparently, Allie Gomez had told the Cassitys what that religious nut judge had said and someone—Mr. Cassity himself?—had called anonymously to rant and perhaps commit a felony by threatening a judge.

Judge Z pushed buttons to get to his voice mail and hit play: "This is for Judge Zenas," a muffled voice said with loud music in the background.

"I am a friend of Mr. Cassity. First of all, you don't know crap about this man. He came from nothing. He worked his tail off after an abusive childhood. You sit up there on your high horse and attach your morals on him? You're a Christian? Really? What kind of Christian are you? What you are is a piece of crap. Not worth wiping off my shoe. Who do you think you are? You better watch out. That's all I know! You better be careful. People are watching you. Every day. Every minute. Who do you think you are, you worthless piece of crap? Who are you to judge anyone?"

Click.

Judge Z listened and smiled. *Who do I think I am? Actually I am a judge. That's who I am,* he said to himself. This was not his first threat. One disturbed man was in prison now for sending a threatening letter.

He thought it over for a minute, then told Karen, "Put the Cassity case back on the docket for next Wednesday. Send a summons for the mother. Also for the aunt and uncle who have the children. I presume this was the uncle on the phone, but who knows. We'll find out."

As he drove home that evening, Judge Z heard a name on the news that sounded familiar. Skipper Johnson. "Victim of a drive-by shooting, the second in the past two days," the radio voice said. "Police suspect drugs were involved. The latest weekend homicides bring the city total to eleven shootings so far this this year..."

He thought, *Skipper. Not many people named Skipper. Oh yeah—Skipper was in court a couple of years ago. The age is right, they said nineteen. Got to be the same kid.*

Not counting J.J., that made three young men he knew—just kids, really—who had been killed in street violence in the past three years.

Judge Z had seen them all in court. All the signs of a bad outcome were there. The gang tats, the drooping pants hanging so low it looked like they had repealed the law of gravity, the hoodies and white T-shirts, the gang signs they flashed to each other.

All were black. All were killed by other young black men.

Jaron was killed on his seventeenth birthday. He was brought into Status Court for "Beyond Control of Parent" by his mom when he was fourteen. His mother always showed up, but as far as anyone could tell he never had a dad. Judge Z finally saw Jaron's father for the first time at the kid's funeral. After that he saw the father on the news, protesting the violence in the streets, demanding that someone do something about it, shedding tears for the cameras. *Where were you for the rest of his life?* the judge had wondered.

The first time Jaron had been in Judge Z's court, he was a textbook definition of "beyond control" of his mom.

"Where is Jaron's dad?" the judge had asked.

With a roll of her eyes she replied, "He's in town. But he's not in the picture."

"Not in the picture? More like the picture was never taken," said the judge sarcastically.

Judge Z wanted to say, *This kid has no chance. Mom complains about no dad around, but in a weird way she's sort of happy he's gone. She knows he is basically a bad guy, with lots of kids by lots of women. So maybe she's right. She's better off without him.*

Every year more young black men were murdered in Lexington. All by other black kids. Not by cops. But the cops were always the targets of protests and accusations about police brutality and excessive force.

Now four of "his" kids had been murdered. Jaron, Chad, J.J. and Skipper.

The funeral for Chad had been quite an event last year. Consolidated Missionary Baptist Church was packed with four hundred people. It was Sunday best for most folks. Pastor Arthur McGaffrey started by asking everyone who was carrying a gun to come put it on the altar. No one did. It was the only funeral the judge ever attended where the deceased was barely mentioned. The service instead was a passionate plea against violence and guns. Chad had never even been in the church. Too late now.

J.J.'s body still lay in a freezer at the coroner's office. Skipper and J.J. might even be together.

The judge knew that if the *Lexington Times* did decide to do anything, the editorial would be about violence and guns and racism and better police-community relations. The publisher was a good man. They had played golf together, and he knew he was a lot more sensible than the unsigned editorials written under his name on the masthead. *I suppose he has about as much control over that newsroom as I have over lawyers and social workers in my courtroom,* he thought.

So the editorial would not be about marriage and family and stability and the importance of giving children a safe home. It would not cite the tragedy of fatherlessness and single parents. It would be written by people who had no clue.

'LUV IS LUV'
November 22

"Okay," said Professor Bertram, as his students settled in for the third class session, "who read the Yale Law Review article by Robert Roche? Or better yet, his whole book, *What is Marriage?* As I told you, don't let the fact that the book is a response to the same-sex marriage debate throw you off. No matter what you think on that, the good news is that we're finally having a conversation about the meaning of marriage. Right?"

Michael nodded his agreement, so Brad asked him, "Michael, can you summarize the Yale article? Remember, a good lawyer has to know both sides."

Michael took a breath and dove in. "It says there are two fundamentally competing views. The conjugal view is that marriage is the union of man and woman, mainly for bearing and raising children. They seal the union with sex." Michael blushed slightly. "That puts a high value on monogamy and fidelity. The welfare of children is why marriage is important to the common good and why the state should recognize and regulate it."

"Excellent summary. And who agrees wholeheartedly with that view? Anyone?"

Only Nicole raised her hand, slowly looking around for support that was not coming.

"Okay Nicole, you also have to be able to argue both sides to be a lawyer. So tell us, what is the revisionist view?"

Nicole stumbled in. "I guess that argument is that love is love. Marriage is the union of two people, no matter the gender, who love and care for each other and share the burdens and benefits of domestic life, enhanced by whatever form of sexual intimacy both partners find agreeable. The state should recognize and regulate marriage because it has an interest in stable, romantic partnerships and any children they may choose to raise."

"Excellent, Nicole. In short, you could almost think about this as children versus love. And obviously, it is very much about both.

"And now, for some late breaking news to enhance the debate, we have these two views specifically outlined in *Bourke versus Beshear,* the same-sex marriage case from Louisville, decided just two weeks ago by the Sixth Circuit Court of Appeals. Judge Sutton's majority opinion—it was two-to-one—gave the rationale for why a state has an interest in defining marriage at all. And confirms that children are at the center of it all. I quote:

"'Imagine a society without marriage. It does not take long to envision problems that might result from an absence of rules about how to handle the natural effects of male-female intercourse: children. May men and women follow their procreative urges wherever they take them? Who is responsible for the children that result? How many mates may an individual have? How does one decide which set of mates is responsible for which set of children? That we rarely think about these questions nowadays shows only how far we have come and how relatively stable our society is, not that States have no explanation for creating such rules in the first place.'

"So," said the professor, "what does that mean?"

Jason Farmer raised his hand quickly, as usual. "It's simply saying that government has a rational reason to be involved in this thing we call marriage. Judge Sutton thinks voters and legislators should define marriage, not judges. And he makes the case that the main reason has to do with having children. Marriage provides a stable environment for children. But honestly, isn't that what gay folks are arguing too? Let us marry so we can provide that same stability." Virtually the entire class seemed to give a silent nod.

Professor Bertram said, "Judge Sutton covers that too. He gave a pretty good definition of the revisionist view when he said, 'Over time, marriage has come to serve another value—to solemnize relationships characterized by love, affection, and commitment. Gay couples, no less than straight couples, are capable of sharing such relationships. And gay couples, no less than straight couples, are capable of raising children and providing stable families for them. The quality of such relationships, and the capacity to raise children within them, turns not on sexual orientation but on individual choices and individual commitment. All of this supports the policy argument made by many that marriage laws should be extended to gay couples, just as nineteen States have done through their own sovereign powers.'"

Judge Zenas, sitting in the back of the room, thought about what had Beulah said: *The greatest tragedy is not that gay people want to get married, but that straight people with children don't want to get married.*

Brad gave the class a five-minute break, and when they returned they heard from Carol Robinson, a professor from Boston University who had written extensively on marriage. She visited the class over Skype.

"Thanks for giving us an hour, Professor Robinson," Brad said. "I have assigned your book, *The Complete History of Love and Marriage*, but I can't guarantee that all of the class has read it."

"I'm not sure I could guarantee that about my own class," she laughed; several students looked relieved. "I suppose you could say it's the history and future of marriage. There has been a truly historic and revolutionary change in the past few decades. My research and study show some real surprises."

"Explain the revolution, please. I'll be quiet and let you talk."

"Sure. The marriage revolution has had so many causes. Divorce and single parenthood are relatively new. The right of women to initiate divorce is also fairly new, and so is the ability of single women to support their children. An extraordinary increase in the economic independence and legal equality of women has reshaped family life.

"Cohabitation and legal gains for unmarried same-sex partners have challenged the ways marriage has organized responsibilities on the basis of gender. And there has been a reproductive revolution, pioneered by married couples eager to overcome their infertility. Now individuals can become parents who would never have been able to do so before. For the first time in history, a child can theoretically have five different parents: a sperm donor, an egg donor, a birth mother, and the social parents who raise the child—not including divorce and remarriage. And maybe another divorce and remarriage or cohabitation. It goes on and on."

Judge Z recalled just such a case, in which a black surrogate mother bore a white baby for a white couple from Florida. The egg and sperm had been joined in a test tube, placed in the young healthy woman, who gladly delivered the baby for a fee. It was all legal in Florida. Judge Z got involved only because the surrogate mother delivered the baby prematurely in Kentucky, where such arrangements are not so legal. The hospital filed a lawsuit to determine who to name as the mother on the birth certificate. *Just another day in family court*, thought the judge at the time.

Robinson continued, "And then there's the increasingly common decision to not have children. Many people who marry choose to remain childless. That's a huge change from the past, when childlessness was an economic disaster and often led to divorce.

"Your law school class may include young people who are delaying marriage until their late twenties or early thirties, not because they are against marriage, but because they are very anti-divorce, from personal experience."

A few of the students nodded on that one.

"As they live on their own for a longer time, the likelihood of remaining single goes up dramatically. The odds of traditional marriage go down."

Brad asked, "Dr. Robinson, when you say traditional marriage, you may mean something different than what I might mean?"

"Yes, my definition is based on the history of how marriage organized our economic and political society. It was a way of raising capital, building political alliances, organizing the division of labor and deciding what claim children had on their parents.

"For the propertied classes, marriage was the main way of consolidating wealth, transferring property, laying claim to political power, even peace treaties. For most men, the dowry that a wife brought was the biggest infusion of cash, goods or land they would ever acquire. For most women, finding a husband was her most important investment in her economic future. And marriage was the most important marker of adulthood and respectability."

After a few more questions by Brad, he asked for questions from his students.

By the end of the hour the word "love" had not even been mentioned, except to point out that it was not a factor during most of the history of marriage.

Judge Z remembered the old Tina Turner tune, "What's Love Got to Do With It?"

Apparently, in the old days, not much. Today, it was everything. And when love was gone, so was the marriage.

BEST MAN AT THE WEDDING
November 23

As he pulled into the church parking lot with Beulah, Judge Z realized with surprise that he was looking forward to hearing the message on marriage. Reverend Hughes was still in the Gospel of John, Chapter 3, the part about John the Baptist.

"How could a man who never married and lived in the wilderness eating locusts teach anyone anything about marriage?" he asked to get started.

"John 3 is typically associated with John 3:16. 'For God so loved the world that he gave his one and only son that whoever believes in him shall not perish but have eternal life.'

"But there's another message in this chapter that is significant.

"When John the Baptist was asked about Jesus, he gave an odd answer: 'The bride belongs to the bridegroom. The friend who attends the bridegroom waits and listens for him, and is full of joy when he hears the bridegroom's voice.'

"John the Baptist was describing himself as the friend of the bridegroom. As the best man at the wedding. The husband in this ceremony is Jesus Himself.

"It was no accident that John 3:16 was backed up immediately by this powerful image of marriage. The Scripture was showing us that the very creation of marriage and intimate relationship between a man and a woman was ordained by God to show us the intimacy that was possible between God and his people.

"And if Jesus was the bridegroom, then who was the bride?"

He looked out over the crowd in the small church. He seemed to be waiting for an answer. He seemed to stare at the family court judge, who felt like the sermon was being directed at him personally.

"You, my friends, are the bride."

Judge Z remembered that from some long-ago Sunday school lesson, but this time the words had fresh meaning. He said to himself, *The bride of Christ? Me? That doesn't feel right.*

Pastor Billy switched gears. "An attack on marriage is trying to wipe out one of God's greatest creations. Evil forces are at work to destroy God's plan for us and his wonderful metaphor."

Judge Z knew marriage might be "irretrievably broken," as the divorce law said. But he never really thought about it in spiritual terms.

"And so, today, I hope you will you hear God's voice asking, 'Will you marry me?'" He went on to explain that a honeymoon was waiting for anyone who believes.

Reverend Billy went on to Mark, Chapter 2 and Matthew, Chapter 9, where Jesus again called Himself the bridegroom.

"Jesus was a bridegroom who came into the world looking for his bride," he concluded. "He says 'Follow me. Trust me.' But even more radical, 'Marry me.'"

Beulah was taking notes.

Reverend Billy closed by returning to John 3:16.

"When God 'gave' his one and only Son, what does that mean? Gave to die? Is that all? What if it means 'gave' to us as a bridegroom? A lover? A husband? This is about more than Jesus' death. It is about His life. And His love."

He paused to let his words sink in.

Driving back to Lexington, Judge Z's head was spinning. He was missing lunch with Beulah. He had scheduled golf with some buddies to take advantage of the last warm day of the year. Sixty two degrees and sunny. Thanksgiving was coming. He was pondering: *God so loved the world that He gave his Son to be a husband?*

He realized that he had done a fair job of believing all the right things, and obeying the voice to serve other people, but he had totally failed to understand the love of God. It almost felt like it was too late to figure it out.

JEFFERSON DAVIS
November 24

Judge Z went straight to a special detention hearing on Monday morning for a new juvenile status case. A runaway had been picked up. The small, bespectacled kid was too young to even have pimples, let alone whiskers.

His name was Jefferson Davis, given by his druggie mom and racist, skin-head dad who proudly displayed his swastika tattoos. Mom was an addict, and Dad had been in prison for years.

The judge had ordered over the weekend that Jefferson should be picked up and detained until a court hearing. He had been found sleeping under a viaduct at 2 a.m., probably drunk.

"Jefferson Lee Davis?" the judge asked with a smile after looking at his birth date in the record, "is this your birthday?"

"Yes, sir," he replied, looking glum and annoyed.

"So you're twelve today. Who is with you?"

"My grandma."

"What is your name, ma'am?"

"Teresa Butler."

"If you don't mind me saying so, you don't seem old enough to be a grand-mother." She looked about thirty-something.

"Well, I'm not really his grandmother. I am his grandpappy's girlfriend. And by the way, we call him 'Jeff.'"

"Okay. And where is Jeff's grandfather today?"

"He couldn't be here. He's not feeling well lately."

"Okay, Jeff, do you know why you're here?"

"Yes," he said. Then, after a pause, "Umm, not really." He knew he was in trouble but was not sure what was going on.

"I'm going to read to you the charges then. And I am appointing a lawyer to represent you. That is the young lady sitting next to you right now. Her name is Adele Harmon."

She reached over, smiled, and handed Jeff her card. She was fresh out of school and ready to save every kid in the world.

"This document has been signed by your grandfather, charging that you ran away from home for more than seventy-two hours in the last six months. Most recently, you were gone from Wednesday night until you were picked up by the sheriff on Sunday night this week. In addition, you've been 'beyond control of your parents,' which is a specific charge stating that you refused to follow orders at home, refused to come home when you're supposed to be there, refused to go to school, and even refused to get out of bed in the morning.

He also states that you have killed the family cat and burned down the shed behind the trailer. There's more, but that's enough for now. You understand?"

"Yes, sir."

"For now, I'm signing an order that requires you to do some basic things. One, go to school every day. Two, make passing grades. Three, obey all rules of your home, including any curfew set by your grandfather. Four, cooperate with the social workers. That would be Mrs. Hollingsworth, who is right over there in the red sweater."

Jeff turned to look at the lady sitting on his left near the wall. She nodded and smiled.

"Five, we will drug-screen you today and then randomly as requested by the social workers. Last, you should have no contact with Lewie Karr who, according to the allegations, gets you into a lot of trouble. Do you understand?"

"Yes, sir."

"Ms. Butler, if he violates any of these orders, you should call the social worker. You will have her phone number. In turn, if you call her, she will call me, and Jeff will be picked up and put into juvenile detention. It is your obligation to make sure that this order is followed. In essence, he is under a form of house arrest, and you are the jailer. Understand?"

With a big smile, "grandma" said yes. Finally someone was paying attention.

"Now, Jeff, tell me, are you having a birthday party tonight?"

The confused kid looked as if the judge was speaking a foreign language. He scrunched his eyebrows, then hung his head. "No. We don't have no birthday parties."

"Is that true? No party?" The grandma's smile disappeared and she shook her head.

He scanned the back row and there was Aaron Morris. He had spent time in a federal penitentiary on a drug conviction. Aaron was now fifty and worked for a local charity to help kids. He wasn't a social worker. But whatever he did seemed to help kids graduate high school.

He claimed that God had changed him eight years ago, and he was never going back to the streets. The judge referred dozens of kids to Aaron's program for summer jobs, basketball and tutoring. Most were black kids, but not always.

"Aaron," the judge said, "it seems to me this boy needs a birthday party. Any chance we can pull that off?"

Aaron gave a big thumbs up, consulted in whispers with one of his associates, and stood up. "Judge, if Jefferson Davis could be at 504 High Street at 5:30 p.m. tomorrow evening, we will have a party."

"Grandma, can you get Jeff down here to the courthouse tomorrow at 5 p.m.?"

"Yes, sir."

"Good. We can walk over together."

TOUGH AGE

Tuesday was a day for thirteen-year-olds.

That must be the toughest age of all, thought Judge Z. When he was thirteen, in the eighth grade at Sadieville Junior High, his dreams of playing basketball at the University of Kentucky had been crushed. He had been cut from the team. Looking back, he realized he had not been ready. He hated wind-sprints. He was lazy. He was just not tough enough. He could shoot free-throws, but that was no good if he was too slow to get fouled.

He took up golf, where slow is part of the game.

His musical career also ended that year. He was so lazy he had chosen the flute because it was easier to carry to school every day than a heavy saxophone or an unwieldy trombone.

So he had genuine sympathy for the thirteen-year-old kids in court.

First was Sharon, an eighth-grader who never knew what it was like to have two parents at home. She was raised in the custody of her dad because her mom couldn't stay out of jail. Now her mom wanted her back, and brought to court Sharon's diaries to show the girl had a crush on another girl and was "turning into a lesbian." This proved Dad was doing a bad job, said the mom.

The dad said Mom's boyfriend was a "pervert."

Both parents were probably right. Judge Z would not worry too much about his ruling because he knew Sharon would do whatever she wanted, no matter what he said. Court rulings have no chance against real life.

Next was the final hearing in a divorce case involving the thirteen-year-old Conway twins, cute little blonde girls who lived with dad because mom's latest boyfriend had a record of domestic violence with other women. The parents had been separated for three years but never divorced because they were "good Catholics." Their religion told them divorce was a sin. Dad had enrolled the girls in a Catholic school, but worried about them "sexting," a word Judge Z wished he had never heard.

One of the twins had sent a message at 2 a.m. to tell some little creep "Spud" what she would do for him. The dad seemed clueless about what to do, but the mom was worse. Sex was inevitable, she said. She only hoped her daughters wouldn't get pregnant. Success was getting her girls to eighteen without a grandbaby. She smiled a nervous laugh, "You know, judge, these young people..."

He decided the girls should stay mainly with their dad.

Next was an emergency removal hearing for young Jeannine, who had just turned fourteen and had a baby the same week. The social worker's report said her own dad was the father of the baby.

"Folks," said Judge Z, "we need the DNA results and we will go from there."

As the dad got up to leave, Deputy Palmer moved in to arrest him. According to the initial affidavit and testimony of the social worker, he had been having sexual contact with his daughter since she was five. He was facing felony statutory rape at a minimum.

The girl's life was destroyed, not to mention her child's. *How will they ever sort it all out?* he wondered. Prison for the dad; adoption or institutional care for the baby; and a lifetime of counseling and therapy and—probably—substance abuse for the daughter.

Some kids grew up too fast. Some never got a chance to be children at all. Maybe his own life at thirteen hadn't been so bad after all.

After a long day of court, he was tired but excited about Jeff's twelfth birthday party. Jeff and grandma showed up right on time. They chatted a while and the judge found out Jeff had a twin sister, Sara, whom he saw only once a month, if that. She was in the custody of an aunt, a hundred miles away in Stanford, Kentucky. It was clear that he missed her.

It was raining, so Jeff and his grandma followed the judge's car to the party in their rust-eaten red Pontiac. When they walked in they were greeted by a huge shout of "Happy birthday!" and the singing began. Jeff was stunned. He even smiled. Grandma was speechless.

A big sheet cake said, "Happy Birthday Jefferson Davis," with twelve candles.

The Judge and Aaron shared a look, winking at the irony of twenty black kids giving a party for a little white boy named Jefferson Davis. None of them had any idea that the original Jefferson Davis was president of the slaveholding Confederacy.

They gave Jeff a basketball, several birthday cards, a gift card for Applebee's, and two tickets to a UK football game. Jefferson Davis' first birthday party, age twelve, was a big success.

Later, as the judge was pulling out of the parking lot, feeling good about the party, he noticed two small legs underneath the old red Pontiac. Worried that something was wrong, he rolled down his window and asked if everything was alright.

"Oh yeah, Judge, that's just Jeff under there," said grandma. "We never can get this car started. He knows how to hotwire it. Thanks. We're fine."

Judge Z went home to celebrate the day's small victory alone. Today had been a good day. He helped a sad, lost kid. He was surprised to find himself weeping. J.J. was dead. His wife, Angelina, was dead. His father, Johnny, was dead. Even his dog Barney the beagle was gone, given away when Angelina died because he had no time to care for him. All he had was Beulah. And he only saw her on Sundays.

Jefferson Davis might make it. He wasn't sure about himself.

He fell asleep on the couch. With no wife, he had no reason to even go to bed.

HOP ALONG CASSITY
November 26

The Cassitys were doing their best to pretend to be sorry about the threatening phone call. The mother, Allie Gomez, sat quietly at the courtroom table with her court-appointed lawyer. Her brother-in-law, Larnelle Cassity, acknowledged that he was the manager of a strip club, Pure Gold. He reminded the judge that it was a perfectly legal business that even advertised in the *Lexington Times* sports pages and on sports radio. Judge Z played the tape from the voice mail.

Larnelle nodded. "Yes, Your Honor, that could be Squirrel, we call him. He's my uncle and one of our bartenders. He was probably drinking. I'm sorry. But now you need to know that my wife takes really good care of them kids. They don't know nothing about any of this."

"Well, I'm glad to hear all that," Judge Z stared at Larnelle. "For today, sir, we will ignore this threat. But you get word to Squirrel that he needs to stay away from me, and he needs to stay away from these kids. In fact, the children are being removed from your care today. You have endangered the kids by allowing them around people like Squirrel. Not to mention being exposed to a place like your strip club."

Larnelle acted upset but the judge knew he was acting. He was half grateful to get rid of the two little troublemakers. His wife had wanted to keep the kids to help her sister, but he was not too keen on kids. Larnelle was just glad the judge was letting him go home. He had been in court enough to know that the look on the judge's face meant that jail was just one miss-step away.

"One last question, Mr. Cassity. We are trying to get Allie off drugs and get her kids back to her as soon as possible. Right?"

"Yessir."

"So tell me, are the girls who work at your place doing drugs? And is your perfectly legal business a place where anyone can get drugs easily?"

Cassity was smart enough to know it was a trap. "Not sure, sir."

The judge gave him a hard stare, then let him go. Cassity scuttled from the courtroom, happy to avoid a night in jail or worse.

Social worker Donna Reese was next with a new case. She raised her right hand and swore to tell the truth, the whole truth and nothing but the truth, so help her God. In this case, the truth was sickening.

Jessica Owens, nineteen, wore an orange jail jumpsuit, facing charges for the attempted murder of her baby, born seven days ago in a toilet. No one knew her side of the story since her criminal lawyer was telling her to stay quiet. Social workers said that Jessica delivered the baby into the toilet, then came back five minutes later, put the little boy into a garbage bag and dumped the bag in a garbage can. One of her roommates, Bonnie, heard a whimper and rescued the child, which was now doing surprisingly well at the University Hospital.

The mother sat silently in front of Judge Z with shackles on her legs and handcuffs on her wrists. The orange suit indicated she was on medical watch.

The father was purported to be Bonnie's husband, Carlton. "Jessica was living with Carlton and Bonnie, who are married," the social worker explained.

"You mean like Abraham and Sarah who had their baby with Hagar?" the judge asked. The social worker looked puzzled—which was exactly how he felt when she used the word "family" to describe Carlton, Bonnie, Jessica and the baby in the toilet.

Carlton declared proudly that he was the father. He was at work when the baby was born and he wanted everyone to know he had nothing to do with "that whole toilet thing," meaning he was a man of high moral integrity.

So Judge Z would eventually have to play Solomon. Who gets the baby? Not the mother. She would undoubtedly be in prison for attempted murder.

The dad? If the DNA test said he was the father, his drug screens and lifestyle were not likely to pass the judge's smell test.

Not Jessica's relatives, who were all on drugs, which was why she lived with Carlton and Bonnie—to escape the chaos with her own family. She did not know the name of her own dad.

That left a foster family. Some married couple that was unable to have kids might make a happy ending to a sad story. Or maybe a young lady without kids who decided that being a single mom was "cool." No man required. The media made single moms sound like supermoms—the new heroes of the new and improved family. And by the time the supermoms found out how hard it was to raise a child alone, it was always too late.

Gay couples also would be available by the dozens. Half of all the adoptions in the past year approved by Judge Z had been for gay foster parents.

"Unknown baby boy," as he was named in the court records, would need a lot of luck to get a good home. He might not be alive at all if his biological mother had been smart enough to visit Planned Parenthood for a late-term abortion—her perfectly legal right to choose her own self-interest over the life of her child. Either way, the child would wind up in the trash, treated like garbage. Her mistake had been waiting too long to kill her baby.

Chapter 7

THE FIRST STONE

"Then neither do I condemn you," Jesus declared. — John 8:11

THANKSGIVING AT BEULAH'S
November 27

The feast at Beulah's house was crazy. The judge could eat himself sick without a worry. There was turkey, of course, but also ham. Not a honey baked ham—real country ham. And all the Beulah sides: mashed potatoes, green beans, sweet potato casserole, corn pudding, asparagus casserole, a real Greek salad with the potato salad on the bottom, and Greek lemon soup. One of Judge Z's favorite parts was listening to Beulah singing and humming her favorite hymns all morning as she cooked.

Present for the feast were Pastor Billy and his wife, Susie, with her parents, Joe and Doris Davis. Beulah was in the kitchen and her son was watching the NFL pregame shows.

"Billy, nice sermon on Sunday," offered Beulah to get some conversation started that did not revolve around the Dallas Cowboys or Detroit Lions.

Beulah had thought about John 3:16 and what it might be like to give up your only son. The love of a parent for a child made the famous verse even more awesome for her. "God gave His only Son..."

"Thanks, Beulah. I was just repeating what my professors taught me," Billy said.

"So Judge," said Joe Davis, "you must have some wild days. Billy has been telling me about your world."

"Yeah, I guess my world is different than yours."

Joe nodded. He was a Nationwide Insurance agent. The worst part of his day was usually a phone call about a fender bender. He liked things to be orderly. "I think the chaos of your world would make me nuts."

Judge Z could see that Joe and Doris had a lot in common with Beulah. "There's not much order in my world," he said. "Mostly disorder. Sex starts at fourteen, with multiple partners. Girls and boys use each other for fun. No one tells them 'no', only 'be careful.' Practice safe sex."

"Now there's an oxymoron," Joe laughed.

"You said it. Everyone assumes sex will happen and nothing can be done to stop it. At sixteen, the first baby comes along. The father is 'not in the picture.' The young girl is often abused but hardly knows it. Her own father is gone so the only males she knows are punks who seem so nice at first. Abortion may solve the problem. But the teenaged mom usually wants the child, to prove someone has loved her. Next, she drops out of school.

"By twenty-one, she has two to four babies or multiple abortions. Her live-in boyfriend is not the father of her kids. Neither has a job. She relies on welfare to pay the bills. If the drugs, chaos and boyfriends cause enough problems, the state gives her kids to foster parents or a relative, usually the same grandmother who raised their mother. So the beat goes on and on."

Beulah frowned and shot him a look, but he was on a roll and missed it. Judge Z had had too much caffeine that morning.

"By the time the kids are in school, problems pop up. Truancy, absences, lice, hunger pains and dirty kids. By the time mom is thirty-two, she is a grandma, raising the grandchildren. At forty-eight, she's a great grandmother, but also the hero of the family. She's the stable one. She has a modest home and no longer uses drugs. She goes to church and praises Jesus as she waits for heaven where it will all get better."

Susie and Doris looked stunned. Beulah shook her head. She knew something was happening to her son. He might not last much longer in his job.

"Enough of that talk," she said. "It's Thanksgiving."

FIVE GUYS
November 30

The Sunday sermon title was "Five Guys," and it had nothing to do with the hamburger joint. Reverend Billy Hughes began by reading from the Gospel of John, Chapter 4:

When a Samaritan woman came to draw water, Jesus said to her, "Will you give me a drink?" (His disciples had gone into the town to buy food.) The Samaritan woman said to him, "You are a Jew and I am a Samaritan woman. How can you ask me for a drink?" (For Jews do not associate with Samaritans.)

Jesus answered her, "If you knew the gift of God and who it is that asks you for a drink, you would have asked him and he would have given you living water."

Pastor Billy explained that Jesus asked about her husband, and she replied, "I have no husband." He read on:

Jesus said to her, "You are right when you say you have no husband. The fact is, you have had five husbands, and the man you now have is not your husband. What you have just said is quite true."

Billy closed the Bible and leaned on the pulpit. "You know, divorce was quite easy in the Jewish culture at that time. Like Muslims today, all you had to say was 'I divorce you' three times and it was done. This Samaritan lady was probably attractive—she had no problem getting five husbands. Her problem was keeping them. We don't know why. But it was legal under the law of Moses to simply say, 'Woman, be gone.' No divorce lawyers, no court hearings," he said, glancing at Judge Z.

"Now today, my friend Judge Zenas tells me, divorce is easier than getting a driver's license.

"The big story in this passage of scripture is that Jesus spoke to this woman at all. It was an outlandish and shocking act. She was surprised. Jewish law forbade Jesus to speak to a woman outside the presence of her husband. And this was a sinful woman.

"But Jesus saw and heard the possibility of change in this sinful lady. Her encounter with Jesus changed her. Jesus seems to have a special place in his heart for women who are alone. Women who give themselves away for a dream of respect, or a few dollars to survive another day—a myriad of reasons. But Jesus says His love can change all that.

"In the case of this sinful woman, she returned to her friends and said, 'Come, see a man who told me everything I ever did.' Her encounter with Jesus changed everything."

The cynical judge thought, *From what I see, most people never change.*

THE PERFECT FATHER
December 1

Judge Z was invited by Nicole's husband, Joe Mason, to a Monday night meeting of the Fatherhood Initiative. This was a federally funded program to try to increase the presence of fathers in the lives of their children, especially men coming out of prison. About two dozen men would be there, and Joe had a message that would be easy to remember: "The Perfect Father."

"'Be ye perfect, as your Father in Heaven is perfect,'" Joe began, quoting from Matthew 5, part of the famous Sermon on the Mount.

The word "perfect" sounded impossible to Judge Z, but he would listen. He got out his favorite pen to take notes, always hoping he might hear a quote or story worth repeating in court.

Joe pointed out that "father" was mentioned nine hundred and twenty-three times in the Bible, so it must be pretty important to God. Then he listed the primary duties of fathers, all beginning with "P." Judge Z wrote down the highlights.

1. Protector. Joe mentioned the Disneyland case which had been in the news, as an example of a father who was not present to protect his children from the fire that killed them.
2. Provider. "Child support payments are a bare minimum," said Joe. "A father's basic obligation to provide food and clothing and shelter should be obvious."
3. Professor. "A dad should be a teacher, but families are too busy with soccer games and drive-through meals, then home to watch television—which teaches all the wrong lessons."
4. Preacher. "Fathers should provide spiritual leadership for their family," Joe said.
5. Prototype. "Kids follow what they see, not hear. They need good models."
6. Prayer. "My dad prayed a lot. And that was more important than any sermon I ever heard."
7. Present. "Even if you're not good at any of the rest, you can still be there—physically, emotionally and mentally. I know that's hard to do when you're divorced and dividing weekends with their mother. But so many men I know are damaged and wounded inside because they feel like their father abandoned them. Just be there—be present."

Some of the men nodded, while others looked guilty because they knew they were failing. "So who is the perfect father here? Anyone get all seven right? Well, here's a surprise: *You* are the perfect father," Joe said, pointing to the men sitting on metal folding chairs.

"God doesn't make mistakes. God chooses the perfect father for every child. Each one of you is the perfect father for your kids."

Judge Z had no kids of his own. But God had chosen him to be "father figure" to multitudes of children in family court. The thought brought him to tears. And then he remembered that J.J.'s body was still in a freezer at the coroner's office and the tears spilled over. Joe noticed the judge's distress.

As the meeting ended, Joe said, "Men, let's lift up this man. He's dealing with all the broken families every day in court. He needs our prayers." They gathered and laid hands on Judge Z as tears ran down his cheeks.

As he got in his car, he called Milward's Funeral Home to arrange a funeral for J.J. He would pay the bill. J.J. needed to be laid to rest.

HER ONLY BEGOTTEN SON

After a busy week of domestic mayhem leading up to the holidays, the judge was ready on Friday to finish *Zhiu v. Yang*.

Florence Bonnard's Guardian Ad Litem five-page report was on his desk, summarizing the status of the young daughter, Meggie. Florence's report confirmed that the mother desired reconciliation. So did the daughter, naturally. The mom and child were in the marital residence, a rented apartment, and dad, a college professor, was paying all the bills in lieu of child support and maintenance. He was living with one of his female students, also from China. Florence reported that the mother had cried throughout her entire attempt to do the interview. She was deeply wounded.

This time, Judge Z had a Mandarin interpreter available to navigate the mother's English that was as broken as the marriage. With no lawyers present except Florence, the judge felt free to ask some nosy questions that most lawyers would find objectionable.

"Sir, who is this girl you live with?" he asked. "When do you see your daughter?" "What is your status to be in the United States?" "Do you plan to return to China?" "Do you have children in China?" "Exactly how much money do you make?" "What are you researching at UK?" "Do you plan to remarry?" "Was this marriage some sort of arranged affair to legalize everyone's immigration status?" "What's going on here anyway?" "Why is everyone on the edge of tears?"

He was getting no good answers. Mr. Zhiu was more nervous with every question, fearful that the man in the black robe would send him back to China or to prison to be re-educated.

Lucky for him, though, the judge was in a hurry. It was late Friday afternoon and J.J.'s funeral was tomorrow. His mind was already there.

"I'm going to find that this marriage is irretrievably broken with no reasonable prospect of reconciliation," Judge Z said, winding up the brief hearing. He did not feel good about this, but he eased his conscience by ordering the husband to pay an outrageous sum of child support and maintenance. If Mr. Zhiu had a lawyer along, the lawyer would scream bloody murder, but it seemed fair to the judge. The divorce was the husband's idea, so he should pay. He ordered staff attorney Clay Henderson to prepare all the paperwork and reminded the parties through the interpreter that nothing would be final until he signed the papers the following week.

The week had gone quickly for Judge Z. His spare time was consumed with planning the Saturday funeral. Deputy Palmer's church and other folks who knew J.J. offered to help. Pastor Billy would assist. Jeremiah Jackson would be buried thirty steps from Johnny Zenas in the small church cemetery just yards from the front door of Sadieville Methodist.

Judge Z chose not to speak at the ceremony. He felt like a failure. What could he say except, "I'm sorry." Instead, he sat with Wanda and cried the whole time. Her pain was just as real as if she was J.J.'s actual mom.

Beulah was there, hugging Wanda, making a difference without a lot of words. Pastor Billy offered prayers and consolation. Deputy Palmer offered words of encouragement and a few comments about his favorite Scripture, John 3:16. "God so loved the world that He gave His only begotten Son..." He told the story about the day when J.J. had confessed his faith and was baptized at the Mt. Gilead Missionary Baptist Church, a small black church in the country. Judge Z had been invited to be there that day. The hope and joy of that day didn't last long for J.J., but it was emotional and gave comfort to those left behind.

J.J.'s father was not there for the funeral. He was in prison. His biological mother was absent too, unaware that her only begotten son was dead.

WILD WOMEN
December 7

Pastor Billy continued the "wild women" theme, this time from the Gospel of John, Chapter 8. His message was that contrary to TV Land, adultery was a sin, but forgiveness was available. He read:

The teachers of the law and the Pharisees brought in a woman caught in adultery. They said to Jesus, "Teacher, this woman was caught in the act of adultery. In the Law of Moses we are commanded to stone such women. And what do you say?"

"It was a trap," Billy said.

Jesus replied, "If anyone of you is without sin, let him be the first to throw a stone at her." And the crowd began to drift away until only Jesus and the woman were left.

Jesus stood up and asked her, "Woman, where are they? Has no one condemned you?"

"No one, sir," she said.

"Then neither do I condemn you," declared Jesus, "go now and leave your life of sin."

Billy closed the Bible and said, "Jesus stood up for the woman because he understands her. He knows her past. He has compassion. He knows being faithful is difficult, especially when things have happened in your past to cause emotional and spiritual trauma."

Judge Z thought that made sense. Typically, some horrible trauma led to disruptive, disintegrating behavior that brought people to court. Abuse, drinking, drugging, cheating, divorce, bad parenting, and on and on. And he often felt like nothing he did could change that. He could try to rescue some of the passengers now and then, but the misery train would keep on rolling down the tracks.

Billy had a different approach: "There comes a time when no matter what happened to you as a kid, you have to be responsible as an adult for your behavior," he said. "Unfortunately, the word 'adultery' means nothing anymore. In fact, as marriage has declined in meaning and importance, adultery means less and less. There are websites just to meet someone else who wants to engage in an adulterous affair—nothing to be ashamed of, right? Just a misdemeanor, a broken promise.

"But if marriage is sacred, covenantal and holy, then adultery should be considered a spiritual felony of the worst kind.

"Before you condemn the hypocrites who dragged this woman to Jesus, take a look in the mirror," Billy said. Judge Z sat up, eyebrows raised. He thought about all the wild women he encountered in court. A man loves a wild woman until she becomes the mother of his baby. The same looseness and drunkenness and tattoos that attracted him on a Saturday night become the evidence he uses against her in court five years later to get custody.

His mind wandered on. *What a word for a child. "Custody." The same word used for jail.*

Billy wrapped up with the final words of Jesus to the wild woman. "Go and sin no more." Sweet and simple grace.

SUNDAY SHOCKER

Beulah looked at her son sitting in the recliner with the NFL pre-game babbling softly in the background, and made a decision. The sermon had sent her deep into some old memories. It was time for her son to hear some big-time truth. The kind that sets you free.

"Atty, was that sermon a bit racy for you? I bet you think every lady at the Methodist Church is a saint?"

"Well, they are a long way from the women I see every week."

"Well, you remember Jane Wright who died last year?"

"Sure. She was a sweet little lady who had four great kids, married to Warner Wright until he died suddenly on the farm. She was a great cook—won blue ribbons for cakes at the country fair, right? Wasn't she on the PTA when I was in elementary school? I'd say she was a saint."

"Hmm. Let me tell you the rest of the story. I recall a sixteen-year-old girl as wild as a hawk, who ran off to get married to a twenty-year-old guy she met, named Pete. She was pregnant and dropped out of school. She came home when Pete hit her and left her alone in a motel in Louisville. The baby went up for adoption. If it had happened two-thousand years ago, Jesus would have had to step in to save her like the lady in the story. And I guess in a way he did."

Judge Z hit mute on the television and turned toward Beulah, his eyes wide in shock. This was not like his mother at all to tell such stories, and certainly nothing like the Mrs. Wright he thought he knew. He thought, *I wonder if her kids have heard this?*

She continued. "At age twenty, Jane came to an old-fashioned revival at the Methodist Church when a young evangelist, Philip Currans, came to preach. She met Christ, found total forgiveness, got married later to a good man who knew her story, had those four kids and became the woman you described."

"I didn't know the Sadieville congregation was more fun than the afternoon soaps," he joked. "Tell me more."

"There's a lot you don't know," his mother said with an edge in her voice that meant this was no joke.

"Okay, I'll tell you one more. There was another girl in Sadieville who stayed in trouble all the time. Everyone called her Virginia. Some people called her Ginny. When she was seventeen, she got pregnant. The boy was Al Peterson, whose father was a deacon at the church. Ginny's parents thought she was safe with a deacon's son, but Al and Ginny went too far. Only takes one time, you know."

Judge Z nodded and sipped his coffee, thinking, *This story sounds juicy. What church lady could Ginny be? Why is mom telling me all this dirt from Sadieville Methodist?*

"Back then, abortion was not an option. And even if it was, her parents would not have allowed it. So, as often happened, Ginny was sent off to 'school' in Cincinnati to have her baby. It was a girl. Adopted by a family that was thrilled to have her.

"Ginny came back, finished high school, and got her life back on track. Her family loved her through it all."

Beulah paused, suddenly struggling with emotion as a tear ran down her cheek. "She was given a second chance. By God," she almost whispered, "and her family."

Judge Z felt like the floor was moving. How could his mother know so many details? Why was she crying? Unless...

Beulah's middle name was Virginia. Ginny.

He stared at his mom, who looked back and smiled through tear-filled eyes. Nothing more needed to be said. Judge Z realized he had a sister somewhere. And now he knew why his mother loved being around little girls.

Beulah said, "Wait right here." She got up from the table, went into her bedroom and came back with an old block of wood with a rock glued to the top. He'd seen it before, so many times he just took it for granted as one of Beulah's treasured dust-collectors along with the porcelain angels and scented candles on her bedroom dresser. Now he looked more closely. On the side was written in large letters, "The First Stone." In smaller letters, it said, "Let him who is without sin cast the first stone."

"Son," she said, laying it on the table in front of him, "there are no saints at that little Methodist Church. Especially not me."

His own eyes were getting blurry with tears and he didn't trust his voice to say anything, so he stood to hug his mother. She was weeping. For the first time, he saw her as that frightened girl Ginny. He felt a love for her that was new and fresh. He wondered how she kept such a secret for sixty years.

His mother told him how she prayed every day that her little girl was happy. "Back in those days, adoptions were permanent and sealed forever," she explained. "And maybe that's for the best."

That evening, he kissed her on the forehead, as usual, and left to drive home, knowing a sister might be out there somewhere. He wondered if Johnny ever knew this story. Probably not.

Chapter 8

GOD'S ARTWORK

God created this organic union of the two sexes. No one should desecrate God's art by cutting them apart.

— *Matthew 19:6*

I WANT A HOME
December 8

The judge made no preparation. Why should he? The case involved two college-educated suburban folks who did not have lawyers because they had enough smarts for a Do-It-Yourself divorce, just like their DIY patio they learned to build on YouTube. Why let lawyers take a slice?

Another judge might let them skip court altogether, but Judge Z had a rule: People too cheap to hire a lawyer should at least come to court one time. They usually made so many mistakes on their pleadings that it was easier to clean up the mess on the record than have them re-type everything.

The Stirlings arrived in the judge's chambers looking nervous and sad.

Judge Z remembered them from motion hour a month ago. Jack Stirling seemed in a big hurry that day, and it had caught the judge's attention.

The husband wore a Jerry Garcia tie that was five years out of style. His new girlfriend had wanted to be there but he had enough sense to make her stay at the apartment this time, which set him apart from some guys who seemed to enjoy putting their new girlfriends on display in divorce court.

The Stirlings were in their forties. He was a little paunchy, probably from piloting a desk all day; she was pretty but stick-figure thin. Anorexia? Genetics? Or just the stress of divorce?

"Nice to meet you both," the judge greeted them. "I have reviewed the record and all seems in order. This shouldn't take long. Both of you raise your right hands."

They did. Mary Stirling looked at her husband. He ignored her.

"Do you swear to tell the truth, the whole truth, and nothing but the truth, so help you God?"

"Yes," they said.

"Okay, Mr. Stirling, you are the petitioner. Your name is Jackson Anthony Stirling?"

"Yes."

"And your wife is Mary Elizabeth Stirling?"

"Yes."

"When did you and your wife separate?"

Jack looked around at his wife, lost.

"When was the last time you lived together as a husband and wife; you know, sleeping together and otherwise behaving as a married couple?"

"It's been a long time," he answered while his wife blushed.

"I need a specific date."

"A year ago today," said Mrs. Stirling with sarcasm and sadness in her voice. Her husband nodded quick agreement.

"Are there any children of this marriage?"

"Yes," said Mrs. Stirling.

"Names and dates of births, please."

Mr. Stirling dove in, providing the details for Jackson Anthony Jr., sixteen, Sarah Lynn, thirteen, and Noah Thomas, five. He looked surprised and proud that he had remembered all three birthdays.

"Do you all have a property settlement?"

"Yes."

"Is this your signature on this agreement? And by your signature, do you agree that it is fair to both parties?"

"Yes," he said. Jack Stirling was relaxing now—he could see the finish line for their marriage, just a few minutes away. He had a night of celebration planned with his girlfriend, Brandi, at the Hyatt Regency, in a room with a Jacuzzi. His mind wandered off.

"Ma'am, are the answers he has given so far accurate?"

"Yes."

"And the agreement? That is your signature and you are satisfied with it?"

"Yes, I was told this is the best I can do."

The judge started to hesitate but kept going.

"Are there any domestic violence orders in effect?"

"Oh, no," said Mrs. Stirling. "Not at all."

"Back to you, Mr. Stirling. Is your marriage irretrievably broken?"

"Yes."

"Is there any reasonable prospect for reconciliation?"

"No."

"Ma'am, do you agree?"

She was silent. It stretched for a full thirty seconds, which seemed much longer.

Judge Z stole a glance at Mr. Stirling and remembered how he had left the motion hour with his new girlfriend. He remembered that the man had hoped his divorce could be finalized without Mrs. Stirling being present. Now he knew why.

Mary Stirling produced a Kleenex to dab her eyes, then seemed to go from tearful to angry and defiant, as if she had reached a decision. *Uh-oh*, the judge thought, *here we go again.*

"I was told it didn't matter what I thought," she said, her chin quivering a bit. "That's what both lawyers I talked to told me. I explained that I wanted to reconcile with my husband. Personally, I can forgive Jack. And believe me, this is not all his fault." She hesitated as she searched for words. "It would be better for our kids. They love us both. They're sick about it. They don't know how to talk to their dad, and they don't understand what's going on, but they all wish he'd come home."

Mr. Stirling stared at her in red-faced disbelief. This was not the script they had prepared with help from Brandi's divorce lawyer friend who said it should be no problem. It was supposed to be like applying for a new credit card. Fill in the blanks, sign a form, check a box, done.

"Mr. Stirling, any hope? What if I send you to a counselor or priest? Is the marriage broken beyond repair?"

"Your Honor, I promise you this marriage is broken. I love my wife but we cannot stay married."

And that's when Judge Atticus Zenas' world changed forever. He had walked in ready to sign the papers and legally sever another marriage. But he just couldn't do it. Not this time. Maybe it was those messages from Reverend Billy. Or maybe he could hear Beulah telling him to trust his conscience and listen to his inner voice—and that voice was saying, *You're the judge—what can you do to protect this woman and her children?*

"Let's start over," he said, stalling. "Ma'am, do you believe your marriage is irretrievably broken?"

"What does that mean?" She looked him in the eye, unflinching. He remembered the Chinese mother asking the same question.

That stopped him cold again. He realized he had no answer. He realized that even after thousands of divorces, he had no idea what it meant.

"Ma'am, if I sent you to a counselor or a priest, could your marriage be salvaged?"

"I just don't know. I didn't know I had any rights at all. I was told it's automatic if he wants out."

"Well, that's mostly true. Only one party has to testify that the marriage is irretrievably broken. Let's ask the second question. Your husband says that there is no reasonable prospect for reconciliation. Do you agree?"

This time, she looked straight at Jack. "What does 'reasonable' mean? What does 'reconciliation' really mean? In fact, what does marriage even mean? What was the meaning of the vows we took in that church?" It was not a question but a statement.

"I married Jack twenty-two years ago. We have three kids. Yes, I signed that settlement, but that's because he gave me everything I could ask for. Custody of the kids. The house. All of our money in the bank. He says I will get six-thousand dollars a month until our baby finishes high school. He pays for college for the kids. Every lawyer I spoke to said it was more than fair, and nothing could be gained by going to court. So I signed it. I thought I had no other choice.

"But I don't want all of that. I want our marriage. We vowed to stay married for better and for worse. Maybe this is the worse. We've certainly had better. But I'm not ready to give up.

"I don't want child support. I want our kids to grow up with a dad. I don't want the house. I want a home."

Interesting. Someone is finally fighting to save a marriage, not kill it, Judge Z thought. "Let's take a short recess," he said. He knew what he wanted to do, but needed to check and re-check the statutes and be absolutely sure. He felt something that was a lot like big-game butterflies—he was nervous and excited as he headed for his office.

Ten minutes later, he came back and asked. "Mr. and Mrs. Stirling, can you come back tomorrow morning at 9 a.m.?"

"Why?" asked Jack, irate, still unexpectedly married. "I was told this is a routine ten-minute divorce. What's going on?"

"I don't do this often, sir, but I am the judge in your case and I am ordering you to come back. I'm sorry to disappoint you, but I'm not just some clerk who rubber stamps your divorce papers. Again, can you come back in the morning?"

"Yes," Jack said grudgingly. "Tomorrow is fine if we can get this done."

As he gaveled the hearing to a close, a voice in Judge Z's head asked, *What are you doing?* But another voice replied, *Something you should have done long ago.*

NO REASONABLE PROSPECT

As he left the Stirling hearing, Judge Z realized that the words that always closed such hearings had gone unspoken: "Both parties are restored to all their rights as single people."

Even rock-solid Karen had looked uneasy.

Back in his office, he called Professor Bertram. He explained the situation and asked, "What can I do? Any ideas? This lady wants to save her marriage. Someone needs to help her."

Brad offered, "For starters, don't forget KRS 403.033, enacted in 1966, six years before no-fault divorce came to Kentucky." He read it aloud verbatim. "'The judge of any circuit court may appoint an advisory committee to counsel with litigants in divorce actions. The committee shall serve without salary or expenses. The court may request the parties involved in these proceedings to appear before the committee at a designated time and place. The committee may make recommendation to the court as to their conclusions from said counseling. These recommendations are not binding on the court.'"

"Sounds like they didn't want judges to give up on marriage in five minutes," Judge Z said.

"That's one way to look at it," Brad replied.

"But does it still apply?"

"It's still on the books. No-fault did not repeal it or change it. As a matter of fact, as I understand it there was a lot of opposition to no-fault, and this provision was cited as a backstop to save marriages and get enough votes to pass no-fault."

"How about the statute on 'irretrievably broken'?"

"That's Section 1 of KRS 403.170," Bertram read. "'If both of the parties by petition or otherwise have stated under oath or affirmation that the marriage is irretrievably broken, or one of the parties has so stated and the other has not denied it, the court, after hearing, shall make a finding whether the marriage is irretrievably broken.'"

"But that's nothing like the way we apply it every day. It sounds like the court can still make a finding that the marriage is not broken no matter who says it is. Especially if one of the parties denies it."

"Right. The court is simply supposed to decide, after a hearing, whether the marriage is irretrievably broken."

"But the way we apply no-fault, if one side says 'I quit,' the marriage is over. This sounds like the judge has to be a real judge."

"Correct. No-fault has been stretched far beyond the original intent."

"Brad, in your research have you ever heard of such a hearing in Kentucky?"

"No. There were a couple of cases in the 1970s that seemed to water down the statute, and after that, no one took it seriously. *Laffosse versus Laffosse* from 1978 seemed to end all the discussion, although if you read the case it really did not end the debate. I was just looking at it for class this week. The case said, and I quote, 'Generally, the law in states with no-fault divorce is that the determination of whether a marriage is irretrievably broken or not is a judicial function based on the evidence in the case.' They then cite several cases from other states. And of course, KRS 403 is unequivocal. Do you have that in front of you?" Judge Z turned to the page and read:

> "If one of the parties has denied under oath or affirmation that the mar-
> riage is irretrievably broken, the court shall consider all relevant factors,
> including the circumstances that gave rise to filing the petition and the
> prospect of reconciliation, and shall: A. Make a finding that the marriage
> is irretrievably broken; or B. Continue the matter for further hearing."

"And don't forget," Brad added, "it says the judge 'may suggest counseling' and can order something called a conciliation conference. Then the judge decides if the marriage is irretrievably broken. As the Laffosse case says, it is a judicial function.

"There's a lot of 'shalls' in there," Judge Z said. "I feel like Paul on the Road to Damascus—knocked right off my feet by a light and a voice from heaven."

"Silly or not, the language is clear," Bertram said. "It doesn't say maybe. It says, '*shall* consider *all* relevant factors, including the circumstances that gave rise to filing the petition and the prospect of reconciliation.' And it requires a waiting period of two months, for cooling off and conciliation."

"Sort of like the waiting period to buy a handgun," Judge Z said. "People should stop and think before they pull the trigger on a divorce. This law has been enthusiastically ignored for over forty years."

"True," said Brad. "The legislators in the 1970s who passed this on behalf of the people of Kentucky wanted some kind of effort to save a marriage. If one party says there's hope, then the judge is supposed to stand with that party to at least give it a good faith effort."

"In other words, marriage is supposed to mean something," Judge Z said, realizing he sounded like Beulah. "Divorce is not supposed to be this easy." Judge Z asked Brad if he had heard of the starfish story. A guy finds all these starfish on the beach and throws one back in the ocean. His friend tells him it's a waste of time, "You can't save them all." And the guy says, "Yeah, but I saved that one."

"Brad, can you meet for breakfast? Tolly Ho, eggs and bacon on me. I may have some more questions."

TOLLY HO
December 9

Tolly Ho did its best business at closing time for the local bars, but it was pretty full when the judge arrived at 7 a.m.— the usual crowd of homeless people, students who dressed like homeless people, nurses in pastel scrubs from the UK hospital nightshift drinking pitchers of beer after work, cops stirring their coffee and a few people with tattoos and pink hair who sneaked wary glances at the cops and stayed as far away as they could.

Judge Z ordered at the counter and waited for his "Four eggs over easy and bacon for Z" to be called out. Brad was waiting at a table for two, working on a cheese omelet.

Over mouthfuls and sips of coffee, they got to work.

"Brad, I have a client for you."

Brad gave him a look that said he knew what was coming. "Judge, you know I have not practiced real law for eight years, and I didn't like it much when I did."

"Yes, I know, but just hear me out. As a member of the bar you're supposed to do so many hours of pro bono work. Well, I have a pro bono case, and this is right up your alley. This situation is the reason you became a lawyer."

"Don't tell me. It's the same case we discussed yesterday?" Brad asked.

"Yes. I need your help. I could always order you—judges can do that, you know. But I'd rather think of it as your idea."

"Whoa, you've got the wrong guy. I would be a disaster in court. That's like asking someone who hasn't picked up a golf club in eight years to play in the U.S. Open."

"I've thought of that. But who else am I going to ask? Everyone else who practices divorce law plays by the same quickie divorce rules. Look, you could use some of your students as your legal team. Instead of teaching theory, you can make it real. Make them your law firm."

Brad looked less certain. But then he shook his head. "So now you've got the weekend hacker in the U.S. Open, helped by a caddy that has never even seen a golf course. Are you crazy? "

Judge Z paused for a bite of eggs and sip of coffee. "Maybe winning isn't everything. Maybe just making a point about marriage—taking a stand—is everything. Or at least everything we can do right now.

"What I know from experience and you know from teaching is that kids do better in homes with both parents, especially when they are married. Mrs. Stirling knows it instinctively, and she is trying to save her children and her marriage. Shouldn't we do something to help her? At least a hearing to make sure the marriage really is over?" He could tell Brad was getting interested.

After a pause, Brad shook his head as if he could see trouble coming and said, "Alright, alright, now that I'm joining Custer's Last Stand, what's next?"

"I plan to give Mrs. Stirling a hearing on whether the marriage is irretrievably broken. I will tell the husband that he needs to come prepared to tell me what marriage means and what it means for a marriage to be broken. He needs to answer all my questions about his marriage and family because, as the statute clearly says, 'the court shall consider all relevant factors, including the circumstances that gave rise to filing the petition and the prospect of reconciliation.'"

"It certainly gives you a lot of latitude."

"Exactly. Relevant factors could be the girlfriend. It covers those three kids who don't want this divorce any more than the wife does. Mr. Stirling may show up today with a lawyer, and she will need one too. I'm talking about you."

"Judge, you can't just appoint me like this. We're friends. We'll both get disbarred, or at least get our wrists slapped."

"I've thought about that too. Remember the scene in *To Kill a Mockingbird* where the judge appears on Atticus Finch's front porch and says, 'Atticus, I need you. That boy Tom Robinson that got arrested needs you too. If you'll let me, I plan to appoint you to represent him. You're the only one around here able to do it.' Well, that's us. If this blows up, I will take the blame. It's my idea. I ordered you, so you had no choice."

Brad arrived at the courthouse as "ordered" at 8:30 a.m. He found Mary Stirling sitting alone in the hallway. It had to be her: forty-something, attractive but too thin, blond, well-dressed. She looked nervous and uncomfortable. Then again, so did everyone who was not a calloused regular in court.

"Mrs. Stirling, I'm Brad Bertram and Judge Zenas has appointed me to be your lawyer in this divorce." He put out his hand and she took it.

"Oh yes, he told me yesterday he might do that. Nice to meet you."

"Can I explain some things to you?"

"Of course. I am sure you have done hundreds of these cases?"

Bertram had a beard, but he still looked like he was in high school. "Actually, I'm a professor and I have not been to court in a long time." He decided not to tell her that he had been to court once in his life. And that was to probate his mother's will.

He could tell his answer made her more nervous, but she pretended to take it in stride. He forged ahead. "Look, Mrs. Stirling, I know you must be afraid and you would like to have a more experienced lawyer. But all I know is this judge, who I respect, told me to be here, and here I am. I teach Constitutional and Family Law at UK. I have degrees from Yale and Columbia, for whatever that's worth. I do know a lot about marriage and divorce law. But most important, I believe in marriage. My wife and I have two little girls. And if you want to slow down this hurry-up divorce and save your marriage, I'm on your side."

She seemed to relax. For the next five minutes he explained what would happen and what they would do. Like nearly everyone who winds up in court, she was reassured to know she had a lawyer looking out for her.

Finally, he asked, "Is that what you want to do?"

"Yes, I do."

"Okay then. For today, trust me and the judge. You will not need to say anything."

"Okay, but what will this cost?"

"Nothing. This is pro bono. In Latin that means 'for free'." She nodded and smiled.

The hearing was in Courtroom G, Fourth Floor. No more conference room hearings. The Stirling case was going to court.

Jack Stirling had asked around and hired the lawyer he had seen in motion hour a month ago. Harry Wolff. Jack was assured by Wolff that the matter would be closed today for a flat fee of five hundred dollars. Jack suffered through a lecture about how stupid he had been to try to get a divorce without a lawyer. But Harry agreed to clean up the mess. He would send his young associate Anna Ollie.

OVER HER HEAD

The hearing started at 9 a.m. It was over in twelve minutes flat. Anna Ollie returned to Harry Wolff and Associates looking like she had been run over by a train. Her straight A's in high school and 3.5 GPA in law school had not helped in court.

She had been hired by Mr. Wolff three weeks ago as a favor to her dad, who spent a fortune on Harry to divorce Anna's step-mother. There was an opening on the staff because Mr. Wolff's tirades had run off yet another young, underpaid associate who could take the long hours but not the abuse.

"So how'd it go?" Harry asked Anna and Jack Stirling as they sat down in his office. "That was fast. I told you it would be routine, right?"

Anna hesitated, but Jack did not. "No, it was not what you said it would be. The judge wouldn't let anyone talk. He went on a rant about marriage being both legal and sacred. He read stuff about what it means to be uncontrollably broken or whatever. Honestly, I don't know what he was saying. He talked about the definition of marriage in Kentucky. And then he ordered me to get counseling with Mary. All I know is I'm still not divorced. I want my money back."

"Anna, is this true? What did you do?" Wolff demanded.

Anna clutched her legal pad and read from her notes. "The judge did three things. He set a final hearing date in one hundred days. He mentioned expert witnesses, and told both sides to exchange witness and exhibit lists. I think he said March second would be the trial.

"Second, he ordered Mr. and Mrs. Stirling to go to counseling. The wife showed up with a lawyer who cited KRS 403-something, that the respondent does not believe the marriage is irretrievably broken and is entitled to a reconciliation conference with a competent counselor," she read from her notes. "The Stirlings have an appointment with a counselor, Don Lathem, next Monday. It was all set up. Judge Z said it would be, and I quote, 'discernment counseling.' This Lathem guy will help the couple discern if they really need a divorce, and help the court discern if the marriage is really broken with no reasonable prospect of reconciliation."

Harry Wolff was fidgeting, waiting for Anna to finish.

"And third, he was considering appointment of a committee—he cited KRS 403.033—to meet with the parties. He ordered us to be back in court at Motion Hour next Friday to get the initial report from the counselor."

"A committee? Discernment counselor?" Harry boomed. "What is Zenas talking about? I've never heard of either one and I've been doing this for thirty years. Anna, you must have made some mistake. Either that sumbitch judge is crazy, or you are the worst lawyer in history. Maybe both."

"Sir, I'm just reporting what he said. It's all here in my notes."

"Your notes," Wolff exploded. "Whaddya think this is, law school?"

Jack Stirling winced as he saw the young woman seem to shrink before his eyes. "Hold on, Wolff, this was not her fault. I was there. She has it right. "

Wolff seemed surprised that his client was still there. He gathered himself with some difficulty and grudgingly said, "Okay, we'll find out about that. Do you have anything else in those magic notes?"

"Yes. Mrs. Stirling came with a lawyer—"

"You already said that."

"—whose name is Bertram."

"Never heard of him. Did anyone get his card?"

"He told me he didn't have any cards."

"Never heard of a lawyer without a card. Anna, call the Bar Association and make sure he's a real lawyer with a real license. It's probably one of the judge's golf buddies."

Jack said, "This Bertram guy hardly said a word. The judge did all the talking. Probably some guy Mary met at church."

"Okay, Anna, I want you to get to work. Start with a motion for the judge to recuse. If he refuses, we'll go from there. Mr. Stirling, you understand I cannot do all this for five hundred. We will have to start billing you at our normal rates."

"Well, you told me you'd finish the case for five hundred. You didn't put any asterisks or fine print on that. This seems like your problem, not mine."

"That was before this nutcase judge screwed it all up. Look, we're going to get you another judge, I hope. And if that fails, we have other options. But none of them were included in a flat no-fault fee."

Stirling realized he was stuck. He needed a real lawyer, now more than ever. His girlfriend, Brandi, was sitting in the Jacuzzi at the Hyatt Regency and she would not be happy. He needed this divorce and he needed Harry Wolff.

But Harry was also stuck. He had emailed Stirling that he would "finish your divorce for a flat fee of five hundred dollars."

It took twenty minutes of haggling and negotiation to finally agree on a rate of one hundred and fifty dollars per hour, half of Harry's normal rate, with a maximum fee not to exceed five thousand. Anna Ollie would work for seventy-five dollars an hour, half her normal fee. No one was happy.

As soon as Jack Stirling left, Harry and Anna got to work. Motions to Recuse were always risky, Harry explained. Judges could get offended. It was, after all, a document telling the judge, in plain English, why the lawyer did not believe the judge could be fair.

There was not a bigger insult to a judge. You could call him stupid. He might agree. His wife did that all the time.

You could call him fat and ugly. He didn't care. The robe covered it all up.

You could call him almost anything else and get away with it.

But unfair? That maligned his integrity, honesty and professional ethics. It struck at the core of a judge's character. An unfair judge was to justice what a crooked cop was to police work. So the lawyer better get it right, or else.

A smart lawyer would couch a motion to recuse in the "appearance" of impropriety. Something like, "Your Honor, I certainly know from being in front of you for many years that you are fair in all your cases and would never do anything even slightly unethical, but my client doesn't know you as I do. Perhaps you can see why he is concerned about your fairness. Therefore, out of an abundance of caution, we need to ask you to step down from this case for your own protection."

Harry told Anna to use the same strategy. But what he really wanted to say was: "Judge Z, you no good piece of crap idiot who almost didn't even get into law school, who do you think you are? I knew you were stupid the first day I met you at UK undergrad twenty-eight years ago, but this takes the cake. You are living proof that judges are too stupid to practice law. And now you're drunk on religion, violating everything about church and state. I suppose next you will order everyone to go to Sunday school."

Judge Z received the Motion to Recuse at 4 p.m. The ink was hardly dry.

RECUSAL REFUSAL
December 12

Harry's motion to kick Judge Zenas off the case was set for a hearing on Friday, during Motion Hour, when a crowd of a hundred would fill the courtroom. Judge Z planned to call it first, to let other lawyers and their clients listen as Harry tried to kick him off the case.

He knew it was creating a buzz at the courthouse. That would give him an audience to make some points about marriage and divorce. He could chastise Harry and every divorce lawyer in Lexington for their total disregard for the law's intent to "preserve the integrity of marriage," which was in the preamble to Kentucky's divorce statutes.

Judge Z started with a smile: *"Stirling versus Stirling."*

"To be heard, Your Honor," said Harry Wolff casually as he sat back down to wait his turn.

"Let's hear it now, Mr. Wolff."

"Now?"

"That's right. Now." Ears perked up from every lawyer in the room. What was happening here?

Harry and Jack Stirling dutifully walked forward. So did Brad Bertram, making his rookie appearance in motion hour, along with his pro bono client, Mary, who was looking sharper today. Jack's girlfriend was there too, sitting on the front row to make sure her man was taking this seriously. She had a nice fish on the line and didn't want to lose him. She had him right up next to the boat.

"Mr. Wolff, I read your motion. I also read between the lines. You think I am the stupidest judge in the history of Kentucky. You probably remember that I only got into UK law school as an alternate. But here's a surprise. I agree with you. I am the stupidest judge in Kentucky. Because I have been presiding in family court for ten years and never read the definition of marriage until four days ago. I never saw the purpose statement of KRS 403. I never saw the section about reconciliation and integrity of marriage.

"Mr. Wolff, let me read you some of our statutes. I wonder if anyone in this room full of divorce lawyers has ever seen this.

"Listen to this, from KRS 403.110: 'This chapter shall be liberally construed and applied to promote its underlying purposes, which are to strengthen and preserve the integrity of marriage and safeguard family relationships.'

"Mr. Wolff, let's stop right there. Let those words sink in." Silence covered the room like a blanket of heavy snow. "It goes on to discuss promoting amicable settlements and mitigating harm to spouses and children. But it all starts with the idea of preserving marriage."

Judge Z shuffled some papers. Harry smirked and glanced around at the confused audience. The room was as quiet as the 18th green with a championship putt on the line.

"The statute is also clear that any person who thinks the marriage may not be broken beyond repair is entitled to a hearing on that. The divorce train is supposed to be a slow train with the possibility of stops, not the Orient Express.

"Your motion for me to recuse is taken under advisement until I have had time to actually read it. I will read the law you cite, I promise. But I am the judge for now. We will have a case management conference on December 22 at 9 a.m. I will rule on your motion then. Mr. Bertram, you should file a response to their motion within the next ten days. Have a nice weekend."

Harry Wolff had not been allowed to speak a word. He smirked and raised his eyebrows at the other lawyers who were all staring at him as he walked away, but he knew his fellow bar members were probably happy to see him take some hits.

BERTRAM, MASON, JENNINGS AND BURCH
December 13

Brad Bertram knew he needed some help in a hurry. So instead of studying legal theory, the class would become a small law firm to help one woman save her marriage.

He had sent each student an email "Final," asking them to come prepared to write for an hour on a fact scenario, pretending to represent either the husband or the wife in a divorce. What would they do? What laws would be relevant? The facts of the Stirling case were presented as the final exam, followed by questions.

The hour went quickly. After the papers were submitted to the professor, he explained that this was a real case, and that he had become something almost never seen on the law school faculty—a real lawyer. "If you would like to help, just see me after class. No pressure. No credit. Just a chance to learn a lot."

Three students stayed behind to wait for him as the rest filed out.

The one he had hoped for was Nicole Mason. She was the daughter of one of the first black judges in Virginia. Brad was sure by her answers and comments in class that she was a strong believer in God's definition of marriage. She was happily married with two kids.

Nicole was clearly excited about the chance to go to court and make Kentucky legal history.

Sally Jennings was also on board. She saw a chance to help a woman in need.

And so was openly gay Michael Burch. Michael's own parents had divorced when he was five, and he still wore the scars. As a child he had dreamed of bringing his mom and dad back together. Finally, he had a small chance to fight for other children.

The next morning, Bertram, Mason, Jennings & Burch, as they jokingly called themselves, had their first planning session over coffee in Styrofoam cups. They divided the papers from the class for review.

"Harry Wolff's motion to recuse is going nowhere, so his next move will be a petition with the Kentucky Supreme Court to have him removed," Brad said. "Our job is to keep Judge Z on this case. We need some research on recusal."

"Sure, I can do that," Sally offered.

"Good. Here's how I see it. The Stirlings have been sent to Don Lathem for counseling. That will likely fail, but Lathem will still likely agree with Mrs. Stirling that the marriage is not irretrievably broken. If so, he can testify that there's still a reasonable prospect of reconciliation."

"What makes you think so?" Sally asked.

"I think the judge picked him for a reason. From what I hear, he's pretty stubborn when it comes to marriage counseling. He believes almost any marriage can be saved with the proper counseling."

"What else?" Michael asked.

"The judge is talking about this crazy committee that's in the statute. Michael, I'd like you to research that, just in case. Meanwhile, we get ready for a trial to decide if the marriage is broken with no hope of reconciliation. And that means we put the burden on the husband to prove the marriage is beyond repair."

"That's a huge burden of proof," Nicole nodded.

"He has to go first," Brad continued. "And under the statute, we have a lot of latitude."

Nicole said, "You mean the part that says, let's see here, it's in my notes... here it is: 'all factors and circumstances leading up to the filing of the petition'? That really covers a lot. It sounds like we can ask him almost anything."

"You've been doing your homework, I see. You're right. This law gives us a loophole like the Grand Canyon."

"So we get to bring in our own witnesses?" Michael asked.

"Absolutely," Brad said. "Here's a list of leading authors, researchers and experts on marriage. I'd like you to start contacting them. Let's see who is willing to help. Make sure they understand we have no money to pay them. "

Chapter 9

LARGENESS OF MARRIAGE

Let the little children come unto me.

— MARK 10:14

JESUS ON DIVORCE
December 14

Pastor Billy's message was about divorce. The timing was good for Judge Z, who was rethinking everything he had thought he knew about the topic.

"Before I start, I know divorce is a touchy subject. I know people sitting here today are divorced. This message is not intended to make you feel guilty."

Judge Z thought, *If anyone should feel guilty it would be me, the guy who has divorced thousands of couples.*

Pastor Billy continued. "But if we are to discuss marriage, divorce cannot be avoided. So let's start by asking: what did Jesus say about divorce? Turn to Matthew 19, where some legalists called Pharisees tried to trick him. I will read from The Message this morning:

One day the Pharisees were badgering Jesus: "Is it legal for a man to divorce his wife for any reason?"

He answered, "Haven't you read in your Bible that the Creator originally made man and woman for each other, male and female? And because of this, a man leaves father and mother and is firmly bonded to his wife, becoming one flesh—no longer two bodies but one. Because God created this organic union of the two sexes, no one should desecrate his art by cutting them apart."

They shot back in rebuttal, "If that's so, why did Moses give instructions for divorce papers and divorce procedures?"

Jesus said, "Moses provided for divorce as a concession to your hard heartedness, but it is not part of God's original plan. I'm holding you to the original plan, and holding you liable for adultery if you divorce your faithful wife and then marry someone else. I make an exception in cases where the spouse has committed adultery."

Jesus' disciples objected, "If those are the terms of marriage, we're stuck. Why get married?"

But Jesus said, "Not everyone is mature enough to live a married life. It requires a certain aptitude and grace. Marriage isn't for everyone. Some, from birth seemingly, never give marriage a thought. Others never get asked—or accepted. And some decide not to get married for Kingdom reasons. But if you're capable of growing into the largeness of marriage, do it."

Billy said, "First, Jesus says marriage is not for everyone. That's because it's not easy." He smiled to take the edge off such a serious subject. "Jesus then finishes by saying that if you're capable of 'growing into the largeness of marriage, do it.' That's interesting—the largeness of marriage. Isn't it much easier to just walk away or quit? He's too much trouble. So I will walk away. She's never going to change. So I will walk away.

"But 'large' people don't walk away. They hang in there to find out what God wants to teach them through marriage. Jesus is saying that divorce is for small people."

Judge Z thought, *That sounds about right. What I see are the people who aren't 'large' enough to fight for their marriages.*

Pastor Billy continued. "One of my favorite marriage books is by John Eldredge, *Love and War*. Eldredge says marriage is a 'love story set in the midst of a war.' For some of us it probably feels like war. But Eldredge also calls marriage a divine conspiracy. We are lured in by love and sex. But then a side benefit comes unexpectedly. God uses your spouse to transform you.

"I have to admit, I eat better because of my wife. Without her, I would be a total bum. Whenever she goes out of town I sleep on the couch because I don't like to make the bed. I eat fried chicken and barbecue for every meal. But she keeps me on track to be the man I am supposed to be."

The women nodded, while the men crossed their arms and looked skeptical.

"So, what is marriage and divorce? Jesus says that the union of man and woman in marriage is a beautiful form of God's 'art'. So, divorce is a desecration of God's artwork. Divorce is splashing graffiti on God's artwork.

"Moses approved divorce, but not because it was a good idea. He approved it only because the people were so hard-hearted that they couldn't see any other way."

Now we divorce people because we actually think it is a good idea, thought the judge as he left after church.

Later at Beulah's, the conversation quickly turned to the sermon topic. "Did you ever consider a divorce with dad?"

"No. Murder? Yes. Divorce? No," she answered with a grin over her shoulder as she worked at the stove. "Remember John the Baptist as the 'best man' at the wedding of Jesus and his bride? You know what happened to John the Baptist? He got his head chopped off. Why? Because he looked King Herod straight in the eye and told him he was sinning by divorcing his wife to marry his brother's wife. He was unafraid to speak God's truth about the sanctity of family."

"What are you saying? You want me to get my head chopped off?"

"No. But someone has to have the courage to say 'This is wrong! Divorce is not supposed to be easier than getting a haircut.'"

Judge Z squirmed. He was catching it from all sides. Beulah. Pastor Billy. The Stirlings. Harry Wolff. Even the Holy Spirit. There was a voice that wouldn't go away, and it kept asking him questions.

HOLD ME TIGHT
December 17

Judge Z had done his research. He knew Don Lathem from a previous case a year earlier. Don had made him aware of Sue Johnson and a book she wrote in 2008 called *Hold Me Tight*, a summary of her theories on reconciling broken relationships. She had developed something called EFT, emotionally focused therapy.

Lathem was a true believer in her EFT theories, which he used to save marriages, according to his website.

Lathem had also educated the judge about William Doherty, a Minnesota counselor and researcher who was proposing that counselors use "Discernment Counseling." This meant that the counselor would help parties discern if a divorce was really a good idea. On the interstate freeway of divorce there were no speed limits. Discernment counseling was a rest stop. Doherty's research showed that 30 percent of all cases in court had some shreds of hope, at least in the beginning when the case was filed.

Now the Stirlings, despite the objections of Mr. Stirling and his legal team, were sitting in Lathem's office. Jack Stirling had his arms crossed, sending a clear signal that he was there only by court order.

Lathem broke the ice by telling Jack, "I know you are only here because you have to be. I understand that." He had a good idea what the problems were. The memo from the judge asked: "Is there a way for this couple to remain together for the sake of the children? Is there any reasonable prospect of reconciliation?"

"Jack, I would guess you are concerned about the effect this will have on your children. Is that right?" Lathem asked.

Jack nodded.

"Tell me about your children," Lathem said, and Jack smiled as he began to describe his kids. But soon he was wiping tears from his eyes.

When Mrs. Stirling was asked how the children were doing, she brought up a conversation with Noah, who had asked, "Mommy, where's daddy?"

"I told him he's not here right now. Sometimes daddies have to be gone. But you will see him again soon. He loves you and would never be gone for long." She looked at her husband.

Lathem turned to Jack. "Jack, did you have a conversation with Noah? How did it go?"

He had no reply. The silence stretched. The facts were sinking in. Jack Stirling began to realize that he was not just divorcing his wife. He was divorcing his children.

After more questions and discussion, Lathem encouraged both of them to be honest with themselves about the guilt and sorrow they were feeling about breaking up their family. Jack said, "I know this will be hard on my kids, but I just don't see any way for us to be happy together."

Lathem closed the session by giving them a book to read. Homework about EFT and the seven transforming conversations that need to happen to reconcile a relationship—connecting, forgiving, bonding and keeping love alive. Jack was leaning with his forearms on his knees, fully engaged, more relaxed and open.

Jack agreed to come back for one more session. He left first. His girlfriend was waiting in the car and worked him over verbally all the way back to the apartment. When they got there she tried to make him remember why he was leaving his family for her. By midnight, half drunk and in Brandi's bed, Jack decided Lathem was a kook. He had forgotten about his children. He decided his wife was a religious fanatic. The judge should be disbarred. Professor Bertram was a punk. Even Harry Wolff was overrated. Why couldn't he get a simple divorce?

PEARL HARBOR BLUES
December 21

Reverend Hughes told the small congregation that his sermon would be short and sweet. He was almost done with his marriage series. But the title was puzzling: "Pearl Harbor Blues." He apologized because the sermon title seemed to have so little to do with Christmas.

"I watched the movie *Pearl Harbor* on TV this week. Picture a quiet Sunday morning in Hawaii. The Navy was mostly sleeping in, recovering from a Saturday night hangover. The admiral was playing golf. While they slept and played, the Japanese declared war and sent planes to destroy the American Pacific fleet. We were at war, but only the enemy knew it.

"Today, the typical American church person is spiritually living in December 7, 1941. They would be shocked to learn that they have an enemy called Satan, who has declared war on marriage and our kids and our very souls. We are living in the middle of a spiritual World War II, but we act like we're in Mayberry with Andy Griffith.

"A few weeks ago I mentioned *Love and War* by John and Staci Eldredge, who say marriage is a love story set in the midst of a war. Satan himself is waging war against us. He takes pleasure in destroying families. He loves it when Christian people get divorced, move on to remarriage or, even worse, just live with someone, giving up on holy commitments in marriage completely.

"Even Christmas takes place in the midst of such a war. Herod was at war with the baby Jesus and killed all those other babies in the Slaughter of the Innocents. Joseph's first decision as Jesus' father was to leave the war zone of Bethlehem and head for Egypt. He heard in a dream: 'Get up. Take the child and his mother and flee to Egypt. Herod is on the hunt for this child, and wants to kill him.'

"Joseph knew his primary purpose on earth was to protect and nurture the baby Jesus. But most of us are like the American admiral in the movie, who said, 'We didn't face facts.'

"So let's take a look at those facts. First, we cannot defeat an enemy if we pretend there is no enemy."

Judge Zenas thought about the time he quoted Beulah in court and said that the devil was real. The social workers and lawyers in court that day rolled their eyes and fidgeted with discomfort. But church people were not all that much different.

"Remember how, in the movie, the Japanese admiral said after the raid, 'I fear all we have done is awaken a sleeping giant'? Well, that giant is you, the church. We put on impressive services and build bigger buildings to draw more people—but for what? What does it take to wake the giant?

"The same devil who tried to kill the baby Jesus is now raging against our families. But the good news is that if we wake up, it is not too late."

Reverend Billy paused a moment, then said, "You're probably wondering what all this has to do with Christmas. Well, it's this: The whole theme of Christmas is about the power of a baby to change everything. Why did God choose to come into the world as a baby named Jesus? He could have come as some mighty unexplainable force, in great glory for all to see. But He came as a baby, in an obscure place, to a simple couple. Why?

"For starters, babies have the power to change people. Babies keep drug addicts clean. Babies change a house into a home. Babies look like their parents, which keeps families connected forever. Babies bring out the best in otherwise messed up people.

"Babies laugh and smile over the simplest of joys, and remind us that we should do the same. Even unborn babies have power. The first witness to the presence of Jesus on earth was an unborn baby, John the Baptist, in Elizabeth's womb. Baby John leaped with joy in the presence of unborn baby Jesus."

As he listened to Reverend Billy, Judge Z thought about Ivory and her little boy. *He's right. Babies really do change people.*

GETTING PERSONAL
December 22

Judge Z began to have second thoughts about scheduling the Stirling case before Christmas. This was the busiest week of the year in family court, helping dysfunctional families decide if Santa Claus will come to mommy's house or daddy's house. He would make his ruling and leave it up to the lawyers to notify the North Pole.

He greeted everyone as he entered the courtroom, sat down and they went on the record.

"Mr. Wolff, let's begin with your motions. But before we get started, let the record show that both parties are present with counsel. Harry Wolff for the petitioner. Anna Ollie is also here for Petitioner. Brad Bertram for the respondent. His Paralegal Assistant Nicole Mason is present. And the court has also invited Florence Bonnard, who may be appointed as a guardian ad litem for the three Stirling children, so they will have their own attorney. They should have a voice."

"May it please the court," Wolff began, with no intention of pleasing the court, "we have several matters. Our motion for recusal is still pending. This court has made statements both on and off the record which indicate a bias against Mr. Stirling and his attempt to obtain an ordinary uncontested divorce. This case—what we're doing right now—is unprecedented in Kentucky. With all due respect to this court, there is no factual or legal basis for us to even be here today. Therefore we respectfully ask the court to recuse."

Judge Z thought he was done, but then Wolff continued.

"We will not even mention that there are rumors that the court has a personal relationship with counsel for Mrs. Stirling, and maybe even Mrs. Stirling herself, and that this court solicited a lawyer to represent her pro bono. If that is true, Your Honor, there is even more reason for you to recuse."

This time Judge Z paused to make sure Wolff was really done. "Okay, Mr. Wolff. For someone who will 'not even mention rumors' you did a pretty good job getting them in the record. You are correct that I know Mr. Bertram. I know hundreds of lawyers in Lexington. Mr. Bertram and I have had discussions about the law from time to time, just as I have had general and hypothetical discussions with you, Mr. Wolff. I have been to Mr. Bertram's class as his guest three times.

"I have also known you for thirty years. We met at UK in undergrad. Remember those days? We had a drink together on occasion. You were even married then, remember?"

Judge Z was moving fast toward sarcasm and bad humor. "I have even attended the dinner every year which you and some other lawyers put on for the judiciary. We hobnob and chit-chat over drinks and filet mignon at Idle Hour Country Club, all paid for by the lawyers who are simply saying 'thanks' to the judges for being so smart and good. I still remember your smile at me last year as you toasted the 'finest collection of circuit judges in the state of Kentucky.' It sounded like you genuinely appreciated our integrity and professionalism.

"So, I cannot recuse from every case in which I know a lawyer. It is also correct that I called Mr. Bertram and asked him to handle this case. I appoint lawyers every day here. I have a panel of a dozen lawyers I appoint to represent indigent parents every day. In fact, if you would like I could put you on my list, Mr. Wolff. It pays about thirty-five dollars an hour. Interested?"

Wolff shifted and raised his gold pen to say something, but Judge Z continued. "As for your hint about my relationship with Mrs. Stirling, do you have any facts to back up your insinuation?"

"Just the word on the street, Your Honor."

"Wow, so now, instead of quoting statutes and law and facts, you rely on rumors from the streets?" Judge Z shook his head.

Harry swallowed his angry reply. He had no choice. He could rant and rave and fire someone if this was his office. He could throw his wife out the door if this was his home. But this was the domain of Judge Atticus Zenas.

"Next, Your Honor, as you might expect, we object to the unnecessary appointment of a guardian ad litem. These parties have already signed a settlement agreement which resolves custody and time-sharing."

Brad responded, "Mr. Wolff is correct that the parties signed an agreement, but the agreement means nothing until it is approved by this court. Our first task is to discover if the marriage is irretrievably broken, and if there is a reasonable chance or prospect of reconciliation.

"As I read the statute, the hearing will involve, quote, 'all relevant factors that led to the filing of the petition.' These three children cannot be ignored. Florence Bonnard needs to tell us what the children are thinking. This case should actually be about them. Not Jack. Not even Mary."

Judge Z nodded. "This divorce is not final until I sign. I am not refusing to grant the divorce. I simply intend to conduct a hearing which was clearly anticipated by the Kentucky Legislature when they gave us KRS 402 and

KRS 403. Just because I'm the first judge in the history of Kentucky to follow the law does not mean I am wrong. If the Kentucky Supreme Court tells me different, fine.

"Your motion to recuse is overruled. Your objection to appointment of the GAL is noted and also overruled. Gentlemen, anything else?"

"Nothing at this time, Your Honor," both lawyers chimed in together.

"Okay. Let's lay down some groundwork for the hearing. You have both received a preliminary report from the counselor, Don Lathem. You can read it later. As you will see, he found that this marriage may not be irretrievably broken and he believes there may be a reasonable prospect of reconciliation. He will see the parties one more time.

"For now, he cited several reasons for possible reconciliation. Mrs. Stirling has forgiven her husband for his indiscretions, she has admitted to her own role in the breakup of the marriage, and the three children desperately want them to stay together. I urge Mr. Stirling to read this report carefully, paying special attention to the opinions of his children. I also order you both, Mr. and Mrs. Stirling, to cooperate with the process.

"Our next step is a full hearing on whether the marriage is irretrievably broken."

Judge Z asked the lawyers how much time they needed to prepare and how many witnesses they expected.

Wolff jumped at the chance. "Your Honor, we're ready today. Our witness will be Jack Stirling and maybe Rev. Donna Cunningham, who counseled this couple for months and says the marriage is over. Both people need to move on. I would be free any time."

"Mr. Bertram, are you ready?"

"Judge, we are interviewing witnesses and believe we will have about eight. We need at least two months."

Harry Wolff rolled his eyes and threw his hands up to show his disgust.

Brad continued. "To prove the marriage is not irretrievably broken, we need to show the court what marriage is. No one has ever actually done that.

"Kentucky's statutory definition of marriage is virtually meaningless, except the part that says 'united in law for life.' For life. So, this is serious to

Mary Stirling. We need at least two months to arrange witnesses. Some are from out of town."

Harry looked like he might have a stroke. He wanted to yell, "This whole thing is rigged," but he had to save that for the office.

The judge confirmed the trial date, along with deadlines for exchanging witness and exhibit lists, discovery and depositions. On March 2, *Stirling v. Stirling* would go to Fayette Circuit Family Court.

Harry walked back to his office faster than usual, forcing Anna Ollie to almost jog to keep up. By lunchtime he had vented on the staff, and Anna and Harry were ready to file a Petition for Disqualification to the Kentucky Supreme Court.

Harry also sent emails to every divorce lawyer in town explaining that this judge was refusing to grant an uncontested divorce. The judge was safe politically, recently re-elected to an eight-year term, without opposition. But Harry could turn up the heat from simmer to scorch. And someone would undoubtedly tip off the press, making his phone ring with calls for comment.

Frustrated by Judge Z's court, Harry would take his case to the court of public opinion, where he couldn't lose. Leaks are unethical, but the press didn't care about the ethics as long as they were first to get the story. The *Lexington Times* never liked Judge Z. They could sell some papers with this story of a judge who refuses to grant divorces. Sunday morning edition. Front page stuff.

Harry also put Anna to work on a Judicial Conduct Commission complaint. He told her to throw the book at the judge. Something would stick. If the Supreme Court of Kentucky didn't force him to recuse, the JCC could issue a scathing reprimand. Meanwhile, editorials and news stories would inflame public opinion and set a fire under the judge's robe.

Harry wasn't about to tell his client, but from here on, he would have gladly worked this case for free.

Since the judge would not recuse, Harry's first strike would be a motion to the state supreme court, pursuant to KRS 26A.015, to disqualify Judge Zenas from the Stirling case. Under Kentucky law, when the judge failed or refused to disqualify himself in any proceeding, any party had the right to pursue immediate relief from the supreme court.

Such motions were rare, but required the Chief Justice to act immediately. They might get an answer the next day.

And sure enough, on Wednesday, an order came in the mail. Chief Justice George Moore had overruled the motion without comment.

Judge Atticus Zenas would be the judge for the Stirlings.

DISBARRED OR DISCIPLINED
January 5

The first Monday morning of the new year was rougher than usual. The sky was gray and low, as if to lean in and remind Lexington that there were three more months of cold, drizzling winter ahead. And though Judge Z should have felt refreshed, the contrast was even worse after nearly two weeks in the Florida sun playing golf, fishing and forgetting family court. He felt like a prisoner being sent back to his cell.

Without his wife to share it, Judge Zenas had decided to skip Christmas and all the mall trips and parties. Instead, he put Beulah and her bags into his SUV and headed for Longboat Key. They both loved the quiet days on a beach without worrying about anything.

But there was the letter—looming low, crowding his thoughts like the winter sky. It had come in the mail while he was gone. Karen handed it to him as he returned to the office. "You should read this."

It was no surprise. The *Lexington Times* had reported a Judicial Conduct Commission complaint filed against Judge Zenas in the Sunday edition. Front page. That was accompanied by an editorial, just in case the readers missed the story or didn't get the point that Judge Z was a menace to society.

The editorial assumed a favorite pose, shaking a finger while wrapped in the self-righteous banner of "the public's right to know," which pretty much covered anything. But somehow they overlooked the public's right to know how they had obtained a summary of the confidential complaint.

"Complaints against judges should be open and transparent," the editorial said. "The cloud of secrecy which envelops all judicial complaints does a great disservice to the public."

After rehashing the most shocking cases of judicial abuse in Kentucky history—judges who were disbarred, removed from office and sent to prison for crimes, drunkenness, drug abuse and sexual offenses—they finally got around to Judge Z—a clever trick of guilt by association.

"Of course," the editorial added with a wink, "we're not certain Judge Zenas has done anything wrong. There is no proof of that yet."

Yet, he thought. He almost had to admire how they could destroy someone's reputation by innuendo, all the while pretending to be fair.

The Sunday headline did as much damage as the editorial: "Family Court Judge Accused of Ethics Violations." Few would read the lengthy article full of anonymous quotes from "courthouse observers." Few would get past the headline to see that the story reported nothing but an accusation and no facts to support it. The rumors were unleashed.

"Did you hear about that judge in trouble?"

"No, what happened?"

"Don't know, but it sounds serious."

And now the letter. He had put it off as long as he could. He unfolded it and began to read. It was dated January 2.

Dear Judge Zenas:

This letter is to advise you that a Complaint has been filed against you for violation of Rule 4.300 Kentucky Code of Judicial Conduct. The name of the complainant is confidential. The complainant states that Judge Atticus Zenas violated all 5 Canons of Judicial Conduct:

1. A judge shall uphold the integrity and independence of the judiciary.
2. A judge shall avoid impropriety and the appearance of impropriety in all of the judge's activities.
3. A judge shall perform the duties of judicial office impartially and diligently.

4. A judge shall so conduct the judge's extra-judicial activities as to minimize the risk of conflict with judicial obligations.
5. A judge or judicial candidate shall refrain from inappropriate political activity.

More specifically:

1. Judge Zenas failed and refused to grant a simple no-fault divorce pursuant to state law. (Canon 3.)
2. Judge Zenas engaged in ex parte conversations with counsel for one of the parties. (Canon 1, 2, and 3.)
3. Judge Zenas has prejudged a case before hearing the evidence. (Canon 1 and 3.)
4. Judge Zenas has injected his religious and political views, violating "church and state." (Canon 5.)
   Your response to these allegations should be received by this office in no less than 14 days.
   Sincerely,
   Hon. Dean Beck, Chairman
   Kentucky Judicial Conduct Commission
   Retired Judge, Fleming Circuit Court

Judge Z didn't wait fourteen days or even fourteen minutes. He didn't waste any time wondering about the source of the complaint. It was the work of Harry Wolff and Anna Ollie. Poor Anna must have worked over the Christmas holiday. Ebenezer Scrooge came to mind. Judge Z got out his portable dictation machine and began to talk:

January 5
Dear Judge Beck:
This will acknowledge receipt of the letter you sent. It has always been my understanding that these proceedings are confidential. If so, perhaps you can explain how this Complaint was referenced in the

Lexington newspapers three days ago (clipping enclosed). Apparently, there has been some breakdown in your own processes. In fact, I first heard about this complaint when I read about it on the front page of the *Lexington Times*.

Until I can get an explanation for how and why this confidential complaint became public knowledge, I choose to not respond specifically to any charges. Perhaps you should investigate the people who made this matter public before you come after me for anything.

In fact, perhaps it would be best for you to simply grant a date for a full hearing. Normally, an accused judge would wish to avoid such a public hearing, where his or her reputation and name could be tarnished. But in this case, since my accusers have already managed to make this public, a public hearing will be the only place to defend myself against the charges.

And by the way, if the charge is that I have decided that marriage is a sacred trust that should not be broken as easily as we have done for the past forty years in Kentucky, I plead guilty. I have done nothing but follow the provisions detailed in KRS 403, to assure that a marriage is truly "irretrievably broken" before granting a divorce.

In fact, I will prove that instead of being the only judge in Kentucky who "refuses to follow the law" (see editorial clipping), I may be the only judge in Kentucky who does follow the law.

With best personal regards, I am,

Judge Atticus T. Zenas

Circuit Judge, 22nd Judicial Circuit, Family Court

CC: *Lexington Times* Editorial Department

Karen got the letter typed in ten minutes. He read it and changed nothing. "Print it for me to sign and mail today."

Karen was worried that her judge was losing it. "You don't want to sleep on this?"

"No. Send it."

HUMPTY DUMPTY HAD A BIG FALL

Despite his brewing issues with the Judicial Conduct Commission, life in family court moved on. The first Monday docket of the year included a review for Serena, twenty-six, the mother of a six-year-old boy. Unfortunately, her drug habit had forced Judge Zenas to take her son, Ray, away from her two years ago. The father was missing, of course. She was on probation for various drug offenses, but drug court had saved her life.

She now saw Judge Z every three months because she still owed child support to the state. During her first appearance, her last name, Murdock, reminded Judge Z of a friend from college.

Judge Z had asked Serena if she knew a Barry Murdock.

"He's my dad," she said without an ounce of affection.

"Really? I remember your dad and mom at Centenary Methodist Church many years ago. They had a little girl." He had looked for a reaction. None came. "Was that you?"

"Yes, it was," she had told him. "But the man you saw at church was not the man I saw at home. He beat my mother. He was a drunk and a coke addict. He can rot in hell as far as I'm concerned."

Someday she is going to have to forgive him, he thought at the time.

But now, two years later, she was in court for a joyous occasion. She was working her plan and had been clean for a year. Her son Ray was coming home to her today.

Her father had reached out to her, she mentioned. He had quit drinking and drugging, had been to AA meetings every night for a year and Jesus was now his Higher Power. "He's not a bad guy when he's sober," she admitted.

Somehow, Serena had found the miracle of forgiveness.

But Serena might have a hard time forgiving herself, he thought, as he read the report. She was pregnant again, living with the same guy for two years, and she was scheduled for an abortion.

Judge Z wrote down a name and phone number. "Serena, come up to the bench please." He wondered if he was going too far this time. Killing babies in the womb seemed so barbaric, but he was not allowed to be political or impose his personal opinions. So even handing Serena a phone number on a piece of paper seemed risky. "The lady at this phone number is someone you should consider talking to. I barely know her, but she knows more about the choices you have than anyone in Lexington. You can make your own decision, but you should do it based on good information. Will you call her?"

"Sure. What's her name? I can't read your writing," said Serena, scrunching her face to make it out.

"Danielle Shirley."

That was all he could do in court. But he would tell Beulah about Serena so she could pray. He would try to pray too, but often he forgot. Beulah would not forget.

Next up was Jalissa, a drug addict with four kids, ages nine to three, all in therapy for sex abuse and neglect. Her new boyfriend, not charged yet, was the likely perpetrator.

Jalissa started crying and complaining. The system was unfair. She missed her children. She only saw them one hour a week. "I'm a good mom," she insisted through angry tears.

"Listen to me," he told her. "It will not be good enough for you to be a normally good mom, with a job and food in the refrigerator and a roof over their heads. These children are so damaged that they all need therapy. A nine-year-old in therapy. A three-year-old in therapy. Think about how absurd that is. I just hope these kids are not Humpty Dumpty."

She looked baffled.

"'Humpty Dumpty sat on a wall, Humpty Dumpty had a great fall, all the king's horses and all the king's men, couldn't put Humpty Dumpty back together again.' Remember that?

"We're using all our horses and all the king's men to try to put your kids back together again, but I'm not sure we can do it. You may get totally sober and clean and still never get your kids back."

Jalissa left angry and confused. She had never heard of Humpty Dumpty and was fully convinced this judge was insane.

Three days later, Karen was waiting with more news from the Judicial Conduct Commission. "Judge, you'd better look at this."

"Great," he muttered, "I stay busy trying to save a few families and the JCC stays busy trying to put me out of business." His blood boiled thinking about it some days.

> Dear Judge Zenas:
> As requested, your case is set for a public hearing on March 27, and the entire Judicial Conduct Commission will hear the case. Hon. Adam Kelly, legal counsel for the JCC, will act as prosecutor of the Petitioner's case. If you have any questions, contact me or Mr. Kelly at this address.
> Sincerely,
> Dean Beck, Chairman JCC

Judge Z knew from personal experience that this could be a tough court. He had once refused to sign an order for a juvenile to get an abortion and had to face a JCC hearing. Planned Parenthood's lawyer petitioned on behalf of a sixteen-year-old under Kentucky's Judicial Bypass, which permitted a juvenile to get an abortion without the consent of her guardian or parents in certain circumstances. Such orders were routinely signed. And just as routinely, the petition was a lie. Usually, it was simply a girl who didn't want her mom and dad to find out she was pregnant.

Planned Parenthood had a cozy connection with Dr. Arnold Cain, the only doctor in town who performed abortions. His part-time receptionist was the sister of Planned Parenthood's executive director. About once a month, Dr. Cain would call Planned Parenthood with a "problem," and their lawyer on retainer would help take care of it by filing a petition for Judicial Bypass, which simply meant bypassing the parents who would not agree to the abortion.

Their first choice to approve those petitions was Judge Robin Newton, who was staunchly and openly pro-abortion.

But somehow one of those cases had wound up in Judge Z's court while Judge Newton was on vacation. And that's when the usual five-minute hearing got complicated. Judge Z asked questions that Judge Newton had never raised, such as, "Is this girl mature enough under the statute to sign her own consent forms?" And, "What do the parents know about this? Are they abusive?"

As it turned out, she was not mature enough to drive a car in Kentucky or sign her own consent to have her ears pierced. And her mom and dad didn't know anything—that was the point. There was no evidence of abuse. So Judge Z denied the petition. An appeal upheld his decision. But he later learned that the girl got consent from her parents and had the abortion anyway.

Then Planned Parenthood filed a complaint. His ruling wasn't the issue. Their objection was Judge Z's speech to the Planned Parenthood lawyer. He accused them of judge shopping, of illegal collusion between the doctor's office and Planned Parenthood, and violating the parents' rights to know what is happening to their child. He had made the lawyer and teenager watch a video of a beating heart at nine weeks. He also said a "womb should not be a tomb," which a *Lexington Times* columnist called "a cheesy imitation of, 'If it doesn't fit, you must acquit.'"

After months of legal wrangling with the Judicial Conduct Commission, Judge Z had agreed to accept a private reprimand that he had "failed his duty as a judge to treat all litigants with respect." He had almost forgotten the whole thing. But he was pretty sure the six members of the JCC would remember. They seemed to enjoy judging other judges. They liked digging into the gossip and drama of complaints. They were busybodies in black robes. And they probably remembered that this judge was a little bit wacky.

Chapter 10

ARRANGED MARRIAGE

But the greatest of these is love.

— *1 Corinthians 13:13*

INVITED TO THE WEDDING
January 19

The trip had snuck up on him. On Monday morning he found himself on a Delta flight from Lexington to Chicago, then London, then Delhi, and finally all the way to Madurai in the south of India.

Thirty-six long hours to think and read and wonder how his world was being rocked by the Stirling case and J.J.'s death.

His friend Ghuna Raja had invited him months ago to be part of the wedding for his son Samuel. At the time it seemed so far off, it was easy to say yes without thinking that it would cost him $3,500 and a week from work. *And I hate weddings*, he reminded himself. *What was I thinking?*

He had been to India once before on a judicial exchange, and he could still remember the smells, the poverty, the sadness of spirit, the overwhelming despair of a religion that said there was no hope on this earth to escape a caste system that held everyone prisoner to the past—don't even try, because you did something bad in the last life to deserve your poverty.

He had met Ghuna on his first visit and they became friends as he visited the local court and mentored a few Indian lawyers, mainly Ghuna and his son Samuel, who was following in his dad's footsteps.

In India, "lawyer" and "liar" not only sounded alike, they were the same thing in public perception. Ghuna and his family were also Christians. And the idea of a "Christian lawyer" was as odd as a "Christian prostitute."

Gandhi was a lawyer, he reminded Judge Z. He studied law in London long before his mission to free India from British rule. The British were gone. But India was still poor and sad. Hinduism was not working.

But Judge Z was about to learn first-hand about marriage in India. Samuel's marriage was a typical arranged affair. Ghuna and his wife, Jaya, were in total control. And Samuel, twenty-eight, accomplished and educated, was fine with that.

Ghuna had found a girl named Preeti to be Samuel's bride. She was also the child of a lawyer, Ravi David from Delhi, who had been looking for the right husband for his daughter for three years.

It was a modern Indian marriage, meaning websites were used to match the bride and groom. The fathers exchanged pictures of their children. If the parents approved, the pictures were shared with the potential bride and groom, who had veto power. This veto was also modern. In the old days, the young couple had no voice at all.

Ghuna had explained India's arranged marriages in his invitation to Judge Z: "We went to the bride's family for a visit. Preeti was there but the meeting was primarily for Samuel to meet her parents, and for the parents to develop friendship. Preeti served tea. She was barely seen, although Samuel watched her closely. Her father and I did most of the talking. At the end, a handshake deal was made for the marriage."

Ghuna had told Judge Z, "After the handshake, Samuel and Preeti talked privately for ten minutes. He shared his dreams with her. She agreed and shared how many children she would like. He agreed and a wedding date was set.

"No contact will happen now until the engagement a month from now. At that time the engaged couple will share some pictures, and once again perhaps ten minutes of conversation. That will be their last contact until the wedding."

According to Ghuna, some Indian couples texted and called; some even dated. But seldom did dating involve physical contact. The marriage would be a full day affair, with a feast that lasted a week, including tandoori chicken, spicy mutton biryani with saffron rice and mango ice cream for dessert.

Judge Z's plane landed in Madurai at midnight. His neck was sore from sleeping on the plane. Ghuna was there to pick him up, along with Samuel. They put wet flowers around his head and shoulders, as always, then took the jetlagged judge straight to his hotel.

Over the following days, Judge Z attended meals and festivities galore. The Indian smells and sounds and busyness rekindled his love affair with India—a mixed bag of love and despair.

GIVE, NOT TAKE
January 24

It was 11 a.m. on the wedding day. In six hours, Preeti would walk down the aisle in a wedding sari more beautiful than any American white wedding dress. Meanwhile, the judge was treated like family, invited to join an exchange of gifts and congratulations over tea and lunch delights. The gathering was at a local traditional Indian hotel, the Pandiyan.

Samuel and his family were there, including his younger sisters and brothers who would soon take their place in line to be married. Like all grooms, he looked more handsome than he was. His attire was perfect. But more than that, his eyes were full of life. He was anticipating new beginnings.

The small room was full with thirty members of Samuel's family. The bride's entourage of twenty-five would arrive any moment. There was huge anticipation of her appearance.

Then a boy, perhaps age twelve, came flying in to announce that she was on her way. And there she was, following her mother and father into a reception room where chairs were set along all four walls. Several people could be heard whispering the same thing, "She is so beautiful." She nodded a hello without speaking. Just a huge smile. Then, a bit shy, Preeti saw her groom and the smile seemed to sparkle and glow.

Samuel smiled back. This would be the love of his life. He had only spoken to her for ten minutes twice. They looked each other over, head to toe. Judge Z wondered: *Could someone really be in love with a stranger, chosen for them by their parents?*

Pictures were taken as a buzz of meaningless chit-chat filled the room. The bride and groom did not exchange a word, but the mystery of sex and marriage and intimacy filled their silent glances with more passion than a bookshelf of romance novels.

He would give himself to her. And she would give herself to him.

Give. Not take.

Thirty minutes of prayer and blessings from the Almighty were sought on behalf of this young couple and their children to come. After an hour, the bride left to change into her wedding sari. Her next appearance would be walking down the aisle with a thousand people waiting in a cathedral, a building worthy of the ceremony.

GOD'S BEST WORK

Bishop Matthew wore a robe and collar that made him appear to be a Catholic priest, but in fact he was a bishop of the Church of South India. Judge Z had to strain to decipher the thick Indian English, but being near the front helped. The crowd was packed into the church in Madurai, home of the largest Hindu temple in the world. But this was no Hindu wedding. This was as Christian as it got. The exquisite bride marched down a center aisle, and Bishop Matthew started, his voice echoing throughout the steamy cathedral, where overhead fans fought a losing battle against the relentless heat.

"Dearly Beloved, we are gathered here in the sight of God and in the presence of these witnesses, to join together Samuel and Preeti in holy matrimony, which is an honorable estate instituted of God at the very beginning of the human race, signifying unto us the mystical union that is between Christ and his church, which holy estate Christ adorned and beautified with his presence and first miracle in Cana of Galilee."

There it is again, Cana of Galilee, Judge Z thought, remembering Pastor Billy's sermons.

"I have three scriptures for you on this sacred occasion. We will not linger long, but neither will we rush through this blessed event."

He read from Genesis 2.

The Lord God said, "It is not good for the man to be alone. I will make a helper suitable for him…

For this reason, a man leaves his father and mother and is united to his wife, and they become one flesh.

The bishop continued. "Is there any doubt that the most beautiful creation of God is the woman?" He invited everyone to again gaze on the beauty of Preeti. No one could see under the veil that the bride was blushing at the thought of two thousand eyes fixed on her splendor.

"Consider this. The first woman came from a man, but ever since then, every single man has come from a woman. Neither can live without the other."

The Bishop paused to let his words sink deep. He smiled at the couple.

Never thought of that, Judge Z said to himself.

"Ecclesiastes 4," continued the bishop.

There was a man all alone. Two are better than one, because they have a good return for their work: If either of them falls down, one can help the other up. But pity anyone who falls and has no one to help them up.

Also, if two lie down together, they will keep warm. But how can one keep warm alone? Though one may be overpowered, two can defend themselves. A cord of three strands is not quickly broken.

"Samuel, you will never be cold again. Preeti, you will never be cold again." Again, the bishop paused to let the wonder sink in.

"What is the cord of three strands? This is the Holy Spirit, because this is a marriage not just of Samuel and Preeti, but the Holy Spirit himself will be with you."

He turned to his final reading. "This wedding is a symbol of the great wedding in heaven which we know from Revelation 19:7-9.

Let us rejoice and be glad and give him glory! For the wedding of the Lamb has come, and his bride has made herself ready. Fine linen, bright and clean, was given her to wear. Then the angel said to me, "Write this: Blessed are those who are invited to the wedding supper of the Lamb!"

"These are the true words of God." He closed the Bible.

"There will be a great wedding in the heavenly realm. Jesus Christ Himself will be our Bridegroom. Today, this beautiful bride, Preeti, reminds us of Christ's church, loved and adored forever. The Bride of Christ.

"Every wedding helps us know God. Many people think of God as just a judge, who can determine your eternal destiny. How sad. A judge has no relationship with the people who stand in front of him.

"The second and better image of God is as our father. That brings the family into the picture. Both Preeti and Samuel are blessed to have fathers who have presented to them a positive view of life and love. A good father is a wonderful gift from God. But you still eventually leave your father, which is what this ceremony is all about.

"So the best image of God is not as Judge or Father, but as our Lover. And He thinks we are as beautiful as Preeti is right now. Indeed, this wedding is a foretaste of heaven itself.

"No doubt there will be difficulties ahead. But there will also be great joy. And in the midst of living your lives as servants of God and raising your own children, never forget your primary relationship on this earth is to each other.

"Preeti, your greatest gift is Samuel. And Samuel, your greatest gift is Preeti. Love each other. Serve each other. Forever."

Bishop Matthew looked at the front row and asked, "Who gives the hand of this beautiful woman to be the bride of this man?" And with that, the wedding vows began. Judge Z picked out the key words: Love, comfort, keep, in sickness and in health and forsaking all others so long as you both shall live.

As expected, the judge was called on for the final blessing. The introduction made him wince: "A judge of the United States Supreme Court." But a correction would have embarrassed the Bishop and ruined the day, so Judge Zenas just stood, marched forward and prayed.

He felt like his words were pitiful compared to what he was observing and had already heard. He sat down. He was embarrassed to be so ignorant of the mystery of God in marriage. He felt small and almost stupid. His prayer would be forgotten because it was like the Kentucky statute that defined marriage: meaningless words. He blessed them, but a judge's blessing seemed very empty. At least he was learning. He wanted to know more about this mystery of marriage.

He would not have to wait for long.

NEW LOVE
January 25

Judge Z's flight home was at 3 p.m. on Sunday, which left time for early morning church. Ghuna wanted him to see a community he worked with in the small village of Oomachikulam, eight kilometers away. Judge Z was expected to say a few words, even preach a short sermon if he could.

Thankfully, the sermons by Billy Hughes gave him something to say. He arrived and sat at the front of a small church which was packed with fifty people sitting on the dirt floor. The twenty in front were all boys, ages six to sixteen, all HIV positive.

Five couples were there, local farmers and laborers from the small village. The women and girls sat on the right; men and boys sat on the left. At the rear were seven older women, also HIV positive. Two of them were blind. None was over forty, but all looked at least sixty. The ladies were destitute women who were saved from the streets, literally thrown out by their own families. They now stayed in the Annie Home, financed by Ghuna and some of his friends. With no government programs in India, helping the poor was everyone's job.

Getzi, his Tamil interpreter, was the director of the home for the HIV-positive boys and the destitute ladies. She may or may not have been accurately interpreting the judge's sermon. It didn't matter. His words were not important. But his presence was special for them. Americans were rare in this little church.

Judge Z was halfway through his fifteen-minute "sermon" about John 2 and the wedding in Cana of Galilee. He made mention of the love of a mother and the need to obey her. As he looked at the orphan boys, and the women in back who were widows or never married, he realized his message was completely out of place. The boys had no mothers. The widows had children who had put them on the streets. As he was about to finish, one of the HIV ladies came forward and stood in front of him. She couldn't wait for the "altar call." She was accustomed to a short sermon and a long time to pray. And she had heard enough. She was ready to pray.

Getzi whispered what was going on. Judge Z wrapped it up, realizing that no one was really listening to him. They wanted to hear from God.

When the final amen was said, it was time to get serious about real prayer. Getzi whispered, "The ladies will expect you to pray for them."

Oh boy. They think I'm a man of God, thought the judge. This was not a request. It was an order. He felt like Jesus being told to turn water into wine by his mother. Or at least like Beulah was telling him what to do.

Getzi tugged him to the back of the small sanctuary, and the woman who had come up for the altar call followed. All seven ladies knelt, waiting for a special touch from this "man of God" from America. He wanted to stop everything and tell them he was a fraud. He was not a man of God. He was a lawyer. A liar. A sinner. Worse. He was a judge who spent his days divorcing couples and wrecking families. This was absurd.

But they expected him to touch them on their heads, which were covered by their Saris, an Indian tradition during prayer. They waited patiently. He had no choice.

He laid a hand on the first lady. She was blind and HIV positive. She was weeping. Her tears seemed to be a combination of pain and joy. Getzi started translating but she was pulled away by one of the boys so Judge Z was suddenly alone. He just dove in with a common prayer.

"Dear Jesus, only you know what this lady needs. Meet her every need today. Hear her prayers." His eyes stayed open, staring at the ladies as he prayed. He realized that they did not understand anything he said, but it did not matter. They wept. They were in love with Jesus, with the Holy Spirit, with God Himself. They certainly had Something the judge didn't have.

He moved to the second lady. Then the third. The fourth was not even five feet tall, bent over, pitiful in every way. As he struggled to pray for her, he heard himself say: "Lord, this lady has a love I know little about..."

What was this? He was praying for himself.

"This lady loves you. She is poor and pitiful, but her tears tell me she loves you. You are her lover. Maybe her only one. Ever. And now Jesus, would you do me a favor? Give me the same love this lady has."

His own words shocked him, as if someone else had prayed for him. Tears stopped the judge from any more words. He was weeping uncontrollably. Did this mean that his prayer was being answered?

When he said "amen," the ladies knew the prayer was over. Everyone was weeping quietly. There was a powerful spirit of lovely lamentation inside these poor afflicted women that the world knew little about. They were married to God Himself.

Judge Z's mind wandered to a new thought. *These people are broken. In fact, they are irretrievably broken.* But the words had a whole new meaning.

He had one last thought as Getzi took him to the airport. *I came to India for an arranged marriage. Did God arrange this trip so I could be married to Him?*

RATED 'R'

Exhausted, Judge Z slept most of the trip home. Madurai to Delhi to Chicago to Lexington.

Somewhere between Delhi and Chicago he decided to watch a movie. *We are the Millers* sounded like an innocent way to kill ninety minutes of a fourteen-hour flight. The star was Jennifer Aniston. So with the sounds of India still in his ears, and the beauty of marriage still in his heart, Judge Z put on the headset.

In the first ten minutes, Hollywood had done its damage. The movie was about a low-level drug dealer named Miller, who lived in Southern California.

He had lots of money and girls. He was cool. He was about thirty, but never had to grow up. He got by selling weed.

Right away, he ran into an old buddy from high school. The poor guy was married, with kids. What a drag. The married guy was just drooling with compliments for the single weed dealer, while Miller looked at the poor guy with complete disgust, glad that his own life had not been ruined by a wife and kids.

Single drug dealer: cool, with a convertible sports car and a good looking chick.

Married dad: fool, with a station wagon and a frumpy wife and two screaming kids.

With liberal use of F-bombs, the rest of the characters were introduced. Aniston was a stripper and neighbor of the drug dealer. She too was super cool. Two teenagers were added, disrespectful of anything involving adults.

Nobody under thirty would want to get married after watching this movie.

Deal drugs? Sure.

Be a stripper? Why not.

Have sex with anyone, even for drugs? Perhaps.

Get married? You got to be kidding. No way. That is clearly for losers.

The guy sitting by the window laughed out loud for most of the ninety minutes, which only made Judge Z more depressed and disgusted.

The wedding in India and the ladies at Oomachikulam had given him hope. But now, halfway back to America over the Pacific Ocean, he sensed he was losing his way again. Jesus had sent his disciples to the "ends of the earth." He used to think that was India or Africa. Now he was pretty sure it was Hollywood—and maybe even Lexington, Kentucky. It was the USA for sure.

Where children were secondary.

Where drug dealers and strippers ruled.

Where the sacredness of life and marriage was gone.

He decided his new mission field would be Lexington, Kentucky, and slept the last four hours to Chicago. He finally arrived back at Bluegrass Airport at 11:22 p.m. on Monday night and realized as he picked up his bags: tomorrow was his birthday.

Chapter 11

NEW MISSION FIELD

I have made you a light that you may bring
salvation to the ends of the earth.

— *Acts 13:47*

HAPPY BIRTHDAY
January 27

Beulah always had a party for Atty on his birthday. This time she invited Pastor Billy and Susie, plus her parents. The ones who usually came to the party were gone. Johnny. Angelina. Even J.J. had come a couple of times when the judge was mentoring him.

The normal Sunday fried chicken was replaced by the judge's favorite: pork ribs, baked beans and coleslaw. It didn't take long for the conversation to turn to India, especially since the judge looked like death itself, jetlagged to the max.

"I thought you didn't like weddings," Billy chided him.

"That's true. But the Lord wanted to get my attention."

"What was it like?" Susie asked.

"It was spectacular. You wouldn't believe the bride's wedding gown. But the best part was the message by the Bishop. He actually sounded like Billy. Beulah would have loved it. He made me realize that, like most people, my first relationship with God was to see him as my judge. But a judge is remote. He wears a black robe. You're not allowed to know him."

"Makes sense," said Susie's dad, Joe Davis.

"And then the bishop said there's God the Father. So we call each other brother and sister at church. One big family. But what about the people who have a poor image of God because of their own father?"

Susie's mother, Doris, chimed in. "My father was... well, a drunk. I don't know how else to say it. I always had trouble praying to 'our Father,' because it made me picture God like my father, as an abusive drunk."

"So what's the third way?" Beulah asked. She knew. She needed to hear Atty say it.

"He said God is our lover. He is our Husband. That means an intimacy that can only be mirrored by marriage on this earth."

"Hmmm. That sounds just like something Billy said in church a while back," Beulah smiled.

Pastor Billy laughed. Apparently it took a trip to India for the ideas to sink in.

"All I can say is that last Sunday in India was the most important day of my life," he said. Beulah stopped and turned around on her way to the kitchen to make sure she had heard correctly.

Judge Z then told about the women in the little rural church, their prayers and amazing faith. How he started praying for them and wound up praying for himself. About his tears of joy and love.

"I don't know if it's permanent or a bad case of jetlag, but I don't want this feeling to stop. I have had a certain 'love' in my head, but it seems to have dropped into my heart."

Beulah's face lit up with joy and a huge smile.

"I even found myself loving and forgiving Harry Wolff. God showed me that He even loves Harry. And so should I." Judge Z laughed out loud at the absurdity.

Billy said, "One way to cement something like this in your life is to speak about it, like you just did. How about if you take some time Sunday and tell your brothers and sisters in church what you experienced? This conversation should not be for just the dinner table."

Judge Z started to decline, but Beulah said, "Sure, he'll do it." His mother had spoken. And he would do it. Just like Jesus in Cana of Galilee.

FIRST SERMON
February 1

On Sunday morning Judge Z felt nerves unlike anything in court. In his robe, he was in charge. Here, he was definitely not. This was God's house. He had to leave his pew and stumble to the pulpit, stand up in front of sixty people at Sadieville Methodist Church and tell them about his new love.

As he told about how he had finally realized the difference between God as judge, father and lover, several women nodded their understanding. So did old man Fitch, a grocery store owner who had been faithfully loving God and people his whole life. The rest of the congregation looked at Judge Z like he was speaking Tamil, one of the languages of South India.

He wondered later: *Is that the look preachers see every Sunday? No wonder they get discouraged and quit. They look at us and see bewilderment, confusion and disinterest, and lots of peeks at the watch or cell phone.*

On the way home he asked, "Mom, have you ever seen the looks on people's faces from up front?"

"Can't say I have."

"As I talked about the ladies in India, they looked shocked. A few women seemed okay. Like Mrs. Davidson and Mrs. Corbitt. And Mr. Fitch was grinning ear to ear. But the other men looked at me like I was crazy."

"Son, it sounded to me like you were pretty shocked yourself the first time you heard it, before it sank in. God is big enough to handle this. Relax."

Judge Z headed home to his condo that evening to watch the Super Bowl by himself. He was alone but not lonely any more. The new love of his life was there with him.

And it was still there on Monday morning. Judge Z had his coffee in one hand, file in the other. His robe was on but not buttoned yet, billowing behind him as he rushed off to a court. It looked like he was going to miss the elevator, but he got lucky. Someone heard him coming and blocked the closing door, holding it for him. It was a young law school intern he'd seen around the courthouse.

"Good morning. You look new around here."

"Yes, sir, I'm Alexandra Sutton. Second-year law student interning with Judge Lowe in criminal court. She sent me off to get some files. And you are Judge Zenas?"

"That's me. Family court. I'm not a real judge according to some. But feel free to stop in and watch anytime."

"I'd love to. Someone told me last week that you are the judge who loves Jesus."

He was caught by surprise. Open talk about Jesus was never heard on courthouse elevators, except among the prisoners in shackles who had just been sentenced to prison. And he couldn't tell if she was mocking him. But her tone seemed sincere.

He almost looked over his shoulder as he replied, although they were alone on the elevator. "Well, thank you for what I hope is a compliment. But let me tell you in two seconds what I know for sure. I really am not sure how well I love Jesus."

Alexandra looked bewildered. Judge Z took off his glasses so he could speak with his eyes as well as his heart. "But I do know this for sure," he said as the elevator door hummed open. "I know He loves me."

Her face lit up in a smile he would remember for a long time.

Saying it out loud made him smile, too. *It's really true*, he thought.

By coincidence—if there was such a thing—his first case was twenty-six-year-old Serena Murdock. The judge was glad to learn she had decided against an abortion and would have her baby. He asked her what changed her mind.

"I did like you told me. I called Danielle Shirley. I really liked her. I had an ultrasound and saw pictures of my baby girl. That was all it took. I saw the positive side of life, and it was nothing like what I heard at Planned Parenthood."

"What did Planned Parenthood tell you?" he asked.

"They told me how life would be hard with a baby. They told me my plans for college, for a career, all of my dreams would be destroyed. They said being a single parent is hard, which I knew already."

"You know it's a girl?"

"No, not for sure. I just think it will be a girl. And I have a name."

Judge Z raised his eyebrows, "What's the name?"

"Grace. I don't deserve this blessing. A little girl. But I am here by God's grace. Just makes sense somehow."

The day has hardly started, he thought, *and already two God-sightings.*

His afternoon was filled with the final hearing for the Dawid divorce. Any hope for settlement had dissolved when the husband would simply not agree that he owned anything. He claimed his brother owned their convenience store, although his own name was on the deed and he had made all the payments.

The wife's lawyer complained that he couldn't get the most basic information from the husband, much less support. During a deposition, Mr. Dawid had answered most of the questions by saying he did not understand, as if he didn't speak English after twenty years in America.

So the judge would have to hear four hours of testimony about property. Every time a difficult question was asked, both parties pretended they did not understand the question. When Mrs. Dawid began to cry, the judge saw that the real issue was not property. This case was about the pain she was experiencing from the destruction of her family.

At the end of the arguments, he asked, "Mrs. Dawid, is there any reasonable prospect for reconciliation?"

What will I do if she says yes?" he worried.

Finally, after wiping tears from her eyes, sobbing and snuffling, she said, "No, I do not believe there is any prospect for reconciliation. He has hurt me deeply. Once upon a time I thought there was hope, just for the children. But he does not love me. I understand. He never did. This marriage is broken. There is no hope."

So, Judge Z signed another divorce decree ending another marriage. She got almost everything. Except love and respect.

STRANGER IN A ROBE
February 4

The first case today was *Lundie v. McConnell,* a custody case involving a beautiful three-year-old boy. The parties had never even considered getting married. In fact, despite the fact that they produced a child, the father had denied that he even dated the mother. "We saw each other, but we never dated," he had said with a straight face. The trial had been a month ago. After a full day of testimony and wrangling, the judge had sent everyone off to settle. But not before they suffered through one of his speeches. He had asked, "Why should a stranger in a black robe be in the middle of your family?"

Usually it worked. Sometimes he got their attention by throwing them out of court and almost yelling, "You don't want me deciding this case. These are your kids, not mine."

Out in the hallway, they might agree on something for the first time: "This judge is crazy!" Then it would dawn on them: "Maybe we should settle this."

The lawyers would wink at each other and smile. They'd all heard the same speech before. As they negotiated in a conference room, Judge Z was already booking a tee time to replace a long hearing he had just avoided.

But this time, settlement negotiations failed. Debby Lundie and Matt McConnell were not the settling type. Both were thirty-something, real adults with good jobs, solid middle class people. But their distaste for each other was real.

Debby had a wild side, with the tattoos to prove it. Matt liked the wild side of her until she got pregnant and ruined everything by having a baby.

Today Judge Z would give them his ruling, in writing. Skipping past twelve pages of "Findings of Fact" outlining testimony, he read his Conclusions of Law and Final Judgment, which neither side wanted to hear. The couple might file an appeal, but once they learned how much it would cost, and that family court judges were rarely overturned, they would probably swallow hard and accept it.

He was fully aware that this order was over the top, very different from anything he would have done even three months ago. But he was not the same judge. It said:

These parents both told the court that they would do anything for their son. The "best interests of the child" is the one and only governing principle in this Court's order today. KRS 403 speaks of endangerment to a child's welfare with four types of endangerment:

Mental endangerment,

Emotional endangerment,

Physical endangerment,

And last but not least, moral endangerment.

During this hearing, it became apparent that these parents have already endangered the health and welfare of this three-year-old boy.

In a better world, which the Court is aware may be gone forever, this child would have been part of a loving, married relationship between a man and a woman. In this case, none of this was even possible.

This case seems so "normal," but truthfully it is a tragedy. This child is actually in danger, as described in KRS 403. Set forth below are the highlights.

1. Marriage. These parents made no commitment to each other of any kind. Parents who are not committed are handicapped in their ability to parent. This child will never have the opportunity to be tucked into bed and hugged by a loving mother and a loving father on the same night.

2. Geographical distance. Soon after the birth, the mother moved to Texas, ignoring the fact that the father would have little time to bond with the child. Sadly, the father never even tried to visit his son in Texas. Only when the mother returned to Kentucky did he show interest.

3. Other partners. Both parties introduced other partners into this so-called family. The father has a steady girlfriend, who is currently married to another man with four children. Likewise, the mother admits she has boyfriends spend the night.

4. Alcohol. The mother expresses concern about the father's drinking, but ultimately agrees that it is okay as long as it is not in the presence of the child. Sobriety is not an expectation of either parent. She says she will continue drinking because she knows "how to control it."

5. Sex. Not specifically stated, but underlying the testimony of both parties, is the idea that having sex with someone is always permissible under all circumstances except for the physical presence of the child.

6. Religion. The father complains that the mother's family is Jehovah's Witnesses and thus will not celebrate Christmas. He wants the child to be a Baptist. Yet neither parent showed any personal inclination toward religion or morality of any kind. Religion is a non-issue in this case.

7. Complete lack of moral direction. This father testified that all couples should go to bed first to determine their compatibility. The mother did not disagree. Both parents agreed that they slept together, had a sexual relationship, but did not date and had no reason to expect fidelity in their relationship.

8. Name. These parents failed on the most basic of all parenting skills: naming the child. The mother gave the child her own last name. The father now complains that he should have his last name. This child's last name will not determine his future. His parents' attitudes and behaviors will determine his future.

In summary, this child deserves a mother and a father who have changed their behavior and their thinking. Hopefully, this will happen with these parents.

Judge Zenas went on to order the parents to keep the name James Russell Lundie for the child, and ordered child support. If the parents had been married, he would have asked if the marriage was irretrievably broken. But in this case, like so many, there was no marriage to be broken. Just children left behind in the wake of parental malpractice.

PRETRIAL MEDIA
February 24

The new year had flown past in a flurry of chaos that had the judge's head spinning. The newspaper was full of Letters to the Editor telling tales of mistreatment in family court under that crazy Judge Zenas, going back ten years. For some reason, the letters sent by his friends and supporters didn't seem to get published.

Both Ms. Lundie and Mr. McConnell had felt insulted by the judge's order. They sent it to the newspaper, which took it out of context to make it sound like Judge Zenas was on a morality crusade.

They also had somehow obtained quotes from his sermon at Sadieville Methodist. Apparently, a reporter had called some of the church members. His testimony at a little country church was now "news." Some said Judge Zenas needed to stop preaching or resign so he could preach full time.

The old story of Ivory and the abortion he stopped was replayed as fiction: The judge had forced a poor young black girl to have a baby she couldn't afford.

They even mentioned that J.J. Jackson had been shot and killed while under the guidance of the judge.

Mr. Fernando had been given plenty of space for his complaints and insults, even though Judge Z had done everything possible to keep him in touch with his kids.

The national news had picked up the Stirling story within the last week. "Marriage on Trial," the TV graphics shouted. "Is Divorce too easy?" Harry

Wolff was getting more air time than Oprah. MSNBC called Judge Zenas the "Bible Belt Marriage Sheriff."

Bill O'Reilly on Fox News tried to be "balanced" by saying "the judge in Kentucky seems to have crossed the line." He did not mention what the line was or where it was, just that it had been crossed. He discussed the matter with two bleached blonde, cleavage-flashing thirty-year-olds called "senior policy analysts" at the bottom of the TV screen. One was a 'Former Prosecutor." For what? A year? The other had worked in the White House, supposedly. One agreed that the Kentucky judge was wrong and was giving conservatives a bad name, while the other one argued that the judge might just be slowing down a divorce that was going way too fast.

Divorce seemed to be sacrosanct, even for so-called conservatives, who didn't stay married any more than so-called liberals. Divorce was a good thing, said the smart people on both sides of the political fence. Many people whose parents had divorced had gone on to have successful lives. Kids are resilient, they said. It wasn't fair to make them live in an unhappy home.

As usual, the media used the story like Silly Putty, kneading and stretching it to pick up the shapes and colors of their own bias. It became a "reminder" of why right-wingers wanted to block gay marriage and keep women shackled to marriage. Never mind that Mrs. Stirling wanted to stay married and the case had no connection to same-sex marriage. None.

Talk shows and reporters called for interviews. Judge Z declined.

Brad Bertram also chose "no comment," knowing he could be next for the media's witch hunt. He already had a target on his back in the faculty meetings, despite getting tenure last year.

Judge Z smiled at the cartoon radical he had become. In fact, he had done nothing really radical his whole life. He was disappointed at how normal he was.

SNOWED IN
March 1

The biggest snow storm in a decade was brewing. Church cancellations included Sadieville Methodist, with eight inches of snow on the ground and more dropping on Lexington like a white lace curtain. Dinner at Beulah's was cancelled too.

At least there was basketball to watch on TV. UK fans were in full-blown insanity and NCAA March Madness would be the only real news that mattered for four weeks.

Judge Z's phone started ringing early. He ignored it until his caller I.D. showed Brad Bertram.

"Judge Z, have you seen the Sunday paper?" Brad asked, without a hello. He was talking about the *Lexington Times* editorial page, of course.

"You know I quit reading newspapers long ago."

"Well, I totally understand, but I think maybe you should look at it."

"Can you send it to my email?"

A few minutes later, Judge Z opened his email and found the editorial. His picture was prominently displayed—the worst photo they could find, showing an angry, contorted look of pain, taken years ago. It made his driver's license look flattering.

"Disorder in Court," the headline shouted. It said:

"Tomorrow could be a sad day for families in Fayette County.

"Jack Stirling will enter a Fayette Circuit Courtroom to accomplish what thousands of people have done over the past 40 years since no-fault divorce became the law of Kentucky. He wants a simple divorce. Both the husband and wife have signed an agreement that was fairly negotiated on the normal issues of property and children.

"But instead of following the rules, Judge Atticus Zenas has refused to grant the divorce and plans to enter an order, which if allowed to stand by the Court of Appeals, could damage simple no-fault divorce forever. One lawyer working on the case said it best: 'We honestly are not sure if this judge has had a mental breakdown or what. But justice in Fayette County cannot be assured if the judge will not do his job, which is simple. Hear the cases. Apply the law. Sign the orders.'

"In short, the concerns we expressed eight years ago about Judge Zenas have sadly and predictably come true. Shortly after his appointment, during his race for re-election, we warned that he might use the court for his personal, right-wing Christian agenda.

"Now Judge Zenas seems determined to lead a misguided, one-man crusade against no-fault divorce. Recently re-elected unopposed, he is safe from being removed by voters. But he should now be retired to his law practice. Removal of judges is difficult, but this is a case of misfeasance which we hope the Judicial Conduct Commission will take seriously. A public hearing is scheduled for March 27. The citizens of Fayette County should pay attention. We certainly will."

Chapter 12

ON THE FIRST DAY

I rescued the fatherless, who had none to help them.

— *JOB 29:12*

JACK'S STORY

The snowstorm was not enough to cancel court. And Judge Z was happy about that. UK had canceled classes. Most businesses would be shut down. But this was family court. Justice could not wait.

He was as ready as he would get, but he didn't feel ready. In fact, he hadn't been this nervous in court since his first case fresh out of law school. All the symptoms were there: the queasy feeling they called butterflies, which felt more like that rubbery-knees nausea he remembered from being on the free-throw line when it counted; his palms were wet, and he kept dropping things—first his keys, then his pen, then he tipped over a take-out cup of coffee on his desk.

He hoped nobody would notice that the bottom half of the paperwork in front of him was coffee-stained mocha brown.

As he came into court he was surprised that the jury box was half full of reporters. "Karen," he said softly, leaning over so nobody else could overhear, "did you tell them they could sit there?"

"Yes," she said. "Do you want me to move them somewhere else?"

"Well, there's a couple I would like to move to the dark side of the moon, but no, let's leave them there. Maybe they will appreciate the courtesy and be fair for a change."

"Don't hold your breath, Your Honor."

Sitting at a table to the judge's left, near the jury box, was Jack Stirling, Harry Wolff and Anna Ollie. Her main job would be to take notes on a long legal pad and make it look like she was an important member of the team. On the other side of the courtroom sat Brad Bertram, Mary Stirling, and third-year law student Nicole Mason, sitting at the table by special permission of the judge. Sitting in a specially designated area behind them was Florence Bonnard, Guardian Ad Litem, acting as the attorney for the children.

This would be the closest thing to a jury trial ever in family court. And Harry Wolff was getting what he wanted: a jury of reporters to try the case in the media. The press was an odd mix. There was Jake Tolliver, the courthouse reporter for the *Lexington Times*, plus four young local TV reporters from the local affiliates for NBC, CBS, ABC and Fox. Marvin Crossfield had come from the *Louisville Post*.

And there was Byron Krause, owner and publisher of the *Georgetown News-Graphic*, the tiny weekly paper that covered all the big news in Sadieville. He was in Beulah's Sunday school class and went to high school with Judge Z. *Well, at least there's one friendly face*, the judge thought.

Judge Z had considered shutting out the press. But that would have defeated his point. He wanted the world to know. So he took the risk of putting his reputation in the hands of people who neither liked him nor understood the law.

After the formalities were read into the record, the hearing got going like all court proceedings—slowly, with stumbles and stutters of elaborate courtesy and stilted offerings "for the record." Judge Z reminded the lawyers that their pretrial conferences had clarified what was at issue. There would be no opening statements to impress the media. Not even the judge would say much.

"Mr. Wolff, I remind you that this is fairly simple, what I would call an IBH. An Irretrievably Broken Hearing. Mrs. Stirling has denied that the marriage is irretrievably broken. The legal burden is therefore on your client to prove by a preponderance of the evidence that the marriage is indeed irretrievably broken. Your first witness please."

"This will be short, Your Honor," Wolff said, standing up with a broad smile. "Presenting our case should only take about as long as the customary five-minute Kentucky no-fault divorce. I call as my first, last and only witness, Jack Stirling."

After Stirling was sworn in, Wolff started slowly: "Mr. Stirling, tell us just a little about yourself." This would be a well-rehearsed performance. Harry had insisted that the girlfriend, Brandi, stay away. But she would not have it. She had snuck in while Harry asked his opening question and sat in the back row, to make sure Jack did as he was told.

"Sure. My name is Jack Stirling. I am forty-five. I graduated from Lafayette High School and UK. I played baseball at UK. I was drafted in the 33rd round by the Reds, and had a two-year run in the minors before it was obvious I could not hit a curve ball. I came back to Lexington, got married, became a State Farm agent and that has been my career. State Farm has been good to me. I get along with people. I go to most UK games, football and basketball. I hear the judge hates Louisville, so we have at least one thing in common." That got a smile from the courtroom crowd and the judge.

"Thank you, Mr. Stirling. Are you married to Mary Stirling?"

"Yes."

"What was the date of your marriage?"

"July 31, 1996."

"Is your wife here in the courtroom?"

"Yes."

"Can you point her out?"

As Jack started to indicate Mary Stirling, who looked mortified, Judge Z interrupted with a pained look on his face. "Mr. Wolff." The stare continued. "Are you serious? We all know the Stirlings by now. They are the reason we're all here. This is a divorce preliminary hearing. I know the media is here, but please…" Judge Z shook his head.

"Of course, Your Honor," said Wolff with a smirk. "I wouldn't want to do anything to extend or lengthen this proceeding beyond normal." He turned back to Jack Stirling.

"Mr. Stirling, this is the critical question: Is your marriage irretrievably broken?"

"Yes."

"As you sit here today, is there any hope, any reasonable prospect, for reconciliation?"

"No."

"Why not?"

Jack Stirling proceeded to offer all the expected answers. The marriage was not working anymore. He was not in love with Mary anymore. Too many arguments had broken their relationship. The children would be better off without the fights. The kids were old enough to understand. He had moved on to a new relationship and he hoped Mrs. Stirling would find someone soon. He made sure to mention Mrs. Stirling's affair with a doctor a few years ago. In his version he made it sound like it happened yesterday. Mary Stirling sat quietly. But she was clearly embarrassed to have her personal baggage unpacked in front of the courtroom and the press.

Harry Wolff let Jack run on and on with the rehearsed complaints. He ended with a typical rationalization used by divorcing parents. "Your honor, I truly believe this will be best for our children."

"No further questions, Your Honor."

It took all of fifteen minutes.

DIVORCING YOUR KIDS

"Mr. Bertram, cross examine?"

"Thanks, Your Honor. Mr. Stirling, I have just a few simple questions. When you and Mary married, did you believe it was forever?"

"Objection, Your Honor. This is so irrelevant," Wolff said, halfway to his feet.

"Overruled. You may be seated, Mr. Wolff. Mr. Stirling, please go ahead and answer."

"Did I think our marriage was forever? Well, I suppose so. No one plans to divorce."

"Do you remember your wedding?" Brad asked.

"Of course. Most of it."

"You remember your vows?"

"Can't say I do for sure."

"Your Honor, permission to play a three-minute video, please."

Brad Bertram had the tape ready to roll. Harry Wolff had lost the battle to preclude the video at a pretrial conference. It was the Stirling wedding, cued up to the vows Jack had made to Mary, preserved by someone's hand-held, shaky video camera.

"Now with your right hands being joined," the pastor's tinny voice said, "let us enter into this pledge of faith, each to the other. Jack, in the name of God, repeat after me."

The priest prompted and Jack repeated:

"I, Jack, take you, Mary... to be my wife... to have and to hold... from this day forward... for better or for worse... for rich or for poor... in sickness and in health... to love and to cherish... till death do us part... according to God's Holy ordinance."

Brad stopped the tape. "Do you remember those vows?"

"Sure, I do now," Jack mumbled.

"And what did they mean to you?"

Jack was not ready for this. There was a long silence, then he stuck his chin out and said, "That was a long time ago."

Brad asked, "Tell me about how you met and dated and decided to marry?"

Jack kept his answer as short as possible, just the facts. "We met in college as seniors. We got married two years later."

"Tell me about your kids."

Jack spent five minutes describing his children and finished by saying, "They are my whole world."

Brad was sitting calmly at his assigned table during the interchange. But now he stood, stared at Brandi Peacock, and said, "Really? Your whole world?" Quiet filled the room.

"Yes, Mr. Bertram. You have any kids? You'd know what I mean if you did," he said, anger starting to boil over.

"Actually, I have two little girls." Brad paused and smiled, then asked, "So why are you divorcing your kids?"

Jack wanted to tell Bertram to go to hell, but instead he said through clenched teeth, "I am not divorcing my children. I simply cannot live with their mother."

"But can we all agree that you will not be there to tuck Noah into bed every night? You will not be there to join your children in prayers? You will see them only on weekends. They will be Ping-Pong balls, bouncing back and forth from mom to dad."

"Objection, Your Honor," Wolff said, standing again. "I don't think this soap opera line of questioning is any of the court's business. It's irrelevant and ridiculous."

Judge Z got out his statute book.

"Mr. Wolff, the statute says the hearing is about, and I quote, '*all* factors and circumstances leading up to the filing of the petition.' So it seems to me that there is virtually no reasonable question that cannot be asked. We're trying to find out if this marriage can be salvaged. Your objection is overruled. Mr. Stirling, you may answer."

"What was the question?"

"Mr. Bertram, please repeat the question."

"Simple. Why are you divorcing your kids?"

"I'm not divorcing my kids. I have been a better dad than ever during the past year."

"Okay, Mr. Stirling. Just one more sort of personal question. Is that your girlfriend sitting behind Mr. Wolff?"

This time, Harry didn't even bother to stand up to object. "Your Honor, to save us all some time and grief, I'd like the record to note my objection to every question from this point forward. Perhaps counsel would like to know what my client had for breakfast this morning."

"Duly noted, Mr. Wolff. But the statute says that we should explore the 'facts giving rise to the filing of the petition.' Whether Mr. Stirling had cereal or eggs for breakfast may be irrelevant, but *where* he had breakfast might be very relevant, and *who* was sitting at the breakfast table would definitely be relevant. Overruled. Mr. Stirling, please answer."

"Her name is Brandi Peacock. And no, we do not live together. She does hair. She loves kids. She's a good person."

Brandi wore a long-sleeved turquoise turtleneck sweater to cover her colorful tattoos. She was smiling politely. She was thirty-two years old, had no children, but had hit the jackpot with Jack Stirling. She could be an occasional mom to his three kids without the bother of childbirth.

"Do you plan to marry Ms. Peacock?"

Jack looked panicked for a split second, then recovered. "Not now. No sir. I am not even sure I can become single again after this circus. I take it one step at a time."

"Circus? Is that what this is, Mr. Stirling? Dancing bears and trapeze artists and clowns?" The question had no good answer. Brad was getting comfortable in court now. He moved on. His point was made. "Let's leave the personal stuff for the moment, Mr. Stirling. What is marriage?"

Harry rumbled, "Note my serious objection now, Your Honor. That calls for a legal conclusion which my client is not qualified to answer."

"Mr. Wolff, I thought you were not going to object anymore?"

Harry opened his mouth to reply, then closed it tight, grinding his teeth, steaming.

"Overruled," Judge Z said. "Please answer the question."

Jack answered, "I guess I'd say it's an agreement between two people in love, to be together."

"So it's not about kids?"

"Sure, I suppose that is part of it for most people."

"So it's just about love?"

Jack gave a shrug and said, "Beats me."

Brad looked at his legal pad while the reporters scribbled to keep up. Then he walked back to his table and sat down. "That's all, Your Honor."

As Jack stood up to return to his seat, Brad stopped him.

"Oh, I'm sorry, Judge. One more question?"

"Sure. Mr. Stirling, have a seat."

"Mr. Stirling, I can tell you love your kids. I imagine you would do anything to make them successful, right?"

"Of course I would."

"What if I told you that Noah, for example, has a two hundred percent higher chance of success growing up in a home with both parents than in a home with a single mom and a weekend dad? Would you stay in your marriage if that was true?"

"That's not fair. Statistics can say anything."

"Fair enough. But let me share a few more. What if Mary finds a boyfriend who moves in after the divorce, and the chances of success for your kids drops even more?"

"All I know is that I hope Mary finds someone. She deserves to be happy."

"Really? So you're okay with another man sleeping in your bed and helping to raise your kids?"

Jack had no reply. He shook his head.

"That's all, Your Honor," Brad concluded.

"Re-direct, Mr. Wolff?"

Even Harry was speechless. For the moment.

HARRY'S EXPERT WITNESS

"The witness may be excused," Judge Z said. "Anything else, Mr. Wolff?"

"Yes, Your Honor, just one more thing for the record. As this court is well aware, I have had a long and respected career handling divorces. I was named the top divorce attorney in town by *Lexington Magazine* in their 'Best of the Bluegrass' issue, and I've won numerous awards and honors for my professional work and as an officer in the local Bar Association." Harry was looking at the judge as he spoke but he was speaking to the "jury" of reporters.

"Yes, we're aware of that, Mr. Wolff, because we get your e-mail newsletter each month," Judge Z smiled back. "I remember that magazine story because it was so clever. They called you the 'Divorce Doberman.' But what does your distinguished reputation have to do with the case before us today?"

"Yes, Your Honor, I'm getting to that. Please bear with me if you can." Judge Z noticed that Wolff winced at being reminded of the "Doberman" award.

"As I was saying, I have extensive experience in divorce and family-law litigation in the Commonwealth of Kentucky. By my reckoning, I have handled more than two thousand divorces since I began my practice, and not once have I failed to deliver the outcome my client hired me to achieve, namely the dissolution of marriage.

"I also have testified as an expert witness on divorce law and litigation. So I think I can be qualified as an expert witness in this case, may it please the court."

"Shall we swear you in as a witness for your own client, Mr. Wolff? And if we do, who will ask the questions on your behalf? Do your professional skills include ventriloquism?"

"No need for any of that, Your Honor. I am an officer of the court sworn to speak the truth fairly. I simply want the record to show that in all my experience as a divorce lawyer, covering more than twenty-five years and over two thousand cases, I have never— repeat, never—been a party to such a..."

Wolff paused, scrunching his eyebrows in deep thought, pretending to search for the perfect adjective while he hoped reporters would fill in their own blanks. Then he continued, "... such an *unusual* hearing as this one. It's unprecedented, irregular, abnormal, unheard of—"

Judge Z cut in, "It's also part of those Kentucky Revised Statutes that you are apparently an expert on."

"Well, Your Honor, I understand that's your interpretation. But for our purposes today, I'd simply like the record to reflect that Mr. Stirling has submitted all of the requisite proof that has ever been needed to obtain a no-fault divorce in Kentucky. He has testified that his marriage is irretrievably broken and there is no hope for reconciliation. I would also remind the court that Mrs. Stirling has likewise signed an agreement which states that the marriage is irretrievably broken. And that is all I have, Your Honor."

"Mr. Bertram?"

"Your Honor," Brad said, rising with a smile, "we have no objection to qualifying Mr. Wolff as an expert witness on divorce."

Wolff beamed.

"Fine. Any questions or rebuttal, Mr. Bertram?"

"Again, not at this time, Your Honor."

"Then let's take a brief recess," Judge Z said. "Let's be back in ten minutes." He rapped his gavel and rose to exit, trying to ignore Harry, who was smiling in his direction the way a shark would smile at a struggling swimmer.

He had to admit, Harry had salted the record with everything he needed to appeal or add to his complaint to the Judicial Conduct Commission.

FIRST WITNESS

After the morning break, Bertram was ready. For the first time in the history of the Fayette Circuit Court since the passage of "No-Fault Divorce," this case would determine if a marriage was "irretrievably broken."

But first, Brad would attempt to define marriage.

His first witness would be Ben Marker, a staff lawyer for the Kentucky Legislature who was a forty-year aide to the Judiciary Committee. That meant he had written the actual language of the bills on divorce in Kentucky. Marker was known at the Capitol as a wizard among wonks. He cared almost nothing about politics. His life was devoted to policy—down to every jot and tittle of state law. He was well into his 70s, but looked surprisingly robust for a single workaholic who lived on Diet Pepsi and cheese nabs. If state government had its own order of ascetic monks, the high priest of policy would look like Ben Marker.

The media and the judge were about to get a lesson in Kentucky statutory definitions.

"Yes, it is certainly correct that there has never been a definition of marriage in Kentucky statutes until 1998," he answered Brad. "For the same reason we don't define the color blue in a statute. We only define words that require definition. We know what blue is, although there are different shades.

"Everyone knew what marriage was, so there was no need to define it. Honestly, if the same-sex marriage issue had not surfaced in the '90s, we still would have no definition."

Brad asked, "So how did we arrive at this definition we have? Let me read it to be clear: 'As used in recognizing the law of the Commonwealth, marriage refers only to the civil status, condition, or relation of one man and one woman united in law for life, for the discharge to each other in the community of the duties legally incumbent upon those whose association is founded on the distinction of sex.' That's KRS 402.005."

Marker laughed out loud. "That's what we call writing by committee. We got the definition by borrowing language from a conglomeration of other states and Black's Law Dictionary. Of course, what happens is that on the floor of the House or Senate, or in the final compromise process, amendments are made. Those amendments are often not even noticed by anyone except the amender. So you end up with nonsense. In this case, the intent was to define marriage for a man and woman only, but then it goes on to say it is 'in law for life,' which seems to rule out divorce."

Judge Z was surprised. No one had ever interpreted it that way, but that's what it said. "In law for life."

That also got Harry's attention. Such a literal interpretation could wipe out his practice.

Brad finished with a question about the purpose of the Divorce statute. "The divorce statute KRS 403.110 starts with interesting language that was written in 1972. Let me read it. 'This chapter shall be liberally construed and applied to promote its underlying purposes, which are to (1.) Strengthen and preserve the integrity of marriage and safeguard family relationships.' Mr. Marker, can you give us any legislative history of this language?"

"Objection, Your Honor, the statutes speak for themselves," Harry tried.

"Overruled. I'd like to hear from the man who wrote it."

Marker preened. "Your Honor, the language is there because the legislature in the early '70s, when this was passed, was still uncomfortable with easy divorces. You see, no-fault divorce was coming to the whole nation, and Kentucky was on board, but most legislators wanted to slow the process down. That explains the sixty-day waiting period, which I know isn't much. Many states have longer waiting periods."

"For example?" Brad asked.

"Even New York and California have six-month waiting periods. Illinois, Pennsylvania and Missouri require two years." The press looked shocked. Marker continued, "It also explains the language about having real hearings on whether a marriage is 'irretrievably broken.' There was specific language, which I remember writing, which mandated a hearing if either party wanted to prove that the marriage could be saved."

Judge Z was scribbling notes as fast as the reporters. Harry stared, turning redder by the minute. Jack glanced over his shoulder at Brandi, who was doing her nails and chewing gum.

"What else can you tell us?" Brad asked.

"Well, perhaps you would find it interesting to know that New York was the last state to pass no-fault divorce as recently as 2010." Brad was the only person in the room, including the judge, who already knew that.

Harry leaned over and whispered to Anna Ollie to check her computer to find out if that could possibly be true.

"And of course, it is also interesting to understand that the very first no-fault statute was signed into law by a California governor, Ronald Reagan, in 1969," said the witness with a smile.

"And don't forget that the language you just read says that our divorce statutes are to be 'liberally construed' and applied to 'preserve the integrity of marriage and safeguard family relationships.' This was vigorously debated and discussed in committee and on the floor of the Kentucky Senate and House. That language was included to make sure the children would be protected and that preserving marriages would always be paramount."

"So this language is not accidental?"

"Oh my, no. It was put there for a reason."

"But it has been ignored now for forty years?" Brad asked.

"I write policy, I don't enforce it. But yes, I would say so."

"That's all, Mr. Marker. The husband's attorney may have some questions."

Harry's cross examination was rough. He made sure the court knew that Ben Marker was single and knew nothing about being married. He also made sure everyone understood that he had never been a "real" lawyer, having worked only as a government bureaucrat for the Kentucky Legislature. He pointed out that twelve states, including Indiana, had no waiting period for divorces. After belittling the witness for five minutes, with a smirk that the reporters enjoyed, he said, "Nothing further for Mr. Marker."

It was time for lunch.

IVY LEAGUE OF HIS OWN

"Your honor, our next witness is Dr. Robert Roche," said Brad Bertram.

Deputy Palmer escorted Dr. Roche to the witness stand. As the witness took a seat, Judge Z noticed that his red bowtie with blue dots was tilted just so—perfectly tied, but just a little bit casual. With his gray tweed jacket, blue oxford button-down shirt and dark-blue slacks, he wore the official uniform of a Yale law professor.

Professor Roche had written law journal articles and books on marriage and family issues for decades. He was staunchly Catholic, but his writing was fastidiously academic, focusing solely on history and the law. "The Death of Marriage," as he called it in one of his book titles, was "America's great tragedy." Contacted by Brad's team, he had volunteered to come to Kentucky to testify.

As Brad qualified Dr. Roche as an expert on "family and marriage legal issues," Harry Wolff objected.

Judge Z replied, "Mr. Wolff, we have already agreed that you are an expert simply because you have divorced a few thousand people. And now, this Ph.D. who teaches at Yale, has a law degree from Harvard, has his undergrad from Columbia, and teaches Family and Constitutional Law is not an expert? Mr. Wolff, do you really object to this man as an expert?"

Harry thought quickly. "No, Your Honor. I have read his latest book. He is a qualified academic. We just disagree with much of what he believes. He does not seem to know how times have changed. But we withdraw our objection."

Bertram began. "Dr. Roche, what is marriage?"

Dr. Roche crossed his legs, straightened the crease on his slacks, adjusted his wire-framed glasses and replied. "There are two fundamentally competing views: One is the conjugal view—marriage is the union of man and woman, fulfilled by bearing and rearing children together. The spouses seal the union with conjugal acts, meaning sexual intercourse. When you get married you are expected to have sex.

"In this view, marriage is valuable in itself, but its inherent purpose is to raise children, and that puts a high value on monogamy and fidelity. The welfare of children also explains why marriage is important to the common good and why the state should recognize and regulate it. Virtue. Fidelity. Monogamy. Faithfulness. Commitment. Lifetime. These are all words that fit under this definition."

The reporters in the jury box were madly taking notes. The judge was too.

"Second is the revisionist view—love is love. Marriage is the union of two people, same sex or opposite sex, who commit to romantically loving and caring for each other and to sharing the burdens and benefits of domestic life. This is a union of hearts and minds enhanced by whatever form of sexual intimacy both partners find agreeable. In this view, the state should recognize and regulate marriage because it has an interest in stable, romantic partnerships and in the concrete needs of spouses and any children they may adopt or raise. Some would say this new view started about a hundred years ago. Some would say it took off in the 1960s. Marriage was considered an impediment to true love by many. But for those who did marry, it was all about being in love."

"So love as we know it is barely part of the definition in the conjugal view, yet love is everything under the new revisionist view?" Brad summarized.

"Yes, but that begs the question, what is love?" Dr. Roche smiled, as if he alone knew the answer. "Is love something you feel or something you do?"

"Where does religion come into this?" Brad asked, anticipating Harry's attack.

"Many would say the conjugal view is purely religious. But with or without religion, this conjugal viewpoint has been the basic view for all of history. Marriage is about order. It's about healthy boundaries. It's about children. It's about a reasonable way to inherit property. It is basic to human life in civilized societies and even uncivilized tribes. It is the way humans have always lived."

Brad nodded. The answer was exactly what he had hoped for.

Dr. Roche continued. "An old U.S. Supreme Court case, *Maynard versus Hill*, said it well one hundred and twenty-six years ago to explain why state legislatures need to say anything about marriage and divorce. I mean, what business is it of the government? Right?"

Judge Zenas had often wondered if maybe the government needed to get out of the marriage business completely. Roche read from his notes, quoting the Maynard case:

"'Marriage, as creating the most important relation in life, as having more to do with the morals and civilization of a people than any other institution, has always been subject to the control of the legislature. That body prescribes the age at which parties may contract to marry, the procedure of form essential to constitute marriage, the duties and obligations it creates, its effects upon the property rights of both, present and prospective, and the acts which may constitute grounds for dissolution...'

"And, 'It is a social relation like that of parent and child, the obligations of which arise not from the consent of concurring minds, but are the creation of the law itself, a relation most important as affecting the happiness of individuals, the first step from barbarism to incipient civilization, the purest tie of social life, and the true basis of human progress.'"

Brad had used this case extensively in his Family Law 301. He was thrilled to discover that Professor Roche liked it too. He paused a moment to let it sink in, then said, "'The first step from barbarism and the true basis of human progress.' That's all, Your Honor."

"Sir," Harry jumped in without waiting to be invited to cross examine, "So what? What does it matter?"

Harry should have known better than to challenge a real expert. It was the first thing they taught litigators, but he couldn't resist the theater of the courtroom.

"Good question, and one we get a lot. It matters for this hearing because if marriage is only about romantic love, as some now believe, then proving that such a marriage is irretrievably broken is a no-brainer. No love. No marriage. Easy come, easy go."

Harry was nodding his agreement.

"But what if…" Dr. Roche paused and looked at the press jury.

"What if marriage is more? What if it's a sacred commitment or covenant, even for non-religious people? As the 1888 Supreme Court case says, this is not just a contract that two people can break. The government has an interest in stable families and successful children. Someone like this judge here today is supposed to step in and make sure the union of two people is never broken in a way that damages people.

"So the definition of marriage makes all the difference in deciding if a marriage is broken."

"And for that you rely on a case from 1888?" Harry sneered. Dr. Roche smiled as if Harry had just walked into a trap. "Is that the best you've got?" Harry had asked one question too many again.

"Well, if you'd like something more recent, consider this quote from perhaps the most liberal member of the Supreme Court in modern times, Justice William O. Douglas, who served for thirty-seven years." He read from his notes again:

"'Marriage is a coming together for better or for worse, hopefully enduring, and intimate to the degree of being sacred. It is an association that promotes a way of life, not causes; a harmony in living, not political faiths; a bilateral loyalty, not commercial or social projects. Yet it is an association for as noble a purpose as any involved in our prior decisions.'"

He looked up at Harry and said, "If you would like to write it down, that is *Griswold versus Connecticut*, 1965. Would you like the citation?"

Harry was not accustomed to being humbled. He had to have the last word. "Did you say 1965?" he asked, as if 1965 was a prehistoric age when dinosaurs ruled the earth.

Dr. Roche just smiled and said nothing.

Harry sat down. "That's all, Your Honor. This witness is free to return to Connecticut."

"Alright, let's take a fifteen minute break."

Judge Zenas went to his office and asked Clay Henderson to print out the Maynard case and the Griswold case. It would give him something to read if the testimony got boring.

DON'T FORGET THE KIDS

"Your Honor, we call Dr. Barbara Rose," Brad said in the afternoon session.

The witness came through the gate carrying a thick stack of files in both arms. She looked about fifty and wore a dark blue skirt and jacket over a white blouse. Her dark hair was cut short and she wore red-framed glasses. "Have a seat, Dr. Rose, and raise your right hand," Judge Z said.

She complied and smiled nervously.

"Do you swear to tell the truth, the whole truth and nothing but the truth, so help you God?"

"I certainly do."

"Mr. Bertram?"

Brad stood. "Your Honor, to speed things up we have stipulated with Mr. Wolff that Dr. Rose is an expert in family studies, based on her career history, the books and papers she has written and the research she has done. She currently teaches at the University of Chicago. Her Ph.D. is from Southern California. Her M.D. is from right here at UK. She has authored over twenty books on family and marriage issues."

Judge Z looked at Harry, who grudgingly nodded agreement. "Just to clarify," Harry said, "we do not agree that she has anything relevant to say about an uncontested divorce case in Lexington, Kentucky. While we stipulate she is an expert on her subject matter, we reserve our right to appeal this entire proceeding."

"Understood, Mr. Wolff. Mr. Bertram, you may proceed."

"Thank you, Your Honor. Dr. Rose, the first thing I would like to cover with you is annual reports by the government on marriage and divorce rates, which I understand you use in your teaching in Family Studies. I have marked the entire document as Exhibit A. Can you please tell us what it is?"

"Sure. This is an annual report by family experts, including me, on marriage in the United States. It covers statistics on marriage and divorce, with polling on what people think about marriage and whether they are happy in their marriages. Cohabitation has recently became a major point of research and discussion."

As she warmed to her subject, Dr. Rose seemed to relax. "The most recent data show that the marriage rate in the U.S. continues to decline. To summarize, marriage is giving ground to unwed unions. A majority of people now live together before they marry for the first time."

"What about divorce?"

"Contrary to what you read in the media," she said with a brief but wary glance at the jury box of reporters, "divorce peaked in the early 1980s. The divorce rate has actually been going down simply because marriage itself is less popular. But there's also good news. Higher income, more education, having children and waiting to have children are all factors that reduce the likelihood of divorce significantly. So does religious affiliation."

"And what were your findings about cohabitation?"

"Objection, Your Honor," Wolff boomed. "This may be relevant in a social studies class at Henry Clay High School, but it's not even remotely relevant to the Stirling divorce. They are not cohabitating, they are married. Still married, unfortunately."

"Overruled," said Judge Z without explanation. "You may answer."

Dr. Rose looked at her notes. "Right. Unmarried cohabitation has increased dramatically over the past five decades. Most younger Americans now spend some time living together outside of marriage. And it is quite common for middle-aged adults who are divorced to cohabitate rather than re-marry."

Jack Stirling squirmed.

"Any theory as to why?" Brad asked.

"Well, the rise in cohabitation corresponds to the increase in divorce and single-parent families. Children raised in unmarried or divorced families are less likely to make the marriage commitment."

Brad asked about statistics that said married people lived longer and made more money. "That's just a fact," said Dr. Rose. "A *Time Magazine* cover story recently asked, 'Do Married People Really Live Longer?' The article said that the short answer is yes. And in fact, not only do married people live longer, so do their children. Statistically, divorce reduces the lifespan of children by five years."

Brad knew that answer was coming but acted surprised. Good lawyers had to be good actors. "Dr. Rose, if that is true, maybe we need the same warning on divorce papers we put on cigarettes? 'This divorce may be hazardous to your health and the health of your children.'"

Judge Z laughed and even the media jury smiled. Brad was becoming a real lawyer. Nicole had slipped him a note with the life-expectancy question. She felt like a football coach who just called the right play.

Dr. Rose chuckled and simply answered, "No doubt about it."

"Okay now, tell us about your book asserting that marriage is on its death-bed in America."

Harry interrupted, "Your Honor, note my objection which I explained in the pretrial pleadings."

"Overruled."

Dr. Rose watched the back-and-forth as if she was at a tennis match, then resumed. "Well, to begin, consider 'The Forgotten Sixty Percent' from the government reports."

As Brad submitted the thick report as evidence, Dr. Rose explained that the sixty percent was defined as "Middle America"—everyone between 25 and 60 who had finished high school but did not have a college degree. She produced a chart from her book that showed the numbers.

"Among these people, marriage is disappearing. Only thirteen percent of their children were born outside of marriage in the 1980s. Now that number is nearly fifty percent. That's thirteen percent to fifty percent. Huge increase.

"And for women under thirty, more than half of all births are outside marriage. In the 1980s, moderately educated households lived pretty similarly to college educated homes, but now this group looks far more like the least educated homes in terms of family dynamics."

Comfortable in her subject, Dr. Rose had a calm confidence. "For those of us old enough to remember it," she glanced at Judge Z, "the 1965 Moynihan Report cited an alarming rise in African-American out-of-wedlock births. But now, whites have surpassed that African-American rate from 1965. What was considered a cultural tragedy in the black community in the 1960s is now the new normal for all categories of ethnicity and education."

"Your Honor, this is just irrelevant to this couples' divorce. What is the point here?" an exasperated Harry griped.

"Mr. Bertram?"

"Your Honor, the statute at issue here gives us wide latitude to determine if this marriage is irretrievably broken and beyond all hope of reconciliation. As we attempt to negotiate unexplored legal territory and apply it for what may be the first time in Kentucky, it's incumbent on the court to first define marriage, so that we can determine what makes a marriage irretrievably broken. This testimony is consistent with that goal."

"Objection overruled. Dr. Rose, you may continue," the judge nodded.

"Thank you. Perhaps this will answer the lawyer's question about why any of this is relevant. Extensive research and human experience make it clear that marriage is not merely a private arrangement. Marriage is also a complex social institution. Because marriage fosters small cooperative unions, otherwise known as stable families, it not only enables children to thrive, but also shores up communities, helping family members to succeed during good times and to weather the bad times.

"But more and more couples that don't make a commitment in marriage still have children—who wind up in unstable homes fractured by cohabitation and breakups. And that's expensive. Our report concluded that the loss of social opportunity for these children and their families, and the national cost to taxpayers when stable families fail to form, is about $112 billion annually, or more than $1 trillion per decade."

"Did you say $112 billion?" Brad asked.

"You heard me correctly. Even if you care nothing about family or morals or decency or good behavior, money alone should make you at least think about this."

"Can you help us define marriage?"

"One way to define marriage is to consider what happens in its absence—sort of like defining George Bailey by the way Bedford Falls turned into grim, unhappy Potterville without him."

Judge Z interrupted, "For those of you who missed it, that's a reference to one of the great movies of all time, *It's a Wonderful Life*. Sorry, Dr. Rose, it's one of my favorites."

"Mine, too. So, what does America look like without marriage? We're beginning to find out. It's not a pretty picture. Cohabitating couples who have a child are twice as likely as married couples to break up before their child turns twelve. People born to married, well-educated parents are much more likely to graduate from college and have a stable marriage. But those born to fragmented families are more likely to repeat their parents' mistakes for a lifetime of heartache, hardship and risks.

"And from previous research, we know that children in cohabitating households are far more likely to be physically, sexually, and emotionally abused. The most dangerous place in the world for children is with a single mom who lives with a man who is not the father.

"To put it bluntly, we've gone from a society that used to say, 'We're going to stay together for the sake of the children,' to a society that now says, 'We're getting divorced for the sake of the children.' But if the children had a vote, they would almost always urge their parents to stay together, especially when we consider the economic and lifelong damage to them in lower earnings, less education, more poverty and more substance abuse. The legacy of what we used to call a 'broken home' is broken children with broken lives."

"And what specifically did you find about child abuse?"

"In another report, 'The Demographics of Child Abuse,' we found that—"

"Objection," shouted Harry. "This case has nothing to do with abuse or neglect. There is no allegation of abuse of neglect against my client. This is outrageous."

"Mr. Bertram. Response?"

"Mr. Stirling has left the home. These children now live in a single-parent home. The witness is giving us perspective on how they may be affected by their changed family structure. We are not alleging abuse. We're exploring how divorce can increase the likelihood of abuse."

"Overruled. Proceed, Dr. Rose."

"Thank you. Let me just read from this report."

Dr. Rose explained how child abuse in the United States followed demographic patterns: "The safest family environment for a child, by far, is a home in which the biological parents are married. Marriage is critical to the safety of children.

"The rate of abuse is six times higher in a blended family in which the divorced mother has remarried. It is fourteen times higher if the child lives with a biological mother who lives alone. And it is twenty times higher for children living with a biological father who lives alone.

"The rate of abuse is twenty times higher living with biological parents who are not married but are cohabiting. And thirty-three times higher if the mother is cohabiting with another man. The overwhelming number of child abuse deaths occurred in households in which the biological mother was cohabiting with someone who was unrelated to the child."

"Marriage is statistically safer for children," Brad prompted.

"It's common sense. Human beings have known for thousands of years that a man and a woman, committed to each other and the children above all else, is the family that provides safety and security and success for kids."

"Last question, I promise. As a culture, what do we do?"

"The answer is the return of the institution of marriage." She shuffled her papers and read:

"If family fragmentation were reduced by just one percent, U.S. taxpayers would save an estimated $1.1 billion annually. But it's not just dollars, it is the human costs—the price paid by the most innocent and vulnerable victims, children. One of my colleagues at Penn State University found, and I quote, 'Increasing marital stability to its 1980 level would result in nearly half a million fewer children suspended from school, about two-hundred thousand fewer children engaging in delinquency or violence, a quarter of a million fewer children receiving therapy, about a quarter of a million fewer smokers, about eighty thousand fewer children thinking about suicide, and twenty-eight thousand fewer children attempting suicide.' We need to revive marriage."

"And how do we do that?"

Harry Wolff objected. "Your Honor, we can all read. It's getting late in the day. Let me suggest we just stipulate that her book on this subject be admitted into evidence and save us all the time of listening to this summary."

"For once, Mr. Wolff, you make perfect sense. So ordered."

"Okay, then. That's all, Your Honor," offered Brad.

"Mr. Wolff, any questions?"

"No, Judge. As I mentioned already, there are no allegations of abuse or neglect by my client. I do not believe this witness has offered any relevant testimony. We renew our objection to everything she has said."

"I understand. Objection overruled. We are done for the day. See y 'all at 8:30 a.m. tomorrow."

Chapter 13

ON THE SECOND DAY

The Lord will call you back as if you were a
wife deserted and distressed in spirit.

— *ISAIAH 54:6*

MISSING FATHERS

Tuesday's newspapers had made the Stirling case front page news.

"Marriage on Trial" was the headline. Page A1. The article by Jake Tolliver was about as fair as the judge expected, although it was still outrageous.

The quotes were accurate, but out of context. Jack Stirling's statement about how much he loved his children was the highlight. The children were not named to protect them, but anyone who read the parents' names and kids' ages could figure out who they were. It was noted that they were excellent students. The story included comments by a sociologist from UCLA, who had written on the "Value of Divorce." Although she was not even a witness in the courtroom, she was quoted saying, "Many children do quite well after divorce." Judge Z thought, *Yes, and many people survive car wrecks.*

The actual witnesses, Ben Marker, Barbara Rose and Robert Roche, were barely mentioned. Most of the article was a rehash of old stories about the "serious charges pending against Judge Zenas" before the JCC at a hearing on March 27. The story made it sound like disbarment, permanent removal, suspension or worse was almost certain.

His blood was boiling as he put his robe on for Day Two. He didn't even glance at the press in the jury box as he entered the courtroom. The TV reporters were mostly gone this morning. This trial was not as exciting as they hoped. No deaths or murders. Better stories were out there in abundance.

The first witness on Tuesday was the Reverend Joe Mason, age thirty-four, associate pastor of Second Street Consolidated Baptist Church and basketball coach at Clark County High School. And husband to Nicole Mason, third-year law student and assistant to Brad Bertram.

Reverend Mason was there to testify about being the father of two children, and being an active volunteer in the Fatherhood Initiative. He was working on his Masters at UK in Family Studies with an emphasis on "Fatherlessness in the African-American Community," and its impact on jail sentences and life expectancy.

Harry Wolff pretended to be surprised that Reverend Mason had no Ph.D. or peer-reviewed papers on his resume. But he quickly realized that his condescending mockery was winning him no friends among the press. Reverend Mason was just too likeable, so he backed off and sat down.

Bertram asked, "Reverend Mason, how important is the father in a marriage?"

"First, marriage exists primarily to attach the father to the family. It is not a gender neutral institution. The same-sex marriage issue misses that point. When marriage breaks down it produces widespread fatherlessness. The father is the weakest link in the family chain, and without enforceable marriage bonds, he is easily discarded. This is obvious. Look at our inner cities.

"Fatherlessness, not poverty or race, predicts social pathology among the young. Without paternal authority, adolescents run wild and society descends into chaos."

"How does divorce fit into all that?"

"I'd say the five-minute Kentucky divorce is a disaster. It's too easy for a man to walk away and also too easy for a woman to throw the father away.

Divorce is the greatest violator of constitutional rights in America today. I know that sounds like a wild statement, but think about it. Imagine a man who works hard, has two kids that he loves and a house in the suburbs. His wife decides to leave him. He is immediately thrown out of his house and told that he can see his children only every other weekend, and can't spend any of the money he earns until the courts and the lawyers get their share."

He gave a pointed look at Harry. Judge Zenas had seen this scenario too often. He realized this young preacher was right. And sadly, he was part of the problem.

"If he fails to pay child support or maintenance as ordered, he will be put in jail without any kind of a real trial."

"Objection," said Harry. "There is no allegation of failure to pay support against my client. In fact, he would like a chance to pay support because that would mean he was finally divorced."

"I don't think that's what the witness implied." Judge Z stated. "Mr. Bertram, can you clarify?"

"Sure. Reverend Mason, how familiar are you with the facts of this case?"

"From what I know, this case is even sadder. The father has not been thrown out or put in jail for not paying. He is walking away on his own. Voluntary. He will not see his kids most nights." Jack Stirling looked stricken.

"The courts need to give a good man like Mr. Stirling time to think about it. Come to his senses. See how much his kids need him. How much they need a father."

Jack looked surprised. *Did he just call me a good man?* he asked himself.

"Divorce court has become a tool for plundering and criminalizing fathers. Not only are the prisons filled with fatherless children, our jails are filled with fathers who voluntarily left their children along with their wives.

"The death of marriage has tragic consequences. On a cultural level, it is well proven that families and their children thrive best in a married two parent home. On a deeper spiritual level, marriage is God's greatest metaphor for our intended relationship with Him. Our ability to understand the love of God is diminished as we lose the concept of sacred marriage."

"That's all, Your Honor."

"Any cross examination, Mr. Wolff?"

"Yes, just one question, Reverend Mason. Your wife is a student in Mr. Bertram's class on family law?"

"Yes sir."

"And you are a high school teacher?" Harry emphasized high school to make it sound like an insult.

"Yes. I had a choice between making money as a lawyer or changing lives as a teacher and coach."

That's a pretty good answer, Judge Z thought.

Harry seemed to agree. "That's all, Your Honor," he said.

THEOLOGY OF THE BODY

At 10:15 a.m., Deputy Sheriff Palmer stepped out to the hallway and called, "Dr. Thomas Weir," then escorted a portly, well-dressed man through the gate to the witness stand. Dr. Weir looked comfortable and ready. He was a Catholic priest, but looked more like a college professor, which was his day job. He wore a blue wool suit over a snow-white shirt and a striped tie in blue and gold.

Brad Bertram was presenting what Harry called the "religious" witnesses. "It sounds like the setup for a joke," Harry had told his friends. "A priest and a rabbi walk into a courtroom..."

Judge Z said, "Dr. Weir, just have a seat and raise your right hand. Do you swear to tell the truth, the whole truth, and nothing but the truth, so help you God?"

"I do."

"You may ask," he nodded to Brad.

"Dr. Weir, my name is Brad Bertram. We have spoken on the phone. Thank you for coming to Lexington. First, what are your professional qualifications?"

"My education includes a seminary degree from Catholic University. My Ph.D. is from Harvard in family studies. I have been teaching for the past forty years, most recently at Georgetown University in Washington, D.C. I'm a Catholic priest but I never pastored at a particular parish. My most recent work has been teaching classes built around Pope John Paul II's sermon series known as the Theology of the Body. I gathered from our conversation that that's what you're interested in today."

"Yes, Dr. Weir, I think it would be helpful if you would simply tell this court what I have asked you to do in this case."

"Sure. You made it clear that you want me to do my best to summarize Pope John Paul II's work on the definition of marriage. I'm not qualified to discuss whatever the law says about the definition of marriage, but I can tell you the Catholic definition."

"And are you qualified to do that?"

"Honestly, yes, I have spent the past twenty years of my life thinking about it every day."

"Your Honor, we move to qualify Dr. Weir as an expert on the question of the definition of marriage for the Catholic Church."

Harry Wolff knew his objection would probably be overruled, but he wanted to let the press know he would not stand for religion in court. "Your Honor, we object. This case involves the legal definition of marriage in Kentucky and what it takes to get someone divorced. Honestly, does the Pope's opinion, or the opinion of this priest, have anything at all to do with this case? I'm sure Mr. Weir—I mean Father Weir—is a fine man. But this is a court of law. I object to having him testify as an expert on anything legal."

"Mr. Bertram?"

"I can see why he would think this is not relevant," Brad replied. "I understand that divorce for the church is quite different than divorce for civil legal authorities. But even though marriage may be defined differently by laws and religion, there is a connection.

"Clergy sign the papers to make a marriage legal. The Stirlings' marriage was approved by a priest acting as an agent of the state. If they were married by a priest in a Catholic church, the definition of marriage by that church is at least partly relevant for our discussion."

"Mr. Wolff's objection is overruled. You may proceed, Mr. Bertram. And Mr. Wolff, you may sit down."

"Or maybe I should kneel, Your Honor?"

Judge Z shot Harry a withering look. Harry had crossed the line. The media loved these moments. "Proceed, Mr. Bertram. As for you, Mr. Wolff, any way you wish to sit or kneel is fine with me." Judge Z said with a frosty smile.

"Dr. Weir," Bertram resumed, "please give us a summary of the Theology of the Body."

"Certainly. I will try to be brief. Genesis 1:27 says simply, 'God created man in his image; in the divine image he created him; male and female he created them.' With this in mind, Pope John Paul II presented his Theology of the Body through short reflections once a week for five years."

As the priest quoted scripture in the courtroom, the reporters in the jury box were so surprised they stopped taking notes and stared at Dr. Weir, then Judge Z, and finally at Harry Wolff, mouths hanging open in disbelief. Then they bent to their notepads and resumed writing furiously.

"They were fifteen-minute sermons," Dr. Weir continued. "He did this because the culture of the sexual revolution was permeating every facet of Western culture. He started with the idea that our physical bodies are a gift from God, part of God's master plan for creation. This means that sexuality is also a great gift from God. This gift is meant to be a means for self-giving love, not selfish entertainment."

Judge Z knew that the Stirlings were casual Catholics—Easter, Christmas and occasional baptisms. He saw Jack Stirling redden and squirm a bit at the "selfish entertainment" part.

It looked like the priest was warming up to a sermon that would put everyone to sleep, so Bertram interrupted. "Reverend Weir, let me stop you and ask you to summarize in five minutes, if possible, what the Pope was saying. And can you bring it down to my level, to the level of uneducated lawyers?"

"I don't know if I can go that low," he replied with a smile, which drew laughter from everyone but Wolff and the press. "I'm not even sure I can bring it down to my own level. But let me try. Theology of the Body tells us what God's love says about how we use our bodies. Basically, Pope John Paul II says it's important to know what our sexuality is for, how it should be used, and what it tells us about God and the way God loves us.

"Sexuality is a gift from God, but it is a gift that can be darkened and turned to evil purposes."

Harry rolled his eyes at the reporters, who raised their eyebrows in appalled sympathy as they imagined their headlines: "Priest Testifies Divorce is Evil." "Catholic Says No Sex After Divorce."

Dr. Weir continued, "Marriage is the proper place to express sexual love because it is a relationship that gives completely, without limits or boundaries. The wedding vows say, 'I promise to be true to you in good times and in bad, in sickness and in health. I will love you and honor you all the days of my life.' Casual sex may seem enticing, fun, and harmless. But what makes it casual is that so much is held back. There is no pretense of sharing life together. Sexual pleasure is separated from the gift of the self. That kind of sex is wrong because it is selfish."

"That makes sense," said Bertram, nodding. Harry was holding his head in his hands, pretending to have a headache, and maybe he did.

"When we indulge ourselves sexually, when we take without giving, we turn the gift of God's love into our own selfishness. The Christian tradition insists that sex should take place within marriages, not because it has a low view of sex; rather, it seeks to elevate and protect the sanctity of sex to maintain its special, divine character."

Jack Stirling turned and looked at Brandi, whose earlier polite smile was turning into a storm cloud frown. Mary Stirling followed the direction of Jack's glance to Brandi, then looked down and gave the merest smile and shake of her head as Weir continued.

"The connection to God's love is the opposite of the superficial and saccharine idea of love as a purely emotional feeling. God's love for us, revealed in Jesus Christ, took on the form of suffering and self-sacrifice and led to the cross. The unselfishness of our own love in marriage should also be willing to suffer, to say, 'Not my will but yours be done.' Love and marriage can have a happily-ever-after-ending, but not without hardship and sacrifice."

Brandi tugged at her short skirt, shifted and crossed her legs, then crossed her arms defensively over her low-cut blouse. She had heard enough. She needed a cigarette.

Brad asked, "So what would John Paul II say about a definition for marriage?"

"Well, I know the definition of marriage that you showed me from the Kentucky statutes, and I'd say his definition would differ. It would include self-sacrificing unconditional love, like the love of Christ for his church. Vows at the altar would be forever. Nothing, and I mean nothing, should break those vows."

"Nothing further, Your Honor."

"Cross, Mr. Wolff?"

"Reverend Weir, have you ever met Mr. and Mrs. Stirling?"

"No."

"So you feel qualified to judge people you have never met?"

"I was asked here to help define marriage. I may not know the Stirlings personally, but I have known many, many couples just like them and I know what they are going through. The two became one at their wedding, and now their marriage bond is being split in half. And whether you do it very carefully with a scalpel or haphazardly with an ax, the result is the same. It's very painful."

"Didn't Jesus tell you not to judge?"

The priest smiled. He had heard this argument before. "No, no, no, you missed my point. I am not judging them individually. I am trying to make a broader comment, judging how our society has lost its way. Failing to judge right and wrong has caused a lot more pain and heartache in our world than an excess of judgment. We live in a world of no absolutes about anything."

"No absolutes?" Wolff asked rhetorically. "I can name one. Jack Stirling absolutely wants a divorce. And he is entitled to that. This is not a mass. This is a trial. This is not a church. This is a courthouse."

"Perhaps if I cited a more secular source? Would that be helpful?" the priest asked.

"Sure, I'd like to hear that," Harry replied, hoping the witness would embarrass himself if he wandered outside his area of expertise.

"Let me paraphrase the famous paradox of G.K. Chesterton, written in 1929, about marriage and the family. Imagine a fence erected across a road. The modern reformer goes up to it and quickly, with little thought, says, 'I don't see the use of this fence. Clear it away.'

"The more intelligent reformer will say, 'Go away and research why the fence is there. If there is no longer any valid reason for the fence, we will tear it down.'

"Chesterton pointed out that the fence did not grow there naturally. It was not built by an escaped lunatic. Someone had a reason. And until we know what the reason was, we don't know if it's still valid. The truth is that nobody has any business to destroy a social institution until he has really seen it as an historical institution."

"How is this relevant?" Wolff grumbled.

"Because even in 1929, the historical institution of marriage and family was under attack. Back then, Socialists and Nazis alike thought that government could do better than families. Chesterton warned that these people would pull down marriage and the traditional home without ever asking what purpose it serves to humanity."

Judge Z thought of how so many Americans were in a big hurry to tear down the "fence" of marriage, which has been there for all of time, to protect children, order, fidelity, virtue, honor, sanity. Sadness crept over him as he thought of the world he was living in, where the fences were torn down already.

Weir quoted Chesterton again: "He said, 'The Commonwealth is made up of a number of small kingdoms. In those kingdoms, a man and a woman are the King and Queen. They exercise a reasonable authority, subject to the common sense of the commonwealth, until those under their care, the children, grow up to found similar kingdoms and exercise similar authority.' That's family—the social structure of mankind, far older than all its records and more universal than any of its religions. It should not be allowed to die without fully understanding why it exists."

Judge Z thought: *Dad is the King and Mom is the Queen of the greatest country in the world. The family.* He asked, "Anything further, Mr. Wolff?"

"That's all Your Honor, unless you think we need a benediction."

Judge Z ignored Harry's sarcasm. "The witness is dismissed. Thank you for coming, Dr. Weir."

THE ROMANCE RABBI

Rabbi Levi Koffler was slender and lanky, all elbows and knees, with thick white hair and a tall, narrow face that looked as if it had been pinched in a vise. He was genial and seemed amused to find himself testifying in court about marriage—as if someone had asked him to define something as obvious as hot and cold.

As he recited his credentials, Judge Z learned that Rabbi Koffler was a professor of theology at NYU in New York City, and before that taught Humanities and World Religions at Columbia. He had had a brief career in business as a stockbroker, then enrolled in Brandeis Seminary when he was thirty-eight, got a Ph.D. in Middle Eastern languages, wrote a thesis on Solomon's "Song of Songs," and became known more recently as an expert on love. Often quoted in newspaper and magazine stories, he was nicknamed "The Romance Rabbi."

But underneath all that he was also an Old Testament scholar who had spent thirty years exploring the academic catacombs of Hebrew language and history.

His book *Old Testament Love* was based on a series of lectures he had given in Jerusalem. It was a textbook for Jewish seminaries, which meant it was hard to find anywhere except on dusty library shelves.

Judge Z asked, "What do I call a rabbi? Father? Rabbi Koffler? Levi?"

"How about the name my wife calls me?" the rabbi replied. "That would be 'Your Most Holy One.'" That drew laughter. "Most people call me Rabbi Levi."

"Okay, Rabbi Levi," Judge Z said. "Mr. Bertram?"

"Rabbi Levi," Brad began, "now that we've established the foundation of your professional expertise, I'd like you to discuss your research on marriage in society and culture."

"I will start by saying we all have a lot to learn. As I look around today, it seems like we have forgotten enough about marriage and love to fill a bookshelf. Also, for those who are squeamish about such things, I need to offer one of those warnings that they require for TV shows. 'The following may contain strong language and adult situations.' I might even quote the Bible, if that's permissible, Your Honor?"

Harry was torn between his impulse to object, at least for the record, and his curiosity. Who wouldn't be interested to learn something from a seventy-seven-year-old expert on love? Curiosity won and he stayed seated.

"Sure it is," said the judge.

"Good. I'm glad to hear the Bible has not been outlawed yet," the rabbi continued, "because it is not possible to discuss marriage unless you understand the Torah. Faith is rooted in history. We study the God of Abraham, the God of Isaac and the God of Jacob. God identified Himself as the God of our forefathers when he came to Moses at the burning bush. Essentially, he said, 'I am' the God of your history."

Jack Stirling shifted uneasily, and Rabbi Levi said, "Please, bear with me. One of the main flaws of Christians is thinking that the God of your Old Testament is the bad guy, the angry old man ready to burn everybody up. They think the good side of God showed up only in your New Testament with Jesus and his mother Mary. Christians take the good God and leave us Hebrews with the angry old man.

"But don't forget what I say next: God is love, and that is a Hebrew concept. Marriage and love were God's idea from Genesis onward. You have heard of Adam and Eve?" He glanced at Harry's side of the room and smiled. "The key that unlocks the door to this great mystery of love is found in a word. But sadly, this word has no equivalent in English. So, let's talk about a Hebrew word, 'hesed.' H-E-S-E-D.

"It is found in the Torah numerous times, meaning a life-long love that is richer and deeper than English words can explain. The New Testament word 'agape' comes closest, meaning selfless, spiritual love.

"Hesed is a steadfast, solid faithfulness that endures to eternity. As it says in Isaiah 54:10, 'Though the mountains be shaken and the hills be removed, yet my unfailing love for you will not be shaken.' That unfailing love is hesed. This love endures beyond any sin or betrayal or adultery. Hesed heals brokenness and extends grace and forgiveness, forever.

"Like many Hebrew words, hesed is not just a feeling but an action. It intervenes on behalf of loved ones and comes to their rescue. It's often translated as 'mercy' or 'loving-kindness,' but neither of these words fully conveys that hesed acts out of unfailing loyalty to the most undeserving."

Harry Wolff could take no more. "With all due respect to the rabbi," he said as he stood to object, "if we wanted a Sunday School lesson we can get that in church."

Before Brad or Judge Z could reply, the rabbi answered, "With all due respect to the gentleman who profits from divorce, I don't think he will get this in church or a synagogue unless he is patient enough to follow the reasoning to its conclusion."

Brad jumped in, "Rabbi Levi, maybe you can explain how this all relates to marriage?"

"Of course I can, but there is no shortcut. May I continue?"

"Let's follow this and see where it goes. Please proceed," said Judge Z.

"Thank you. Consider the story of Hosea. He was a prophet requested by God to marry a harlot. There was a spirit of harlotry and prostitution in the people of Israel. They were unfaithful to God. But for our purposes, just consider the story. Hosea is told to go marry a prostitute named Gomer." Judge Z smiled as he heard the familiar story, which always made him picture a woman who looked like Gomer Pyle.

"So he marries this unfaithful woman. The fact of her sinfulness does not stop Hosea from marrying her and loving her. Not love the way we think about it now. This is something more. God says 'be faithful' to her. And he is. He shows hesed. Hosea Chapter 6 explains that human love is always temporary. *'Your love is like the morning mist, like the early dew that disappears.'*

"But hesed is quite different. Today's love lasts just a few days or weeks or years. Maybe decades. It is closer to the morning mist and early dew than a loyal sacrificial love that never leaves. Never.

"That," he said, looking at Harry and Jack, "is what God intended for marriage. For thousands of years, that has been the standard. And measured against hesed, a marriage is never irretrievably broken. Never. There is always—always—hope for reconciliation."

The courtroom was spellbound by the tone of his deep, rich voice as much as his words. For once, Harry was speechless and Jack was paying attention.

"Rabbi Levi," Brad asked, "based on your experience and scholarship, how can a marriage be restored?"

"My answer may not be what you expect. I don't have a policy or a program or a clever counseling gimmick. I have hesed. But some of you may still not quite 'get it.'" He made air quotes around the words with his long, bony fingers. "So let me offer some practical examples.

"Hesed is a mother who cuts her career short to be sure her Down Syndrome baby has full-time care. For thirty years or more, as long as it takes.

"Hesed is a father who drives all night to bail his drug-addicted son out of a county jail. Again.

"Hesed is a wife who stays up praying all night for her husband, who went off on Friday night to have a beer with his friends and came home Saturday afternoon with no money in his pocket. She cooks him dinner.

"Hesed is a sister who prays for her alcoholic brother. And then uses all of her savings to send him to rehab.

"Hesed is a husband who welcomes his wife even after she has listened to her friends who told her to go back to an old boyfriend.

"Hesed does not care what wrong has been done, what sin has been committed, what trust has been violated. Hesed is a judge," he looked at Judge Z, "and a lawyer," now at Brad, "who have the love in their hearts to fight to save a marriage when it seems like the whole world wants to destroy it."

He turned to Jack. "Hesed is the husband who loves his children unconditionally and refuses, for their sake, to let his marriage be broken."

Then Mary. "Hesed is the mother who protects her family by opening her heart to find reconciliation, even after her husband has wounded her deeply and says he wants to walk away from her."

In the stillness that followed, Mary rummaged in her purse for a Kleenex. Jack Stirling's chin was on his chest, like a man who has been condemned by his own conscience. Harry Wolff would not look up, either. He was scribbling something on a legal pad. Judge Z wondered: *Is he just doodling? Framing another complaint? Preparing his scathing quotes for the evening news?*

"No more questions, Your Honor," said Brad, quietly.

"Mr. Wolff, any questions for the witness?"

"Yes, Your Honor, I have just one." He approached the rabbi, put an arm on the railing around the witness box and waited, drawing out the moment, building suspense. Then he asked, "Rabbi Koffler, is it not true that you were divorced from your first wife, Rachel, in 1976?"

A murmur rippled through the courtroom like a breeze across a pond. Judge Z rapped his gavel, turned to the rabbi and saw the twinkling light in his eyes dim for the first time since he had walked into the courtroom. The rabbi was hesitating, hoping the judge would bail him out. "Please answer the question," Judge Z said, hating himself for it.

"Yes," the rabbi answered, regret in his voice. "That is true. It was the worst mistake of my life. My children never forgave—"

"That's all, Your Honor," Wolff broke in, turning his back abruptly.

Rabbi Levi sat for a moment, then slowly stood to leave, as if his personal failures had put a heavy burden on his frail shoulders.

Harry smirked.

Judge Z glanced at his watch, saw it was after five o'clock and said, "Adjourned until 9 a.m. tomorrow."

BREAKING NEWS

That evening, Judge Z turned on the local Eye Witness News, feeling like a gawker at the scene of a car wreck. He didn't want to watch but couldn't resist.

A pretty young reporter was on the steps of the courthouse, wearing a businesslike gray skirt and jacket over a light blue blouse. She looked like a corporate lawyer.

"…Dan, Judge Atticus Zenas heard testimony today from a priest, a rabbi and a Baptist pastor. It felt more like an ecumenical gathering of religious leaders than a courtroom."

Dan the anchorman chuckled as if she had told a joke. "What did they have to say?"

"Basically, Rabbi Levi Koffler said marriage is ordained by God in the Old Testament. He did not say God would strike divorced couples with lightning, but some undoubtedly left the courtroom with that impression. One observer said that with all the scripture reading today, he didn't know if he was in Judge Zenas' courtroom or at a tent revival meeting. The rabbi testified that divorce is a sin and a mistake, but he was forced by Jack Stirling's well-known divorce attorney, Harry Wolff, to admit that he himself was divorced."

"Christy, that sounds like Mrs. Stirling's effort to force her husband to stay married against his will is coming unraveled."

"Dan, I think that would be a fair conclusion, although most observers think the judge has already made up his mind."

"Sounds fascinating, Christy. What about tomorrow?"

"Dan, they have a counselor who spent time with the couple, and Mrs. Stirling will apparently testify about the marriage, the children, and her desire to, and I quote, 'save her family.' Should be quite a show."

"Thanks, Christy. Tonight at eleven, Melissa Bryant interviews two former Kentucky lawmakers who helped pass Kentucky's no-fault divorce law—and they have quite an objection for Judge Zenas."

Judge Z turned off the TV.

He arrived early at the courthouse the next morning, made his coffee and sat down in his favorite office chair. He turned on the TV again, choosing CNN so he could avoid the local news.

"…And now a Lexington, Kentucky, family court judge, Atticus Zenas, has ignited a controversy by turning a simple uncontested divorce into what some observers call his own personal crusade for traditional marriage. Legal experts in family law seem to agree that his efforts to delay a no-fault divorce are unprecedented in the nation—once again focusing national attention on Kentucky's reputation as the backward buckle on the Bible Belt. Back to you…"

CNN. ABC. CBS. FOX. Even NPR was giving Judge Z the full media X-ray treatment. Maybe they thought it would stop the spread of his conservative cancer. More likely it would make him so radioactive that nobody would get near him for years.

So this is what it feels like to get my fifteen-second dose of fame, he thought. *Ten years on the bench and all anyone will remember is that Judge Z was the guy who tried to outlaw divorce in Kentucky. It might even be worth it if they reported any of the actual trial, or even a little bit of the truth.*

But the camera crews and reporters were there mainly there waiting for him to say something stupid—anything that could be used to make him sound like a backwoods Bible Bozo.

There was no Miranda warning from the media, he was learning. Anything you say can and will be used against you as often as possible in the court of public opinion.

The trial would probably end today. Three full days for a simple uncontested divorce. Even Judge Zenas began to think he might be going crazy.

He watched on TV as Mary Stirling and Brad Bertram said "no comment" and kept moving up the courthouse steps. Then he watched Harry Wolff stop to look into the camera and say, "Mr. Stirling just wants a simple divorce. He loves his kids but the marriage is not working. This is America. This judge is on some sort of crusade."

He switched the channel and there was Christy again on the Eye Witness News. "…Experts from around the country have been here to testify about the meaning of marriage. Later this afternoon we're expecting to hear from the wife, Mary Stirling, about why her marriage is not already broken beyond repair."

"I understand the judge and the so-called 'Divorce Doberman' Harry Wolff are not on good terms?"

"Yes, exactly, Dan. It's well known around the courthouse that there is bad blood between the two. This could get very personal. Emotions are high and, as you know, Dan, Judge Zenas has a reputation for making intemperate statements. One courthouse regular who is knowledgeable about this case told me that one of the exhibits suggests that Judge Zenas is attempting to blame, quote, 'unmarriageable young black men' for broken families, divorce, even crime. You may recall that his own trial for malfeasance will be later this month."

Dan put on his patented anchorman frown of troubled concern and said, "Thanks, Christy, we'll check back at noon. Sounds like a big day in court."

Chapter 14

ON THE THIRD DAY

Noah, in holy fear, built an ark to save his family.

— *Hebrews 11:7*

DISCERNMENT COUNSELOR

Don Lathem always made a good impression in court. He didn't look like a marriage counselor. He was fit and tall, a former UK walk-on basketball player, and he moved with the athletic grace of a guard, which is what he had been, and still was in his church league. He had a boyish face that made Judge Z want to call him "Opie," with freckles and a big smile that he flashed often.

For a guy who has seen more wrecked marriages than I have, Judge Z thought, *he sure seems happy. How does he keep his good humor when the rest of us get burned out?*

That humor would be tested today, though. Lathem had never met Harry Wolff.

Brad Bertram first established Lathem's professional credentials and experience counseling hundreds of married couples. "Mr. Lathem, please tell us your impression when you first met the Stirlings."

"Well, the Stirlings were sitting in front of me for their first session in December after being court ordered by Judge Zenas to see me. I was supposed to assist the parties to determine if their marriage was irretrievably broken. Even during our first visit the trouble in their relationship was obvious by their body language and behavior toward each other."

"Can you elaborate?"

"We see this all the time, so we learn to spot the signals. He doesn't hold the door for her. He goes and takes a seat immediately, without waiting for her. She looks at him, but he won't look at her. He folds his arms across his chest—classic oppositional defiance behavior. She folds her hands in her lap and hangs her head—a signal of defeat, submission or resignation. This is not a happy marriage. Do you want me to go on?"

"No, Mr. Lathem, that tells the story. What was your professional opinion at that point?"

"On the surface of things, any reasonable person could conclude that this relationship was over. As we discussed their situation, I learned that Mr. Stirling had a new lover. Betrayal of trust like that is the classic cause of broken marriages. But while most might figure this is a done deal, that's where marriage counseling starts. Where others see an ending, we see a beginning."

"Can you describe your basic theory?"

"Sure. I've been trained in Emotionally Focused Therapy—known as EFT in our business. Over twenty years it has a research-documented success rate of seventy-three percent, meaning almost three quarters of couples who stick with the entire course of treatment are still married. Among the ones I've successfully treated, most form a secure emotional bond, the bedrock of a lasting marriage. In other words, they learn what it takes to love each other."

"Did you see that kind of hope for the Stirlings?"

"Yes. My opinion, based on our interview, is that Mr. Stirling was seeking a relationship that made him feel valued, accepted, understood, cared for and loved. It is the same thing Mrs. Stirling is looking for, and that you and I and everyone on the planet needs and desires.

"To figure out why this desire can be destructive, I had to listen to the music of their lives. I know that sounds sappy, but it's a good analogy. Like music, their lives are made of many parts that blend together. When they are in tune, it's a symphony. When they are not, it sounds like one of those third-grade band concerts."

"I'd say that's a good analogy, too," Brad said. "I've been to a few of those concerts. So where does the marriage music come from?"

Harry was shifting and fidgeting, about to jump in with another interruption, but Judge Z seemed to read his mind and shot him a warning look.

Lathem continued. "The music comes from parents, loved ones, siblings, all of the important people in our lives who have been there for us at critical moments or let us down when it counted most to us. We ask if this person we're counseling experienced a profound and painful experience of being alone. Did someone they depended on abandon them? Has their faith been destroyed, or their trust been betrayed? When this happens, it creates an off-key chorus, if you will, that repeats again and again."

"How do you stop that broken record?"

"Once they understand the cause, they begin to understand how their hurt and disappointment is being replayed and causing more pain for themselves and others. That's where the healing can begin."

"Did you see that possibility for the Stirlings?"

"Very clearly. The hope was still there, within their hearts. It is always amazing to me how powerful the bond of marriage can be, how almost everyone I see really wants their marriage to work, but they just don't know how. My job is to find that place within Mr. Stirling and help him find it, too. Then show them how."

"Can you explain that?"

"Well, one of the positive things that I saw right away was that Mr. Stirling loves his children very much and feels very protective toward them. Anyone who can attach to a child is capable of attaching with an adult. EFT is a roadmap to find that again. I spent a significant amount of time with the Stirlings, listening to their story. Mrs. Stirling is emotionally wounded and in distress at being left, feeling unwanted and rejected."

"How do you repair that?"

"I ask her what that's like, and she says, 'It makes me angry.' Then all her husband sees is her anger, not her hurt and pain, her need for his love. So the accusations fly. Anger feeds anger. He feels her criticism and contempt. She feels his rejection. They told me, 'This is where we end up every time.' And Jack—Mr. Stirling—said, 'This is why I finally just had to leave. I couldn't take it anymore.' They are both alone."

"So what can they do about it?" Brad asked. Jack Stirling had his head in his hands; Mary was wiping her eyes.

"We can learn to change all that. We can learn to be aware of our emotions and stop ourselves before they get out of control and become destructive. EFT teaches adult love and bonding, with definable steps such as forgiveness. When I find a couple that still has hope, I tell them they can always get divorced, but at least postpone it and give your marriage a chance."

"And it's your professional opinion that the Stirlings are such a couple? Their marriage has a chance?"

"Absolutely. I've seen reconciliation in marriages that were far more damaged. Jack and Mary have good prospects for saving their marriage if they will commit to work with a good counselor. A few hours of counseling can spare them a lifetime of regret and also save their children from replaying the same sad music of broken relationships. As Mr. Stirling knows from the divorce of his own parents, divorce is hereditary."

"In your opinion, he is still hurt by his own parents' divorce?"

"Yes. That's typical. Those wounds can last a lifetime."

"Mr. Lathem, I understand there is now research to back up the idea that not everyone who makes it to the courthouse is headed toward a divorce?"

"True. A study by Dr. William Doherty at the University of Minnesota shows that thirty percent of couples who have already filed for divorce are what he calls 'mixed agenda couples', meaning that one or both of them sees hope. This is based on a four question simple assessment form he uses.

"Dr. Doherty calls it an Ambivalence Assessment. His research shows that in ten percent of all cases, both parties are 'ambivalent.' And when that happens, the parties should go to a counselor trained in discernment counseling.

It is not 'reconciliation' counseling. No one is forced to reconcile. But it slows down the process, lets people breathe and analyze if this is really what they should do."

"And you are available for such counseling?"

"For sure."

"That's all, Your Honor."

Judge Z nodded at Jack Stirling's table. "Mr. Wolff?"

"Only a couple of questions, Your Honor."

A 'couple' meant a dozen as Harry tried to pepper the record with insinuations that Lathem was another crony of the judge, planted to come up with a pre-determined opinion.

As he wrapped up, he couldn't resist trying to get in the last word. "Mr. Lathem, you testified that seventy-three percent of couples that come to you can save their marriages. But doesn't that also mean that twenty-seven percent cannot?"

"Well, yes and no. The correct way to phrase that is 'will not.' Ultimately, they have to make a commitment to finish EFT counseling. If they don't, their chances of divorce rise, as you would expect."

"So," Harry said, brushing aside the answer. "Can you state in your professional opinion, with full certainty, that the Stirlings will never get divorced if they submit to this ESP treatment or whatever you call it?"

"That's EFT. And no, of course not. People are, well, human. But I can tell you that the chances rise dramatically if—"

"That's all, Your Honor," Harry said in a rush. "This man obviously is delusional about his ability to save marriages."

Don Lathem just smiled at the insult and left the witness stand. Jake Tolliver followed him out the door, hoping for a comment. The newspaper photographer snapped fifty pictures, to make sure he would have one that made Lathem look like a goofball.

"Let's take a brief recess and come back in fifteen minutes," said Judge Z.

As he got up to leave, he saw something that almost made him stop in his tracks. Jack Stirling was looking at Mary, meeting her eyes for the first time since the hearing began two days ago. Was that a spark of love he saw—some code signal of mutual understanding and support in the secret language that every married couple shares?

The walk-on may have just scored a buzzer-beater, Judge Z said to himself.

MARY V. HARRY

Next up was perhaps the only witness that mattered. Mary Stirling. The same person who just three months ago had asked Judge Z to define "irretrievably broken." She was still waiting for an answer. So was Judge Z.

For a full hour, she provided a full history of her relationship with Jack Stirling. She was a cheerleader at UK. National Champions, in fact. She came to UK as Mary Massey, from Clay County, where she had been a pretty good softball player. She was a mountain girl. Her dad was a retired coal miner. Her parents had been married fifty-two years when her mom passed away a year ago. Her dad was sitting in the gallery, and she looked at him with a smile.

She knew Jack a little bit at UK. He played baseball. They went on a few dates, but they were never serious, meaning no sex. When Jack's career in baseball flamed out, they reconnected and the spark was quite sudden and real. He had no hesitation when she made it clear that marriage was on her agenda. Her very Baptist parents were not too crazy about the Catholic wedding, but they figured there were worse things than being married to a Catholic. Mary was a nurse but hoped to have kids and be a stay-home mom. It all worked out nicely for a long time. Two great kids. And then she got cancer. She survived non-Hodgkin's Lymphoma. Prayer and wonderful doctors got her through. And Jack had been super through all that—a caring, loving husband.

But she later learned he was not being faithful during that time. There was an affair and regular visits to strip clubs. She forgave him to save the marriage and moved on. She admitted she had a brief and unhappy affair with a doctor she knew when she was nursing at UK Hospital in her twenties. She regretted it. And then came a total surprise at age thirty-nine: Noah, now age 5. The perfect reason to keep going.

"And why did you name him Noah?" Brad asked.

"Two reasons. One, my grandfather was Noah Baker. A good old Clay County name. And two, when Noah was born, I must admit our marriage was on rocky ground. It was not irretrievably broken. But it was shaky. Our communication skills were gone. And a friend told me about the story of Noah in the Bible, that Noah 'built an ark to save his family.' It was sort of nuts, but the combination of grandpa Noah and my hope that this baby would help us save our family—that's why he is Noah."

That rang a bell in the back of the judge's mind. Something from one of Billy's sermons about Noah.

Mary went on to say that she would forgive her husband and start over, in spite of her obvious pain and humiliation caused by his betrayal.

"His settlement offer was generous?" Brad asked.

"Yes, he offered to give me whatever I wanted. But I don't want money," she said through tears. "I want my family. I don't want a house. I want a home."

The courtroom was quiet. Brad let the silence stretch, then said, "Mary, anything else you'd like to say?"

She turned to her left and looked straight at her husband. "Well, I thought I loved my husband before today." She paused and coughed. "But after hearing about 'hesed' yesterday, for the first time I know I still love him. It all makes sense. Yes, this is about the kids. But it also is about us. I need Jack and he needs me. We are one, and no court order can change that." She held up two fingers crossed to show that she and Jack were still one.

"No more questions at this time, Your Honor," Brad said as he sat down.

Harry was ready to go after Mary. These were the moments he was made for: cross examining a spouse. He couldn't wait to discuss her affair. Her nagging. Her failures. Her screaming at Jack. The time she drank too much and threw a lamp at her husband. All the times she told Jack that she was leaving. Or told him to leave. "Isn't it true, Mrs. Stirling," he began, just warming up, ready to go on and on until she was broken down in tears again. Harry knew how to find the raw nerves; like a surgeon with a scalpel, he could expose the wounds and drag out the pain until everyone could see that the marriage was dead. If Mary had hired him to divorce Jack, he would have enjoyed making the husband implode. He was good at it. Nobody was better.

But Jack leaned over and clamped a hand on his arm. "No questions, Harry," he said in a firm, hoarse whisper that could be heard in the quiet courtroom. "She's had enough." Harry could tell he meant it. Jack was visibly shaken.

Harry looked back at Brandi in the first row. She looked stricken. She had been briefed on the plan and was looking forward to watching the Divorce Doberman attack Mary, to finish the marriage for good. But something was happening. Jack seemed to be stopping Harry.

The jury of reporters were leaning forward, hoping they would not be disappointed. They were waiting for the big scene starring Harry's brilliance. They would enjoy it almost as much as Harry would enjoy building a cage of questions, then slamming the door and locking it. But not today. Jack's grip on his arm tightened. No, not today.

"Let's take a recess for lunch," the judge said, breaking the awkward silence, bailing out Harry.

When they returned, Judge Z asked Harry if he still wished to cross examine Mrs. Stirling. "No, Your Honor. No questions." Mary was relieved and bowed her head in silent thanks as Brad put a reassuring hand on her shoulder.

"Mr. Bertram, call your next witness."

Brad surprised everyone, including Judge Z. "I call as my next witness Harry Wolff," he said.

There was a stunned silence while it sank in, then Wolff jumped to his feet. "Objection. I am counsel for Jack Stirling, not a witness. What possible legal foundation does Professor Bertram have to call me as a witness? This is not a classroom exercise in moot court. I'm not going to—"

"Mr. Wolff, your objection is noted," Judge Z broke in. "I can hear you. Please use your indoor voice. Before we call in the National Guard, let's find out what Mr. Bertram has to say."

"Your Honor," said Brad, "I may be just a law professor with no court-room experience, especially compared to my esteemed colleague Mr. Wolff. But I can take notes. So can Nicole. And our notes show that on Monday, we stipulated that he was qualified as an expert witness."

"Well," said Judge Z, "No doubt about it. Mr. Wolff, you said you were an expert and Mr. Bertram stipulated. Please approach the witness stand."

Harry walked to the stand like a man being dragged to the electric chair. Judge Z swore him in. "Do you swear to tell the truth, the whole truth and nothing but the truth, so help you God?"

"Your Honor, I object," Wolff said, red-faced. Judge Z waited. Wolff seethed, started to say something else, took a deep breath and finally replied, "Alright, yes, I swear to tell the truth—under protest."

That drew a chuckle from the press gallery and Judge Z said, "There you have it, breaking news. A lawyer has agreed to tell the truth—but only under protest."

Wolff did not think it was funny.

Brad began, "Mr. Wolff, I only have a couple of questions. In fact, my first question is the same one you asked Rabbi Koffler. Have you been divorced?"

"Your Honor, my personal life is not relevant to this hearing. I object again. This is outrageous."

"Overruled. Answer the question."

"Yes, I have," Harry said softly.

"How many times? And please speak up."

"Three times."

"Did you have children by your previous marriages?"

"Judge Z?" Harry said, pleading.

"I'm sorry, Mr. Wolff, please answer the question."

"Yes, I have three children. Two by my first wife. One by my second wife."

"Mr. Wolff, when's the last time you spoke to your twenty-four-year-old son?"

"None of your damn business."

Brad was ready. "His post on Facebook says it's been six years. Sound about right? And your nineteen-year-old daughter has—"

"Your Honor, please. These questions are not appropriate. This is enough," said a suddenly humbled Harry Wolff.

Judge Z agreed. "Okay, we've heard enough. We get the point. I think that's as far as we need to go down this street."

"Thank you, Your Honor," Wolff said, quickly getting up. He gently carried his dented dignity back to his seat next to an astonished and confused Jack Stirling.

NOAH'S ARK

Brad concluded, "Your Honor, that is all we have. But I know the Guardian Ad Litem has a report."

"Ms. Bonnard?"

"Yes, first of all I have prepared a report that details the wishes of the children. May I approach the bench?"

"Sure."

Florence Bonnard handed the judge a fifteen-page report on her investigation and interviews with the children. She had been instructed to zero in on the best interests of the children. She summarized.

"Jack Jr. is sixteen. They call him 'Jay.' He loves baseball. His team made it to the Little League World Series five years ago, which apparently consumed an entire summer for the family. He is a really good pitcher, thanks entirely to his dad working with him. He told me he needs another five miles an hour on his fastball to get a Division One offer. He is a junior at Tates Creek High School.

"Sadly, at this time, he wishes his dad would stay away. He says he hates Ms. Peacock, even though he has never met her. He loves his dad but he is angry right now. Both times I have seen him, his body language was not good.

"Sarah Lynn is thirteen. It is a difficult age. Frankly, this girl does not fully understand anything that's happening, but in my opinion, Sarah Lynn needs time with her father. Whether they are divorced or not, she will need a daddy in her life for the next few years. She could go either way. I know she admitted she has already smoked marijuana and has a boyfriend. Those are not good signs in middle school. She is also angry at her dad. But she thinks Brandi Peacock is 'cool.' She wants a tattoo. She has no extracurricular activities now, which is not good.

"Current visitation for the older kids has been unstructured. They are both busy kids, so Mr. Stirling just calls one or both and works it out. Mrs. Stirling has told the children to always answer the phone when Dad calls and do whatever they want to do. That normally has been a visit once a week for a meal, usually fast food. Mr. Stirling went to most of Jay's games until the season ended last fall. Baseball is just getting started again.

"On average, the kids see their dad once a week for a couple hours. There have been no overnights. One, the apartment is too small. Two, Ms. Peacock is usually there. I know he says she does not live there, but she is there most nights.

"Last, Noah. Age five." Florence smiled.

The Stirlings were not smiling. Mary looked hurt and angry to hear her family picked apart in court. Jack was also uncomfortable.

Harry Wolff had on his poker face. The reporters were tuned in. All that other stuff from the priests and rabbis and counselors and Ph.D.'s was too hard to report, and their editors didn't like it. But this was the good stuff—someone crying, telling a story everyone could understand. It was "good TV." The kind of emotion and drama that could move their bylines to Page One.

Florence Bonnard continued. "Noah might be the cutest kid I have ever represented. And smart. He's doing well in kindergarten. As you might expect, he adores his older brother. He, too, wants to be a pitcher. He started T-Ball last fall. He knows how to aggravate his sister. Like most five-year-olds, he has no idea what's going on and hopes this divorce thing is a bad dream. He wants his dad home. He says his daddy can fix anything."

Florence paused and looked straight at Jack Stirling, who looked down. Harry looked like the only person in the room who was not moved. Judge Z wrote down on his notepad: "*Daddy can fix anything*." Those words might make it into his written order.

"Your Honor, I have the video we discussed," Florence said.

"You know my objection, Judge," Harry said. "This is bordering on child abuse to put a kid in front of a camera like that."

"I understand the objection," Judge Z said. "Normally this falls under my Santa Claus rule. If a child believes in Santa Claus, they obviously are not fully mature enough to testify. But this is just a video of a kid doing what kids do, talking about his life and family. Children are the forgotten ones in divorces, aren't they? Not today. Maybe Noah's thoughts will bring a little sanity to our courtroom."

Florence hooked up her laptop to the courtroom system and hit the play button. There was Noah, age five, looking like Jack Stirling must have looked at that age. He was wearing his favorite T-Ball cap. Cubs. His tee shirt had stains from spaghetti that ended up in the wrong place. He was sitting on the stairs going up to his upstairs bedroom. He had started kindergarten at Glendover Elementary School. He had no clue what was going on. He had never heard of the Peacock lady. He knew nothing about sex. He believed in Santa Claus. All he knew was that daddy was gone. Judge Z now knew the statistics and said to himself, *The only thing stopping this child from making it will be his parents' divorce.*

"Hi, Daddy." He looked away from the camera, distracted by whatever distracts a five-year-old, which is anything. He was thinking. Then, "Daddy, can you come home? Please come home. All I want is for everybody not to be mad. Can't we all just be nice? I pwomise. If you come home, I will be nice."

In the background, Mary's voice could be heard, saying, "Tell daddy you love him. He loves you."

Noah looked back into the camera, "I wuv you. Come home, Daddy. I pwomise. I will be nice." The five year old turned and ran up the stairs to his bedroom.

Florence stopped the tape.

Harry plunged in, "Your Honor, you heard Mary Stirling in the background of this video. She clearly has coached this child. This entire video should be stricken."

"Mr. Wolff, interesting argument. Most arguments about coaching kids for court involve 'parental alienation,' with one parent telling the kids how bad the other parent is. But I think I heard Mary Stirling say, 'Tell daddy you love him. He loves you too,' or something like that. If that was coaching, don't we need more of that?"

Harry started to speak but the judge said, "Objection overruled. Mrs. Bonnard, anything else?"

"Just a simple statement. This is not a love that can be explained by Ph.D.'s and lawyers or even theologians. I know this father-son love can be extremely awkward and complicated by the time the child is thirteen. But now he is five, and it's simple. He wants daddy to come home. And in all honesty, it would be in his best interest. There is no evidence of domestic violence in this home. There is nothing that would seem to prevent this couple from raising these kids together. Jay and Sarah Lynn need their father just as much as Noah does. In short, if this divorce happens I will have to make recommendations about where the children should live. But for today, the children's best interest is in this marriage staying intact."

Three days in court probably could have been shortened to a two minute video, Judge Z thought. And everyone in the room knew it. Jack Stirling knew it. Eyewitness News knew it. The *Lexington Times* knew it.

A verse came to his mind: *"And a little child shall lead them."*

Chapter 15

ON THE FOURTH DAY

Let us not love with words or speech but
with actions and in truth.

— *1 John 3:18*

FINAL ORDER

The trial had ended on Wednesday, just in time for TV reporters to break the news of Mary Stirling's testimony and Noah's video on the five o'clock news.

Harry had planned to put Mr. Stirling back on the stand to rebut all the wife's testimony, to get the last word. He even briefly considered using Brandi Peacock, depending on how the trial went. Anna Ollie had rehearsed testimony with Brandi, to show the judge how she would be a great stepmother. She would not show the judge her tattoos. They would be covered by a conservative dress that would make the judge, or at least the media, think she was teaching Sunday school somewhere.

But Jack Stirling had refused to testify any further. And Harry had decided that without Jack, he was not going to let Brandi Peacock anywhere near a courtroom.

So the trial ended with Noah's video.

The video had gone viral on YouTube, with 300,000 hits since it was played in court the day before. CNN had shown a brief clip. Megan Kelly. O'Reilly. Greta. All showed the thirty-second clip.

Maybe Noah really did save his family, Judge Z thought with a smile.

Everyone had been ordered back in court on Thursday at 1 p.m. Now it was time to decide. The case was being tried in the media, but they didn't matter now. Judge Atticus Zenas spent Thursday morning putting the final touches on an Order that would undoubtedly be appealed by Harry Wolff. Like most judges, knowing an appeal is likely made him more careful than normal. He would dot every "i" and cross every "t".

Was this marriage irretrievably broken? Custody and timesharing, property and debt division, maintenance for the wife, all these could wait. First, before any of that could happen, the judge had to make a finding that the marriage was "irretrievably broken with no prospect of reconciliation," words that he had spoken thousands of times, usually without a thought.

But everyone knew this was different. This was not the same judge. He looked the same. His hair was a little grayer than a year ago. His robe was still black. His smile was still there, although not as often. He still drove the same Buick, went to the same Greek restaurant and ordered the same moussaka, followed by vanilla custard bougatsa pastries for dessert. He lived in the same too-quiet condo and played golf as poorly as the rest of his hacker foursome at the same Keene Trace course on Saturdays. His name was still Atticus Zenas. He was still Beulah's son.

But this was serious business. The jokes were gone. This marriage decision felt like the future of all families was at stake.

When all the lawyers and parties were assembled, Judge Z announced "*Stirling versus Stirling*," and dove into reading his "Findings of Fact." He got right to the point. "I find it to be a fact that this marriage is not irretrievably broken. I also find as a fact that there is indeed a reasonable prospect for reconciliation."

He saw Jake Tolliver scribbling furiously, so he carefully built a wall of evidence to support his findings, brick by brick. He cited all the experts. Rabbi

Koffler, Reverend Weir, Joe Mason, Professors Roche and Rose. Ben Marker. And especially Don Lathem, the counselor.

He explained the purposes of marriage from the divorce sections of the Kentucky Revised Statutes.

He found himself quoting his mother, as usual.

And he reviewed the history of this one family, the Stirlings.

He recalled the testimony of Mrs. Stirling, about Jack and Mary falling in love at age twenty-four after college. Planning a life together. "For better and for worse, till death do us part." How they wondered what their children would be like. The joy of their first home together. Jack playing Santa Claus to thrill the kids, going to school events together—including lots of ballgames and ballet concerts—and covering the front of the refrigerator with the kids' artwork and handmade letters on Father's Day and Mother's Day. He recalled Mary's testimony about Jack's honeymoon promise that he would always be there for her.

The children had turned the couple into a family. A divorce would be devastating for them. They deserved both parents, a stable family, not the broken wreckage of a suddenly single, struggling mom and a part-time dad who arranges visits when it's convenient for him and his girlfriend.

Then Judge Z talked about forgiveness. "If Mary can forgive Jack—and nobody would blame her if she could not—then this court should stand with her and slow down this divorce. We are not denying divorce. We are just putting speed bumps in the road. Divorce court should not be an interstate or autobahn. It should be a neighborhood street, with 'Children at Play' signs and 'Beware Children Crossing' signs."

He pointed out that there were no concerns about domestic violence. No control issues. No emotional or physical abuse. No reason for this man and woman not to try again. And again, if needed.

He cited the recommendation of Florence Bonnard. It was in the best interests of the children for these parents to give it another try, she had said.

Unspoken was what the judge was thinking. "*Save this family*" kept ringing in the his ears. "*By faith Noah, when warned about things not yet seen, in holy fear built an ark to save his family.*" To save his family.

He thought of *Schindler's List*, when the hero had whispered, "I could have saved one more." Judge Z couldn't save the human race or even a single neighborhood in Lexington, but he could save the only family in front of him now.

Mr. and Mrs. Stirling and three kids.

A SECOND CHANCE

Judge Z turned to Jack, whose face was red, from anger or maybe remorse. "Mr. Stirling, perhaps this ruling sounds like the worst day of your life. You may think this is a nightmare. You wanted a simple no-fault, uncontested divorce. It was supposed to take sixty days and a hundred dollars for a filing fee. You didn't even need a lawyer, you thought. The final hearing was supposed to be five minutes. Your opinion was the only one that was supposed to matter. By now, you expected to be on a beach in Cabo with the new lady of your life, while your first love was at home raising your three kids.

"So, in a sense, I truly do apologize for making you part of my experiment, a long overdue application of the law as it was written. But I have real hope for you and Mary. I heard you testify. I saw your tears as Mary talked about her love for you. I heard you speak with true affection and pride about Jay, Sarah Lynn, and Noah.

"I saw the real Jack Stirling. He is a good man, a good father who may need to be rescued from his own mistakes. I saw your tears as the video played, so I know you get it, you see how important you are in their lives, how it would hurt them forever if you leave.

"Maybe that's the other side of the coin. An irretrievably broken marriage would also mean irretrievably lost happiness for those children. The sadness of divorce would never go away. Never. It would mean you failed at the most fundamental human level. Family.

"And then I thought, I hope correctly, that all I am doing today is actually helping *you*," the judge said, emphasizing it with a pointed look at Jack Stirling. "I'm helping you do what you really want to do yourself. Save your family. I'm sure you remember, as I do, what little Noah said to the guardian ad litem: 'Daddy can fix anything.'"

Judge Z took a sip of coffee. He shuffled his papers. Harry Wolff was fidgeting. "You heard the testimony. We don't need to go over all those statistics again. But now that you know how the odds are stacked against kids from a broken family, wouldn't you do anything to increase your kids' chances of success by two hundred percent?

"I don't know what is going through your head now, but I do not believe that Jack Stirling at age sixty will think it was a good idea to sit on a beach with his girlfriend when he could have been sitting at home on the couch with his three children.

"As some reporters have pointed out, I don't have any children. In their eyes, that makes me unqualified to judge this case, I guess. But from where I sit, it makes me qualified to say I would have given anything for the love and joy of a family that you are trying to throw away.

"If that seems too personal and emotional, well then, welcome to family court. This is where life really happens, for better and for worse."

Judge Z paused, undecided if he would finish saying what he wanted to say or just stop right there. *Oh, what the heck*, he thought, *if they're going to hang me in headlines I already gave them plenty of rope.*

"I'll probably regret this," he began, causing both Clay and Karen to give him an alarmed sidelong glance. They'd heard that before, and he was always right—he most certainly did regret what he said next, every time. "But as you all can tell, I've done a lot of thinking about this case and the greater issues that surround it. When we set out to define marriage, I had no idea just how profound that question would be.

"For what it's worth, here's what I've learned from the witnesses we've heard, who are a lot smarter than I am. First, if marriage is only about love, which seems to be the modern view, then it takes almost nothing to be married and almost nothing to break it. Under that theory, cohabitation serves all the purposes of marriage. I would almost say it is broken before it even starts. The wedding vows mean nothing. It is a lie to say 'forever.'

"But what if it's more like a covenant, something more sacred than a legal contract? Just listen to the language of our own Supreme Court, not to mention the sacred traditions. Covenant symbolizes a union of two people in a pact of life-long love and loyalty. 'Forever' should not be an easy promise to ignore.

"All the witnesses testified that a child will do better with two parents in the same home. We already knew that, didn't we? It's just Hollywood and our friends in the media who tell us otherwise," he said, glancing at the jury box where reporters had their heads down, writing on notepads to keep up.

"So shouldn't the law do more to keep parents together for the sake of the children, as they said in the old days? Isn't that what was intended when this law was written, to allow real judges to decide if a marriage is irretrievably broken?

"And what does broken mean? Drop a plate on the floor and it breaks. Is it irretrievably broken? Could you glue it back together? Maybe, if it's not shattered in a thousand pieces.

"What about a broken bone? Is it irretrievably broken? No, because it can heal. Some doctors will tell you the bone will be stronger than it was before.

"I'd say marriage is more like a bone than a plate, because it can heal. Healing is painful. It takes patience, even some therapy, perhaps. But when it's healed, it's stronger than it was before. That's what orthopedic doctors tell me.

"And this word 'irretrievable.' I play some golf. Is a golf ball that is lost ever irretrievable? I suppose if it's hit into the ocean at Pebble Beach, maybe. But usually it is just in the woods, or the bottom of a small pond. It's lost, but that's a lot different than 'irretrievable.'

"And the word here in this statute is clear. Irretrievably broken. That is strong language. So here is my final order:

"Pursuant to findings required by Kentucky Revised Statute 403, this marriage is *not* irretrievably broken. There is a reasonable prospect of reconciliation. This matter is set for further review on June 26. That's about one hundred days from now.

"No specific orders will be entered requiring either party to engage in counseling or other action facilitating any possible reconciliation, but the Court encourages both the husband and wife to consider the best interests of their three children as they contemplate their future, either together or separately. In short, after all this attention and expert witnesses and tears, my order is simple: wait. Give this marriage time to heal.

"I could dismiss the case under the law, but I will wait until June 26 to decide whether to dismiss the case or proceed with the divorce."

Judge Z looked up from the written order he had been reading and said, "Mr. Wolff, I see by your agitated state that you may have something to say at this point?"

"Your Honor, obviously we will appeal this ruling. When can we expect a final judgment to be signed?"

Judge Z waved his Order at Harry. "I just signed it so you can expedite whatever appeal or complaint or protest you wish to file."

As Judge Z was speaking, Mr. Stirling grabbed his lawyer's sleeve roughly and pulled him down to whisper in his ear.

Wolff stood again and asked, "Your Honor, could I have a moment to speak with my client?"

"Of course, take ten while I get a cup of coffee."

'YOU'RE FIRED'

Ten minutes turned into an hour. It was now 2:30 p.m. Judge Z was in his office, preparing to start another hearing at 3 p.m. when the call came from the courtroom that the parties had reappeared and were ready to reconvene.

"Remain seated," said Deputy Palmer, with an outstretched palm to motion all to stay in their seats as the judge entered again. The media were gone. They had their story. No reason to stick around for administrative details. They had left as soon as the judge entered his order. TV people were outside preparing for the five o'clock news. Jake Tolliver had rushed back to the newsroom to file his front-page story. Same for Marvin Crossfield from the *Post*, who had a long drive back to Louisville. They were all gone and missed the really big news. Harry had been fired.

Wolff stood, looking like he had just been mugged. "Your Honor, I need to make a motion to withdraw as counsel for Mr. Stirling. You may have found a reasonable prospect of reconciliation with the Stirlings, but we have developed an irretrievably broken relationship in our attorney-client relation-ship. May I be excused?"

Stunned, Judge Z looked first at Jack Stirling. "Is this correct? You agree for Mr. Wolff to be released from his duties to you?"

"Yes, sir."

"Alright, the motion to withdraw is sustained. Mr. Wolff, you are excused. Please prepare an Order of withdrawal for me to sign."

"Of course, your Honor, as soon as I get to the office." Harry Wolff packed up his remaining papers, turned and headed back to his office, a beaten man.

"Your Honor, may I say something?" Jack asked.

"By all means Mr. Stirling, but would you like to obtain new legal counsel first?"

"No, sir, I can represent myself. I'd like to ask you to dismiss this action. Completely. I think daddy can fix anything. My children deserve both par-ents at home."

Judge Z was stunned. "Wow," was all he could say. Then, "Can I ask what changed your mind? You've spent a lot of time and money trying to divorce your wife. Why the sudden change?"

"Well, Your Honor, it was lots of things. Noah's video of course. But mostly I just can't forget what that Rabbi Levi said."

"You mean the part about the concept of hesed?"

"Well, that too. But what really got my attention was at the end, when he said he had to confess that he had been divorced and it was the greatest mis-take of his life. He said his children had never forgiven him."

Brandi Peacock was still seated in the second row on the left side, unaware of the dramatic changes in Jack Stirling's heart over the last few hours. She was being fired too, and was just now getting it.

She quickly got up and stalked out of the courtroom on high heels that clicked and clacked like curses as she shoved her way past the courtroom doors. She tried to slam the door, but it only hissed on its air springs—mak-ing a loud sigh of furious frustration. That was followed by a muffled string of obscenities as she reached the outer hallway. Jesus was mentioned but she wasn't praying.

Jack glanced at Mary in embarrassment, and she looked at him with an expression all husbands know and dread—the raised-eyebrows wince of pity and disbelief, as if to say, "Oh, Jack. What could you have been thinking to trade your family for that?" Everyone else pretended to ignore it, but they were asking themselves the same question.

Judge Z was not done with the legal matters. "Mr. Stirling, I realize that you wish the case to be dismissed but I think the best option honestly is for you to take your time. You and Mrs. Stirling should take advantage of Don Lathem's offer for counseling. Go home. See how this works. I will keep the case on my docket. If you don't show up on June 26 I will know everything has worked out. Or feel free to come tell me how it is going on that day. For now, our next hearing is still set for Friday, June 26 at 9 a.m."

Meanwhile, Harry Wolff, followed loyally by Anna Ollie, had exited quickly out the back door. He usually made sure to walk past the TV crew so he could give a comment. But this time he took the long way back to his office, hoping no one would notice him. This was the first time in his life that the Divorce Doberman had failed. He was worried. This could hurt business. He had lost a simple no-contest divorce, an absolute impossibility according to his own opinion just four months ago.

Brad Bertram had packed up his papers. Nicole Mason was smiling the biggest smile possible. She had been told by her professors, by her dad the judge back in Virginia and by even Judge Z himself that "No one ever wins in divorce court."

But boy, did this feel like a win. She decided she liked being a lawyer. Nothing beats the feeling of helping someone. Especially to save a family. To save a marriage.

READ ALL ABOUT IT

Friday's media coverage of his decision was perhaps the most bizarre Judge Z had ever seen. The headline, front page, said: "Judge Denies Divorce." The article that followed recounted three days of testimony and included quotes and comments mostly from Harry Wolff and another one of those anonymous "courthouse observers". It was duly noted that Brad Bertram had no comment. The Stirlings could not be reached for comment, the story claimed.

The facts that Judge Zenas may have saved the marriage, that Harry Wolff had been fired, and that the Stirlings left the courthouse holding hands, were completely missing. Completely.

Jake Tolliver had left the courthouse and missed the last hour of reconciliation. The TV reporters had also left early, missing the real story. The media only reported the decision by the judge: The marriage was not irretrievably broken and there was a reasonable prospect of reconciliation. Divorce would not be granted in the Stirling case. And according to the press, that meant this judge was a right-wing nut, refusing to follow the law and allow a divorce.

It was implied by various quotes in the stories that the judge's order would have a chilling effect, striking fear into the hearts of hundreds of couples who were seeking divorces in Fayette County.

There were quotes from local "experts," none of whom were anywhere near the trial. "This is a disaster for domestic violence victims," said a women's rights advocate who taught a course in Gender Violence at UK. She predicted that Judge Z's ruling would force abused women to stay with abusive men. She had not seen one second of the trial.

Judge Z wondered: *Should I call the paper and set the record straight? Should I write an op-ed or letter to the editor to point out the distortions and errors?* No, he decided. He would keep a low profile and see how long it took the media to figure out what really happened. Maybe Brad would call and straighten it out.

Friday and Saturday were a welcome break. The UK basketball team was still the big news, finishing off a historic undefeated season. But even the Wildcats' 31-0 regular season did not keep Judge Z out of the Sunday paper, where his picture was on the editorial page.

He knew what most readers probably did not: The likely author of the unsigned editorial, Josephine Conrad, had been divorced three times and had given up on marriage long ago. Judging by her signed columns, she believed that the only rule was no rules: People should be free to do whatever felt good, and Judge Zenas was an intolerant Neanderthal who needed to crawl back in his cave.

Judge Z was surprised that three full days later they still had failed to report that the Stirlings had fired their lawyer and reconciled, meaning Judge Z's crusade to save this one marriage had actually been successful. He read the editorial again:

We Object:
Conservative Judge Orders
Unhappy Couple to Stay Married

Fayette County Family Court Judge Atticus Zenas is no longer married and has no children. But he apparently thinks he knows more about other people's marriages than they do.

Judge Zenas singlehandedly—and unilaterally—overturned 50 years of divorce-law precedent in Kentucky this week when he ordered Jack and Mary Stirling to "try again" at their failing marriage. The Stirlings had sought a routine Kentucky no-fault divorce—the same granted to countless married couples every year, usually in "30 minutes or less," as they say at the courthouse, and with minimal or no attorneys' fees. "Access to Justice" initiatives over the last few decades have made divorce accessible and affordable for the first time in history.

But when Mary Stirling had second thoughts, Judge Zenas rushed in where no judges had gone before—insisting he had the authority to make them remain married under an obscure provision of law.

After a week-long trial that featured a priest, a rabbi and a Baptist minister—no, this is not a joke—Judge Zenas issued a ruling that quoted scripture, social science, a marriage counselor, and the ultimate authority in his courtroom, his own mother.

Judge Zenas did not respond to our call for comment, but that's nothing new with this judge, who insists that he speaks through his orders. So let's take a look at what his order said.

In his ruling he stated that his goal was to keep the family intact for the sake of the Stirlings' three children. But if he really cared about those kids, he would let the couple go ahead with their plans for an amicable split, to avoid the domestic rancor that has made so many children the unhappy victims of unsettled homes, even domestic violence.

His judicial activism is the kind of thing conservatives usually deplore. It is especially rich to see Judge Zenas, who holds down the right wing of the courthouse all by himself, using his authority to have government dictate what should be a personal, private, family decision.

How many other couples will be intimidated from exercising their rights to a no-fault divorce after witnessing what Judge Zenas has done?

His behavior will be reviewed by the Judicial Conduct Commission on March 27. The Kentucky Supreme Court may want to also consider sanctions, up to and including removal and disbarment. The citizens of Fayette County deserve better.

Judge Z shook his head. There were so many errors, lies and misrepresentations he didn't know where to start. "Second thoughts" for Mary Stirling? She never had the first thought in favor of divorce. *What call for comment?* he wondered. He checked his iPhone. Sure enough, there was a voice message asking for "a statement" from the *Lexington Times* at 10 p.m. on Saturday night, after he had gone to bed. Calling for comment just before the deadline was a classic trick to make the target of a story look uncooperative and guilty.

And that line about his mother. That was just unforgiveable. *How do these people look at themselves in the mirror,* he wondered. He was glad Beulah didn't read the paper.

Somewhere in the back of his mind, an exhausted part of him was saying, *You don't have to put up with this. You can resign.*

Chapter 16

BEULAH LAND

Listen, son of my womb. Listen, my son,
the answers to my prayers.

— *Proverbs 31:2*

FINAL SECRET
March 8

Sunday was back to normal, if there was such a thing. Church at Sadieville was a respite for the judge. Reverend Billy was surprised to hear that the Stirlings had reconciled. Beulah knew all about it after peppering her son with questions. He had decided not to tell her about the Sunday editorial. She was already worried enough by the upcoming JCC hearing.

After church and Beulah's fried chicken, he was ready to watch some basketball but fell asleep in Johnny's old chair. UK finished off a perfect season while the judge slept soundly. He woke up just in time to wonder how the former Mr. and Mrs. Jones were getting along with their UK tickets, laughing with his mom about such nutty fans.

But today, Beulah had something more serious on her mind. It was time to show her only son another secret. "Atty, come with me," she said. Groggy from his nap, he followed upstairs to her bedroom, where she opened a closet door and invited him to peek in.

No clothes. No hangers. No drawers. Just a lot of pictures and letters taped to the walls. A rocking chair sat in the middle. "This is the chair I used to rock you in," she said, taking a seat in the chair and slowly rocking back and forth. The old rocker was painted green and made a comforting creak that he remembered from his childhood.

"I cleaned out this closet a long time ago, when I heard you should pray in secret. Jesus said 'go into your closet.' So I did. At first, I prayed for your dad to quit drinking and follow Jesus. He did. Then I prayed for a baby. And I got pregnant. I often prayed the prayer of Hannah in I Samuel 1:10. You can look it up." She smiled at the pictures of him and Johnny taped to the wall.

"I sang songs of praise as I rocked in this chair, knowing that praising the Lord seems to go with asking Him for answers. I prayed for the baby to be a boy who would someday be a God-fearing man, and maybe even a God-fearing lawyer. That took a while." She glanced at her son who sat down on the floor to gaze at all the pictures and letters.

"Mom, I don't know what to say," he said. Beulah saw him squinting to read the writing on the walls.

"Those are letters to God on behalf of some people who needed help," she said. "And the pictures are to remind me of who to pray for. I forget who's who, especially these days."

He was in a lot of the pictures. And there were yellowed newspaper clippings to remind Beulah that her son was under attack. She was praying for the world. Israel. India. African missionaries. But mostly family and friends in Sadieville. And last but not least was a picture of Harry Wolff—a newspaper "mug shot." And another of the Stirlings. She had been praying for them.

Judge Z got up, kissed Beulah on the top of her head, and asked, "Why did you never tell me about this?"

"Well, number one you never asked. And number two, Jesus said to pray in secret."

Judge Z now knew where all the power and wisdom had originated. His mother had prayed in secret, and she had been rewarded in full measure.

GOING HOME

In spite of his nap, or maybe because of it, he was exhausted as he drove home and was sound asleep in bed at 9 p.m. The call twenty minutes later was not alarming. He was on call, and it was not unusual for court clerks and social workers to phone at night to ask for emergency custody orders or emergency protection orders. He just had the usual thought when he was forced awake by a ringing phone: *Is it time to quit?*

He expected a clerk to read him allegations of child abuse or domestic violence, or offer to email the paperwork to his smartphone so he could push the button for reply, give instructions and go back to sleep. At first, those calls kept him awake as he replayed the ugly details of beatings, injuries, drunken violence and arrests. But now he'd seen and heard most everything—it was no big deal. He'd be back asleep in two minutes.

But this call had nothing to do with court.

A nurse at the small Scott County Hospital was on the line, saying, "Your mother, Beulah Zenas, had a stroke at approximately 8 p.m."

Beulah had managed to call 911, and was now in the intensive care unit.

In a daze, hardly knowing what he was doing, he yanked on some pants and a shirt, put on shoes and a jacket, hurried to his car and got to the hospital in thirty-five minutes. They directed him to the ICU, where he found her with a young doctor and two nurses. Machines showed numbers and squiggly moving lines; she had an oxygen line and mask over her face. She looked like she was asleep, but her forehead seemed creased by worry, as if she was having a bad dream. They told him she had not regained consciousness since the rescue squad found her on the floor by her phone.

Dr. Jeannine Raleigh gave some instructions to the nurses, then turned to him with a kind smile. "Sir, will you please step out with me for just a moment. You're her son, right?" Her demeanor was exactly what you would hope for in such a situation. Somber but polite.

"Yes, of course. How is she?"

"This is very serious. I'm sorry to tell you this but frankly, she probably will not make it, and if she does it will be in a diminished capacity. You need to be aware that some decisions may need to be made. It will be your call as we go along."

Judge Z's head was spinning. He was struggling for traction like a car on ice. This was happening too fast. "What do I need to decide?" he asked, immediately realizing the answer was obvious.

"We will need to know what her wishes were."

"She has a living will that covers that. No extraordinary efforts." He gulped back the lump in his throat. He remembered her words. *I am ready for heaven. Don't slow me down if the time is right.*

"Okay. We'll tell you everything we know as soon as we know it, to help you out. I know this is a very difficult time. If there's anything we can do, let us know."

"Thank you," Judge Z said. He walked back into the ICU unit where his mother looked like she was being attacked by plastic tubes that were draining her life away instead of keeping her alive. She was so gray.

The room felt surprisingly comfortable after he sat down awhile in a chair by her bed. There was a sweet aroma. It couldn't be flowers because there weren't any yet. So it had to be in his imagination, but it was real to him. He remembered a sermon from somewhere, *Faith is just holy imagination. It is just as real as anything you touch.*

This was not the smell of death, he realized. This was the smell of life. It dawned on him that Beulah was entering into the presence of the two loves of her life: Johnny and Jesus.

He found her hand and held it. He thought she responded with a slight squeeze, but it may have been only wishful thinking. He didn't want anyone to come in and interrupt her beautiful transition. As he sat, holding her hand, his sadness was turning to inexplicable joy.

His tears of sorrow were turning to tears of happiness, not grief. It was totally unexpected. Her voice was speaking to him, with some of her kitchen wisdom. He remembered how she would smile and say, *"Jesus, come soon,"* after one of his horrific family court stories.

Where is this joy coming from? he wondered, feeling almost embarrassed by the smile that he couldn't contain. As if she answered him, he realized it was coming from Beulah. She was already there, telling God not to let her son "mourn as the world mourns." Her reunion with Johnny was happening right now. At 12:15 a.m. on March 9. Beulah had gone home.

RING THE GOLDEN BELLS
March 12

Beulah's funeral was at 11 a.m. on Thursday at the Sadieville Methodist Church. Pastor Hughes would lead, but Judge Z knew he would have to speak for Beulah.

The organist played softly as people filed in. The service opened without introduction with the tenor voice of Harold Whitmoor, singing "When They Ring the Golden Bells."

"Don't you hear the bells a ringing, can't you hear the angels singing.

"Singing Glory Hallelujah Jubilee.

"In that far off sweet forever just beyond the shining river

"When they ring those golden bells for you and me..."

Harold was one of the judge's childhood friends who sang once a month at the church. Beulah loved him. He was not overly faithful at church. But he could sing.

The plan was for an opening prayer by Reverend Hughes, followed by a medley of her favorite hymns, then the eulogy by her son. Then it would close with the obvious musical choice, "Beulah Land."

As the hymns were sung and a prayer was offered, Judge Z hardly heard a word. He stared at the wedding picture of Beulah and Johnny propped on the casket, which was closed at Beulah's request.

On the front row, in the area always designated for family at funerals, Judge Atticus Timothy Zenas sat alone.

Johnny was gone. Angelina was gone. Aunts and uncles were all gone. Now Beulah was gone. Even J.J. was gone. Some cousins sat on the second row.

As he heard his name called by Reverend Hughes, he got up and walked to the pulpit, then stood there and looked out over the crowd. It was a packed house, stretching the seams of the little Sadieville church. He started to speak, but had to stop and gather himself. His voice wasn't working right. He looked out through tears at the faces in the crowd. There were several social workers and lawyers he knew. Divorce lawyer Eleanor Day was there with her husband of forty years. Even Harry Wolff was there, looking uncomfortable, sitting with Anna Ollie on the aisle where he could get away quickly if necessary. Judge Z was surprised and genuinely touched.

Near the back—was that Jefferson Davis with his grandma? It sure was.

Sitting on the third row was Serena, six months pregnant with Grace, and her son, Ray. She had told Judge Z that, sure enough, it was a girl. Sitting next to her were Ivory and two-year-old Jeremiah. Wanda was there, still wearing her funeral sadness from the service for J.J. He noticed some of his fellow judges of the Fayette Circuit Court. A few rows away were Brad Bertram and his wife, with Nicole Mason and her husband, Joe. Sally and Michael from Family Law 301 sat with them.

Judge Z recognized a couple of reporters. He saw the publisher of the *Lexington Times*, who nodded with sympathy. The last time Judge Z had stood in this pulpit, five weeks ago, he had been misquoted and blasted by the paper. For some reason though, Judge Z was not mad at anyone. He remembered Beulah quoting Jesus' words to him when that happened: *"Forgive them Father, for they know not what they do."*

Then, just as he opened his Bible to read and drew a breath to speak, a well-dressed couple came through the back door. Being late was always embarrassing at a funeral. Inevitably, the door squeaked or banged and the sound of shoes on a hardwood floor caused everyone to turn and glance with varying shades of disapproval. But this couple brought an immediate smile to the judge's face. Jack and Mary Stirling were holding hands, looking for an empty seat somewhere near the back of the church. He smiled and thought, *Better late than never.*

BROKEN JUDGE

"Thanks for being here today," Judge Z began.

"Beulah Virginia Zenas was a friend to all of you. Mother, wife, Sunday school teacher, greatest cook ever, gardener, preacher at times, always humming in the kitchen, always ready with hugs for anyone in need."

A few heads in the crowd nodded as if to say "amen" to their memories of Beulah's humming and hugs.

"Most of all she was a teacher. And what did she teach me, perhaps the worst of all her students?

"One: she taught me that her son was *not* the most important thing in her life. 'Of course,' you're thinking. 'God was the most important thing in her life.' Well, yes and no. Beulah loved God. She loved this church. But as Jesus would say, those who have 'ears to hear' will understand what I say next. The number one love of her life was actually her husband, Johnny. I saw it with my own eyes.

"She taught me by her actions that marriage was important and children like me were created by the love of a man and woman. I finally realized that to save a marriage…"

Judge Z choked and stopped. He swallowed hard, cleared his throat and continued.

"… is to save a child. It only took me fifty years or so to figure that out." He hoped they would all understand. "Bear in mind, my father Johnny was far from perfect. In fact, Beulah could have left him many times during the first ten years of their marriage, so I am told. But she stayed. And her patience and prayers were rewarded when Johnny Zenas gave his life to Christ and was set free to become a good father and a good husband.

"I saw them kiss. I saw them hold hands. I saw them love each other. They didn't even know they were teaching me. But they were. I felt secure because of who *they* were, not just individually, but also together. Johnny and Beulah were a piece of God's artwork.

"Second and related to the first point: Beulah loved family. She often quoted Psalm 68:6. It tells us that God puts lonely people in families. God had a great idea, didn't he? He could have made the universe any way he wanted. But he made it with families.

"Men. Women. Babies. Growing together. God's system was all about families. But now, we have messed it up so much that we need courts to sort out all the family mess, with courtrooms full of people making money off the anguish of broken families."

He could have aimed a glance at Harry Wolff, but he was no longer angry, just sad.

"It's nothing new, I guess. Cain killed Abel. And from there we end up with families that are so chaotic and evil that God sent a flood and started all over again. But He finds one good man and wife, one good couple like Beulah and Johnny. He asks Noah to save his family, and by saving his family, Noah saves the entire world. Hebrews 11:7 was a favorite of my Mom's. 'Noah built an ark to save his family.'

"Here is the greatest and simplest truth taught by Beulah. It is so simple that it should be taught to a third-grader, yet it is so profound that no one ever says it. Let me quote her just four days ago at dinner on Sunday afternoon."

Judge Z spoke slowly so his words would be heard clearly.

"She said none of us would exist if God's plan in the Garden for a man and woman to love each other intimately had not been fulfilled. A man. A woman. So intimate that their bodies come together and children are produced. If that system stops, the human race stops.

"And that's how God gives order to our lives. Children look like their parents, act like them, learn from them without even trying. Wild young men grow up when they commit to marriage and become fathers. Girls become mothers and turn into responsible women who save the world with their grace and beauty. The government can't do it."

This time he heard a couple of quiet "amens."

"The family is no accident of evolution. God did not just wind the clock and walk away, letting it all work itself out. No, Beulah was sure, and I am more certain every day, that God is very intentional about us. And he started with a family.

"Why? Love. God wanted more than anything to love and be loved, and so he used the family to show us that love. And he gave us free will so that our love would mean something. It's a choice.

"As Reverend Hughes has been telling us, marriage became God's greatest metaphor of the intimate relationship he desires with us. Intimate love produces offspring, who become a sacred family. It has worked for thousands of years. Without the sacredness of a system that says one man and one woman having children, the world is total chaos.

"And that is why marriage matters so much. It leads us to God.

"Now, the closing hymn is obviously 'Beulah Land.' Let me just say a few words about it. 'Beulah' is found only once in the entire Bible. Isaiah 62:4. Most people think it means heaven, but no." He paused to make sure everyone was listening. "The name Beulah actually means married." He read the scripture:

No longer will they call you Deserted,
or name your land Desolate.
But you will be called Hephzibah,
and your land Beulah;
for the Lord will take delight in you,
and your land will be married.
As a young man marries a young woman,
so will your Builder marry you;
as a bridegroom rejoices over his bride,
so will your God rejoice over you.

"The people of God would no longer be destitute and lonely. They would be married to God. He would be their Lover. Their Savior. Their Redeemer. Their Provider. Their Husband.

"In the past few months I have finally learned that God wants to be more than a judge. More than a father. God wants to be your lover.

"The notion of Beulah Land was made famous by John Bunyan in 1672 in *Pilgrim's Progress*. He described it not as heaven, but the land just before heaven. You can see heaven from there. You can smell it.

"There is this idea, deeply imbedded in the story, that just as Beulah Land is on the borders of Heaven, so marriage is on the borders of Heaven. Not everyone has to get married to find God, obviously, but the relationship of marriage is given to us as the perfect metaphor, leading us to Heaven.

"Listen to what Bunyan wrote about Christian's journey through Beulah Land:

"'The air was sweet and pleasant, and their way lay directly through it. Here they heard continually the singing of the birds, and saw every day new flowers appear on the earth. In this country the sun shone night and day because this was beyond the Valley of the Shadow of Death. It was also out of reach of Giant Despair. Here they were within sight of the City they were going to. Here they met some of the inhabitants of the country. The Shining Ones commonly walked in this land because it was on the borders of heaven. In this land the contract between the bride and the bridegroom was renewed. There was no want of corn and wine, for in this place they met with abundance of what they had sought in all their pilgrimage.'

"'As they walked in the land, they had more rejoicing than in parts more remote from the Kingdom to which they were bound. And drawing near to the City, they had a more perfect view of it. It was built of pearls and precious stones. Also, the streets were paved with gold, so that by reason of the natural glory of the City and reflection of the sunbeams on it, Christian fell sick with desire to dwell there.'"

Judge Z closed the book by Bunyan with a soft thump like a punctuation mark in the quiet church. Then he looked over the congregation and said, "This week, Beulah Zenas was met by the Shining Ones who escorted her out of Beulah Land into the City of God. We should not weep. We should rejoice. Like the pilgrims, Beulah Zenas was homesick for Heaven. Today she is there."

Judge Z smiled through tears. He stepped down from the pulpit and took his seat alone in the empty front row.

The organist played and they all stood and sang. Reverend Hughes was back in front, as Harold Whitmoor led congregants in singing the original

'Beulah Land' written by Edgar Stites in 1875—the same hymn her own
mother sang as she rocked Beulah to sleep.

"O Beulah land, sweet Beulah land!
"As on thy highest mount I stand,
"I look away across the sea
"Where mansions are prepared for me
"And view the shining glory shore
"My heaven, my home forever more."

The normal procession of cars to a cemetery would not be needed. Beulah
would be buried in the church cemetery, just fifty yards from the back door of
Sadieville Methodist Church. She would be next to Johnny Zenas. Angelina
and J.J. were there too. Sadness overwhelmed the judge as he walked with
Pastor Billy, followed by the entire congregation. Not only was he burying his
mother, his sweet memories of life with Angelina were also coming to the surface. He knew his marriage had kept him sane and healthy for twenty-eight
years. But only now, too late, did he fully comprehend the deep meaning of
it all.

Another headstone said Atticus Timothy Zenas (1964-). He realized that
the "dash" was all the room anyone got on a grave headstone to tell the story
of their life.

Beulah's headstone had already been filled in. Her dash stood for Atticus
and Johnny. Beulah had devoted her life to her family.

The sun was shining brightly. It was one of those rare warm days in
March when it finally felt like spring was really coming. A few patches of
snow remained. But they were melting, along with the hearts of everyone who
loved Beulah.

After all had assembled under the tent, Pastor Billy read John 14:2-4:

My father's house has many rooms; if that were not so, would I have told
you that I am going there to prepare a place for you? And if I go and

prepare a place for you, I will come back and take you to be with me that you also may be where I am.

Judge Z remembered the Jewish wedding traditions, and that he too was a bride. Jesus had prepared a place for him too. As he stood next to the graves of everyone he had ever considered family, it occurred to the judge that he was finally broken himself.

In fact, he hoped he was "irretrievably broken." It would be a good thing. The trials of the last few months had placed him square in the center of Beulah Land. His path to faith and heaven had been cleared by circumstances beyond his own choosing.

It included his upbringing by Beulah and Johnny. The wisdom of Beulah's dinner table. His marriage to Angelina. His endless days of chaos in family court. His decision to follow the law and have a hearing on whether the Stirling marriage was irretrievably broken. His trip to India and the ladies at the little church. His final Sunday with Beulah and her closet.

Finally, he understood "hesed." His heart was singing that old hymn, *"Love lifted me, love lifted me. When nothing else could help, love lifted me."*

Pastor Billy offered the benediction and everyone moved down to the basement for a classic church potluck dinner. The only thing missing would be Beulah's fried chicken.

Chapter 17

EPILOGUE

Your land will be called Beulah; for the Lord will take
delight in you, and your land will be married.

— ISAIAH 62:4

JUDGE ON TRIAL
March 27

By the time his own "trial" finally arrived, it was almost a relief. The Judicial Conduct Commission hearing had been loitering in the back of Judge Z's mind now for more than four months, like a bully waiting for him after school.

But Judge Z was living in Beulah Land now. The stress had been gradually disappearing. And it wasn't just that the Stirlings had reconciled. It was not just that he had "won" the showdown with Harry.

The love he found in India had magnified in his heart since Beulah died. He had a prayer closet now. On the Friday after Beulah's funeral, he had cleared out a closet at his office and now the crazy judge was spending an hour a day in his closet, praying for people like Harry. And all the children and families of family court. Judge Z smiled and thought, *I wonder what the ACLU would think about a prayer closet in the courthouse?*

Back in January, before this new love, he woke up many nights at 3 a.m. and watched as all the worst possible outcomes paraded down Main Street of his imagination, banging drums and crashing cymbals. Disbarment. Crash! Impeachment. Boom! Disgrace. Crash-Boom! Maybe even jail?

He knew that the whole complaint was bogus, but still, he was nervous.

As he arrived on Monday morning he discovered that the hearing would be held, ironically, in the very same courtroom where the Stirling case had been heard. Were they trying to rub salt in the wounds of disbarment by "sentencing" him in his own courtroom? It didn't matter. He was at peace, even smiling as the hearing got started. He had decided not to say much and just let the record speak for itself. Let the reconciliation of the Stirlings speak louder than words.

The original complaint, filed in early January, had been simple.

1. Judge Zenas failed and refused to grant a simple no-fault divorce pursuant to state law. (Canon 3)
2. Judge Zenas engaged in ex parte conversations with counsel for one of the parties. (Canon 1, 2, and 3)
3. Judge Zenas has prejudged a case before hearing the evidence. (Canon 1 and 3)
4. Judge Zenas has injected his religious and political views, and violated "church and state." (Canon 5)

But now there was more. Since the original filing, the JCC prosecutor and investigator had added numerous documents and reports. The complaint had started with Harry Wolff and Jack Stirling, but now there was more, including some accusations added the day before the hearing. *There's a joke,* he thought. *Judges give everyone due process—except other judges.*

He had no lawyer to defend him. He would call no witnesses. His only defense would be plain truth from his heart. If they wished to retire him, he would actually be quietly happy about it. He was trusting in a much higher power than the Commonwealth of Kentucky.

The file with his name on it was more than he could stand to read, a full two inches thick, crammed with attacks on his character, competence and integrity. He had flipped through it that morning over eggs and bacon at Tolly Ho. There were newspaper stories, letters of complaint from a disgruntled litigant he had long forgotten, briefs and a complaint by Planned Parenthood about the Ivory Smith case. The judge had allegedly interfered with her right to a legal abortion. Another complaint pointed out that he had marched in a pro-life rally. They forgot to mention it was before he was even a judge. An affidavit from a student in Family Law 301 alleged that he made some politically incorrect statements in class, about marriage making a better family than unmarried parents.

He was surprised to find a report on his sermon about the ladies in India. And there was a report, added the day before, quoting his eulogy at Beulah's funeral. The implication was that no judge should ever speak publicly about religion, that such comments were proof that he could not remain unbiased toward people who had no faith or those of other faiths. Affidavits from Dr. Patel and Mr. Dawid were added to claim that Hindus and Muslims had been treated unfairly.

None of the additional information was relevant to the original charges by Harry Wolff. But it would make great theater for the press. Jake Tolliver was at the hearing, along with local TV reporters, almost writing the headlines in advance of the judge's comeuppance. Marvin Crossfield from the *Louisville Post* was there, too.

But three weeks after the Stirling case was final, there still had been no media reports about the couple's reconciliation and firing of Harry Wolff. Judging from his file, the JCC was still in the dark about that too.

Their investigator, Adam Kelly, had been so hard at work, drumming up more charges against the judge, he forgot to check the final record.

The commissioners sat at a long table in business clothes, but somehow managed to create the impression that they were elevated on a bench above everyone else, wearing black robes and powdered wigs. Being on the wrong side of that was an eerie feeling for Judge Z, like being in the principal's office, waiting for his parents to arrive.

The Honorable Dean Beck, chairman, rapped his knuckles on the table to begin the hearing and read the complaint number into the record. He looked like that folksy old guy who sold oatmeal on TV. Beck was retired from Fleming County, where "urban renewal" meant buying a new stoplight for the main intersection down by the Dairy Queen.

They started by inviting Kelly to deliver a summary of the complaint. He painted Judge Z as a renegade, a one-man vigilante against divorce. "Not since 1972," he said, "when the no-fault divorce came into existence, has a judge refused to grant a divorce on the grounds that the marriage was not irretrievably broken. The improper, unusual and unethical actions of Judge Zenas have caused irreparable damage to Mr. Stirling."

As Kelly droned on, Judge Z began to feel more confident, which defied logic. *This is weird*, he thought. *I'm supposed to be intimidated and scared by all this. But instead I feel calm, almost relieved. The worst that can happen is that I lose my job, and that's no big loss. Heck, I'm halfway out the door already. The rest is just pride.*

JUDGING THE JUDGE

Just as Kelly was finishing his twenty minute opening statement, the door to the hearing room huffed open and Judge Z turned to see Jack and Mary Stirling enter. He had not told them about the hearing, but they had apparently read about it in the paper.

As they entered, everything stopped. Kelly stopped in mid-sentence, then fidgeted and shifted from foot to foot, impatient to continue with his prosecution. The commissioners stared at the Stirlings with varying reactions of concern and annoyance, probably assuming this nice but clueless couple had just stumbled into the wrong room. No witnesses were allowed in the room. The first witness to be called by the prosecution would be Harry Wolff, who was waiting in the hallway. The Planned Parenthood lawyer was standing by to come down if called by Kelly. Most of the prosecution's case was a video of the entire Stirling proceeding, made a part of the record by stipulation with Judge Zenas.

"And whom do we have here, Mr. Kelly?" Presiding Judge Dean Beck asked as the Stirlings took a seat near the front of the room.

"I'm sorry, sir, I don't—" Kelly stopped, turned to the Stirlings and asked, like an annoyed, harried store clerk, "Can I help you?"

Jack stood. "We're Jack and Mary Stirling."

Mr. Kelly had never even met the Stirlings. In theory he was protecting Mr. Stirling's right to a divorce, but he had never even talked to him. He had taken Harry Wolff's word for everything. Since Mr. Stirling's testimony from the trial would be played on video as evidence, Kelly saw no reason to even speak to the man who signed the original complaint. "Your witnesses, Mr. Kelly?" Beck asked. "If so, they need to step out until you call them."

"No sir. Harry Wolff will testify on behalf of the Stirlings. There must have been some mistake."

Beck turned to the Stirlings. "Folks, you will need to step outside."

Jack ignored Beck, stuck his chin out and spoke up. "I am responsible for this hearing. This complaint was brought on my behalf as the petitioner in our divorce case. I don't know the rules or procedures, but I'd like to say something, if I could."

Kelly squirmed. "Your Honor, this is irregular. Mr. Wolff is here to speak for Mr. Stirling."

Jack replied, "Sir, perhaps you and this commission are not aware that I fired Mr. Wolff on the final day of our trial. Mary and I have reconciled."

That got everyone's attention. All the commissioners were wide awake now, coming out of the coma induced by Kelly's monotonous opening statement. Jake Tolliver looked like he might have a panic attack. The TV reporters were looking at each other as if to ask, "How did we miss this?" Then, "And how do we explain how we missed it?"

Jack took advantage of the stunned silence. "Honestly, I don't know how this works. I thought when I fired Harry Wolff that this complaint would be automatically dismissed. We only knew about this hearing today when we got a call at 8 a.m. from a friend who saw the newspaper today. We came down to see what we could do to help Judge Zenas."

The commissioners turned to Adam Kelly for answers. "Mr. Kelly, did you know this?" Beck asked with a sharp edge in his voice.

"No sir, but it still does not resolve the case. There is more to this than the Stirlings."

"Well maybe, but I would note for the record that the only signature on this complaint is Jack Stirling's. Right, Mr. Kelly?"

The prosecutor stumbled and mumbled and shuffled through his papers to find the actual complaint. Before he could answer, Chairman Beck saved him the embarrassment of an incoherent response.

"Why don't we make sure these folks can say whatever they need to say so they can go back to their lives. So what would you like to say, Mr. Stirling?"

Jack and Mary stood together this time, holding hands for moral support. Jack started, "Only this, Your Honor. Judge Zenas saved our marriage and brought me to my senses before I destroyed our family and ruined the lives of my children. Harry Wolff did everything to try to destroy our marriage. Yes, I hired him, and I blame myself for that. I also paid him way too much, but that's another complaint. All we want to say is that if not for Judge Zenas..." Jack was overcome by emotion and struggled to continue.

"All we want to say," Mary stepped in, "is that it would be a terrible injustice to punish Judge Zenas for saving a marriage and protecting our children."

Jack cleared his throat and added, "All this judge did was slow down a divorce that was going way too fast. He put some bumps in the road that gave us time to think and remember why we got married and had a family."

The Stirlings took a seat as if they had no intention to leave. For a few moments, nobody spoke. Then Kelly stood to address the commission. "As I was saying—"

Beck, who had been furiously paging through the file, cut him off.

"Mr. Stirling, I notice that this entire complaint was filed by you. Your signature is on the complaint. I must admit that I presumed you would be a witness today for the prosecution. Can you please clarify your position? You do not wish to proceed?"

"That's correct, sir," Jack replied.

"You have no complaint about Judge Atticus Zenas?"

"No sir, absolutely none."

"Well then. The lawyer who filed the complaint was fired from the case. The case was decided by the judge. And the complaining party, Mr. Stirling, has no complaint about that decision. There are no appeals planned. Do I have a motion to dismiss?"

Tanya McCoy, a retired judge from Harlan County who had been feuding with Beck since she joined the commission, leaned forward. She had led the charge and voted to sanction Judge Zenas for his original Planned Parenthood case. "Mr. Chairman, we should not forget that the Stirling case is not the only charge here. This record is full of allegations against this judge that have nothing to do with the Stirlings."

"I hear you," said Beck, "but I will remind you and all the commissioners that those extra added charges were never made an official part of any complaint against this judge. From what I read, they are mostly rumors and innuendo paper clipped to newspaper articles, and angry letters from people who left a courtroom unhappy—which describes just about everyone who winds up in family court. Some were filed so late they might even violate Judge Zenas' basic rights of due process. I would suggest that if someone wishes to make charges against him that are unrelated to the Stirling decision, they should file a separate complaint, granting him the opportunity to be heard."

Judge McCoy started to reply, but one of the lay commissioners, Diane Williams, saw the chance to collect her per diem, end the day early and go back to work selling real estate. She jumped in with a nod from the chairman. "I move we dismiss this complaint."

"All-in-favor-say-aye-the-ayes-have-it-case-dismissed," Judge Beck said in an auctioneer's rush while McCoy sputtered. "Judge Zenas, you are free to go, but first I would like to apologize on behalf of the Kentucky Judicial Conduct Commission for the leaks to the newspaper that tarnished your reputation. I can assure you, I will get to the bottom of that and it will not happen again."

Jake Tolliver and Marvin Crossfield were busy whispering to each other, plotting how they would inform readers in Lexington and Louisville that all of their stories over the last three weeks about the Stirling case now required massive corrections. They agreed, without spelling it out, that their next stories on the Stirling case would be the last, and very short: "Judge Complaint Dismissed on Technicality." It would be on Page C3, buried as deep as possible.

Harry Wolff was still waiting in the hallway, wondering what the delay could be, impatient to see Judge Z embarrassed or even disbarred and get back to delivering divorces as fast as possible. He grabbed Adam Kelly on the way out; when Kelly quickly explained what had happened, he shouted, "What?"

As Judge Z passed him and got on the elevator with the Stirlings, Harry flashed an angry glance at the judge. And the judge looked back at Harry and remembered how that morning, in his new prayer closet, he had prayed for Harry to someday find the same love that had changed him. He asked the Stirlings to wait and turned back.

As he approached them, Harry was agitated and Kelly looked nervous. Before Harry could say anything, Judge Z said, "Harry, I meant to thank you sincerely for coming to my mother's funeral. That was very thoughtful. Thank you." He put his hand out to shake. Harry looked surprised, recovered and shook hands as he mumbled, "Sure. I am sorry for your loss."

"Well, I guess I will see you in Motion Hour next week. Y'all have a good day." Judge Z headed for the elevator as Jack Stirling held the door open. He had "won" his case without saying a word.

On the elevator, Judge Z thanked the Stirlings for coming and asked, "Can I take you to lunch? I know a little Greek place."

NATASHA'S DONUT SHOP
June 27

Summer was in full bloom as Judge Z locked the door at 7 a.m. on Saturday and left his new home, which was his old home—Beulah's place. He had kept his official residence at his condo, since he had to live there to be a judge in Fayette County. But most nights were now spent in Sadieville.

He headed for a Saturday morning cup of coffee a block away at Natasha's Café on Pike Street. He could almost smell the fresh-ground house blend.

Natasha's husband, Eddie, was an addict. First alcohol, then pain pills, then when the pain pills dried up his friendly neighborhood pusher gave him a free trial on black tar heroin. The stuff was everywhere. Even here in sleepy little Sadieville. Natasha was edging closer and closer to throwing Eddie out, and had hinted that she might want to discuss a divorce with Judge Z. But Natasha and Eddie had children.

"Hiya, Judge," she said as he entered the café. The bright plaid curtains on the front door fluttered in the gentle spring breeze as it swung open, and a tiny silver bell tinkled at the top to announce the arrival of a customer. A guy in a sleeveless neon yellow shirt, work jeans and muddy boots was just leaving with a big box of donuts for the county road crew. He nodded and smiled at Judge Z, who held the door and returned the greeting, caught by surprise once again at the routine friendliness of small-town life.

"Good morning, Natasha," he said. "I'll have my usual."

"Chocolate covered fried cake and black coffee, on its way. And this one's on the house."

"I know I'm a good customer, but you can't pay your bills giving donuts away."

"No, Judge Z, this is just my way of saying thank you for some good advice you gave me last time we chatted. You know, when you talked the other day about how kids in single-parent homes struggle through life, how divorce can wreck their future."

"Well, all that stuff about the damage of divorce is true, but that doesn't mean it's not necessary sometimes. Sometimes you absolutely have to protect your kids and yourself. Every case is different."

"Boy, do I know it. These last couple of years have been hard." She looked around at the empty shop and decided she had time to wipe her hands on her apron and pour a cup for herself. She leaned a hip on the small counter where Judge Z took his usual swivel stool nearest to the front window. "Look, I don't talk about this with anyone else much. Well, my mother, of course. But that's different. You just have a way of listening, I guess. And maybe you don't even know it, but the things you said really made me think. I went home and looked at my kids."

"Three, right?"

"No, four," she laughed. "So I tried to pray that night after I put the kids to bed. And the message I got loud and clear was to hang in there. I'm telling you, Judge, with those kids' lives and their future at risk, I just have to keep hoping we can make our marriage work."

"But that takes two, right?"

"Well, sometimes I think even half of a man would be a big improvement. Another woman, I can handle that. But the drinking and drugging, that's something I just can't tolerate. He has to win that battle himself."

"But does he even want to?"

"Thank God, yes, I think so. That night we had a long conversation. I told him I would stand by him. I told him all that I could remember from what you said about how our kids would never be the same if we split up. I told him I was considering divorce and talked to a lawyer about it—meaning you—but that I had decided to try everything to save our marriage and our children. That gave him a scare. He could tell I was serious. There were lots of tears. And he agreed to get treatment."

"Fantastic. That's a huge first step. But you realize, of course, it's only a first step."

"Yes, we've been down this dead-end street before. But this time feels different. I feel like I have a new attitude. It's not about me, not about Eddie anymore. It's about Amy, Ben, Hope and Faith."

Judge Z laughed and shook his head. "Perfect," he said. "That sounds just like something my mother would have said. 'It's about Hope and Faith.'"

That made Natasha laugh too. "I never even thought of that. But I guess we named them that way for a good reason."

She went to top off his coffee but held the pot over his cup and paused.

"Judge, I guess you know your mom's letter really meant a lot to me." Judge Z had almost forgotten about Beulah's letter. He had read parts of it to Natasha the week before.

It was a letter he kept in his desk, written in 1956 by Beulah to her sister Pauline, to explain why she would not leave Johnny, even though he was a drunk. Her whole family was telling her, "You need to leave Johnny. He's no good."

As if to prove they were right, Johnny had stayed out all night after refereeing a Friday night basketball game in December 1956. He had stopped off in Lexington for a drink on the way home. Then it was Saturday afternoon and still no Johnny. He finally staggered in, reeking of bourbon on his breath and lies on his lips.

There was no logical reason to stay with a man like Johnny. But Beulah saw something that no one else saw. Her letter was all about why she would hang in there with Johnny. She had listed his good qualities. She even mentioned what a great dad he would be someday. She had faith to believe. She referenced the promise of Acts 16:31: "Believe on the Lord Jesus Christ, and you will be saved, you and your household." Beulah had taken the "household" part seriously. She believed, not just for herself but for Johnny and any children to follow.

All that had contributed to Judge Z's standard speech for men, who would hang their heads in court while the mother of their kids listened and nodded. It ended with, "I wouldn't be here if my dad had not quit drinking, and my dad would've never quit drinking if my mom had not believed that he could change."

The bell over the door jingled and Natasha poured him some coffee, then left to take care of her customer.

Judge Z finished his second donut and coffee. Natasha was busy talking to a man in coveralls with "Mike's Mower Repair" written in red script on the back, so he just waved and said, "Thanks, Natasha" on his way out the door.

"No, thank *you*, Judge," she replied with a big smile.

As he started down the sidewalk he glanced at a newspaper rack displaying the front page of *USA Today*. Judge Z had quit reading papers, but he couldn't miss the giant bold headline. He was not altogether surprised.

"Supreme Court Redefines Marriage," it said. Same-sex marriage would now be the law of the land. The headline was bigger than the day Kennedy was shot. Almost as big as "Japan Attacks Pearl Harbor." A big picture above the fold showed a judge in Michigan marrying two lip-locked men before the ink was even dry on the U.S. Supreme Court's 5-4 opinion. *In fact,* the judge thought, *it's technically not even final, although no one would mention that. The revisionists have won. Luv is luv.*

Judge Z shook his head, then smiled. He decided that for his own mental health he would not to read the article. Instead, he would read the actual opinion from the Supreme Court next week.

The old Judge Atticus Zenas would have fumed and fretted. But the new Judge Z was broken. Irretrievably broken in the eyes of God. His walls had been torn down so that love could pour in. And being broken this way sure felt good. He was humbled. Contrite. But stronger. At peace. The doors of heaven on earth had been opened for him.

He didn't need the Supreme Court to define marriage for him.

He moved on toward his Buick and headed for the golf course, where a small dose of paradise would be waiting on the first tee.

As he walked down the sidewalk in the sunshine, he could hear a lawnmower droning somewhere in the leafy neighborhood that started a block back from Pike Street. It was a reassuring sound—the background music of summertime.

As soon as he got in the car, his phone rang. It was Brad Bertram's number, calling no doubt to discuss the Supreme Court case. He was not in the mood and let it go to voice mail. A few minutes later, another call came in. The number was "Unknown" so he decided not to answer.

As he pulled into the parking lot at the golf course, he dialed voice mail. First up was Brad: "Judge, no rush. Just call me. You know my number."

The next call was the perfect antidote for anything ailing the judge today. It was from Serena Murdock.

"Judge Zenas, this is Serena. I hope you remember me. Just calling to let you know that my little girl was born yesterday, June 26. I told you I was going to name her Grace. Well, I did. But after going to your mother's funeral, I decided to change it just a little. Beulah Grace Barnette was born at 9:22 a.m. You may notice the last name is different, too. Sam and I got married last week. Better late than never. Anyway, thanks, Judge."

Yeah, thought the judge. *Better late than never.*

Judge Z popped the trunk for his clubs and climbed out of the car. The sun was shining bright on his ol' Kentucky home. Beulah was smiling.

"A dead thing can go with the stream, but only a living thing can go against it."

— G.K. CHESTERTON

ACKNOWLEDGMENTS

First I want to thank my wife, Sue. We have been married forty-four years. She is the only person who really knows me and tells me what I need to hear. She loves me. And I love her. And it is getting better all the time. Thanks to some things I learned as I wrote this book, I now know what love is. The inspiration to write a book on marriage comes entirely from the love of Sue for me.

Next, I offer my thanks to a gifted young man, Thomas Cothran. He and I worked together on a serious scholarly work defining marriage, both legally and spiritually, for two years before I decided that a novel would be a better approach. Thomas pointed me to resources and books I did not know existed. The books and blogs he suggested changed my life for the better, and eventually made this novel possible. Thomas helped me with invaluable research. His father, Martin Cothran, has been a primary source of information and inspiration on the family for twenty five years.

Thanks also to Dr. Dennis Kinlaw. Now a lively 93 years of age, he is an Old Testament scholar whose own thoughts on the love of God changed my life. He has been my favorite preacher for decades, and most of my own "sermons" were stolen from him. The idea that God is a judge, father and husband came entirely from sitting at his feet. I have followed Dr. Kinlaw as he has followed Christ.

I'm also grateful to a group of men that meet regularly for spiritual insight: Al Coppedge, Robert Coleman, Stan Key, Danny Corbitt, Jerry Coleman, Ron Smith and John Oswalt have had a major impact on the ideas in this book. The entire concept of "hesed" came from Dr. Oswalt. Everyone needs a small group like ours. I found my niche when I started to meet with these brilliant men who know the love of God.

Thanks, of course, to Ford and Virginia Philpot. My parents were married for more than fifty years and taught me without even trying. As I often say in court, I learned almost everything I needed by just eavesdropping on their conversations with each other. So, thanks to Mom and Dad, my best teachers.

Thanks also to a small group of young married couples in Monroeville, Alabama, who met with me two years ago to let me practice the ideas in this book. That weekend got me off the ground in exploring "Why Marriage Matters."

I must also thank my "coach," Greg Salciccioli. I would still be telling people I was writing a book if Greg had not encouraged me to finish, and given me the tools to make it happen.

Thanks also to some unnamed destitute ladies in India who transformed me with their love of God in 2012. I am living now on the borders of heaven because God showed me love on a hot day in India. Women like them continue to be a primary source of inspiration for me, which makes sense since "wisdom" in Proverbs is always gender specific and female.

I thank everyone under thirty who is married and determined to stay that way. You are inspirational outliers in today's world because you are swimming upstream.

Thanks to Peter Bronson, who has been my primary editor on this project. He is not only a gifted writer, but also loves God and loves his wife. He has protected me from saying a lot of stupid things in this book and so, Pete, thanks for saving me. Again.

Also, Emma Davis for her valuable copy editing, which helped me feel confident that this book is done the right way.

Thanks to a group of men who gather in the bar at Keene Run Golf Club every Thursday to study the Bible and hear each other's stories. Those twenty or so men have a combined six hundred-plus years of marriage, an amazing statistic and proof that, as G.K. Chesterton said, "Marriage is a duel to the death which no man of honor should decline."

Last, thanks to my writer friends who provided valuable feedback: Todd Wright, Gregg Lewis, Angela Correll, Steve Flairty, Jeff Hopper, Ben Witherington, Mike Henderson and Wayne Jacobsen. And to anyone I missed, my sincere apologies.

My final thank-you is to thousands of people I have never met. They are families who do *not* come to court. They have worked hard at their marriages and realized that a courtroom is not a good place for solving family problems. They loved their children enough to keep them away from court. They have been selfless in a selfish world.

FURTHER READING

Knowingly or unknowingly, these authors and their excellent books have contributed to this work of fiction. I am grateful for their research and expertise. -- Tim Philpot

Coontz, Stephanie. *Marriage, a History: How Love Conquered Marriage*. Reprint edition. Penguin Books, 2006.

Doherty, William J. *Take back your marriage: Sticking together in a world that pulls us apart*. New York: Guilford, 2001.

Edwards, Gene. *The Divine Romance*. Reissue edition. Tyndale House Publishers, 1993.

Eldredge, John. *Love & War*. Colorado Springs, Col.: WaterBrook Press, 2011.

Esolen, Anthony. *Defending Marriage: Twelve Arguments for Sanity*. 1st edition. Charlotte, N.C.: Saint Benedict Press, 2014.

Fox-Genovese, Elizabeth. *Marriage: The Dream That Refuses to Die*. 1st edition. Wilmington, Del: Intercollegiate Studies Institute, 2008.

Girgis, Sherif, Ryan T. Anderson, and Robert P. George. *What Is Marriage?: Man and Woman: A Defense*. 1st Edition. New York: Encounter Books, 2012.

Kinlaw, Dennis F. *Let's Start with Jesus: A New Way of Doing Theology*. Grand Rapids, Mich.: Zondervan, 2005.

Weigel, George. *Witness to Hope: The Biography of Pope John Paul II.* Updated edition. New York: Harper Perennial, 2004.

Whitehead, Barbara Dafoe. *The Divorce Culture: Rethinking Our Commitments to Marriage and Family.* New York: Vintage, 1998.

Bible verses are quoted from the *New International Version* and *The Message.*

Also by Tim Philpot:
Ford's Wonderful World of Golf
www.fordswonderfulworld.com

CPSIA information can be obtained
at www.ICGtesting.com
Printed in the USA
LVOW12s1311260417

532265LV00015B/393/P